Somewhere
Only We
Know

Erin
LAWLESS

Harper*Impulse* an imprint of
HarperCollins*Publishers* Ltd
1 London Bridge Street
London SE1 9GF

www.harpercollins.co.uk

A Paperback Original 2015

First published in Great Britain in ebook format by Harper*Impulse* 2015

A catalogue record for this book is
available from the British Library

ISBN: 9780008139643

This novel is entirely a work of fiction.
The names, characters and incidents portrayed in it are
the work of the author's imagination. Any resemblance to
actual persons, living or dead, events or localities is
entirely coincidental.

Automatically produced by Atomik ePublisher from Easypress

Моей лучшей подруге
KSENIA

and also,
to LONDON
a home of my heart

People are like cities:
We all have alleys and gardens and secret rooftops and places
where daisies sprout between the sidewalk cracks, but most of the
time all we let each other see is a postcard glimpse of a skyline
or a polished square. Love lets you find those hidden places in
another person, even the ones they didn't know were there, even
the ones they wouldn't have thought to call beautiful themselves.

Hilary T. Smith

Chapter 1

Alex

The weight Donnelly was putting on was definitely starting to show; his paunch was forced to rest on top of the boardroom table, his straining lower shirt buttons pointing to the ceiling. He looked as though at any minute he was going to start stroking his stomach like a Bond villain with a cat. The new graduate trainee to Alex's left was enthusiastically taking notes; Alex had stopped bringing a notepad and pen to this sort of meeting after his first six months. He tilted his head to see what he'd missed whilst distracted by Donnelly's chub. *Attention to detail*, Newbie had jotted down. *Asking the right questions. Adding value to your day* was underlined neatly. The thing that would add most value to his day, Alex thought, was not having this pointless team meeting scheduled for a Friday afternoon.

After a few more motivational mantras, Donnelly released them back to their desks for the final twenty minutes of the working week. Alex shook his mouse to wake up his PC and had to hurriedly smother his office-inappropriate smile at seeing he'd received an email from Lila.

It was only a couple of lines asking him if he fancied spaghetti bolognaise for dinner or if he had other plans. Like he'd have other plans! Seeing Lila was, no exaggeration, the very highlight of his week. Just getting to eat a meal she'd put together, sit with her in companionable silence as they watched a DVD. Being madly in love with someone made the mundane magic.

Then, as usual, his flatmate, Rory, came straight to the front of his mind, putting a bullet in the brain of Alex's enthusiasm. "Hey, Lils," Alex typed, with a sigh. "Spag bol sounds great! Thank you! What are you and Rory up to this weekend?"

Nadia

Nadia was almost certain the police were coming for her. It made it difficult to relax.

She made herself yet another cup of tea, but that just made her jittery, so most of it went down the sink. She tried to distract herself with a little Facebook stalking, but – for some reason – other people's lives weren't as fascinating as they usually seemed. Television was a lost cause since daytime TV made her want to poke her eyes out with a fork, so she ended up just sitting and fretting for hours. By the time Holly got home from work, Nadia was in a right state and had been waiting in the hallway for twenty minutes.

"I'm having second thoughts," she admitted, without preamble, before Holly had even got fully through the flat door.

Holly arched an eyebrow at her as she kicked off her shoes. "Bit late for that, hun, the stuff's in the post."

"I know. I know. But, I was thinking, maybe we can call Royal Mail, or the sorting office, and get them to, sort of, pull it?" she said, hopefully.

Holly's eyebrow arched higher. "Pull it?"

Nadia waved her hand vaguely. "Yeah. You know, take it out of the system and… return it to sender."

"'Fraid it doesn't work like that," Holly said, moving past her flatmate towards her bedroom. "Don't worry about it; everything's going to be fine."

"But… I've lied," Nadia said, miserably. "On an official document. I could get in some serious trouble over this. Things are bad enough already. I don't know what I was thinking."

"Calm down," Holly instructed, as she attempted to tame her heat-frizzed hair with a brush and pull it up and away from her flushed face and neck. She'd had a long, hot journey home on the stuffy Tube. "People lie on these things all the time. Besides, I wouldn't even say you've lied, per se."

"Oh yeah? Well, what would you call it, then?"

Holly considered her response. "You were just a little bit preemptive," she said finally, scooping up an armful of dirty clothes from the hamper in the corner of her bedroom and moving past Nadia into the hallway again.

"Pre-emptive?" Nadia echoed, as she trailed Holly to the kitchen. "How's that? And stop it with that! I know very well that you only ever do laundry when you're putting off doing something else." Holly shot her a guilty expression as she shoved her load into the washing-machine drum. "Seriously, Hol, I am freaking out here."

"You don't need to be!" Holly reasserted, standing straight and slamming the drum door shut. "It's not like you told them you'd been happily married for ten years and are pregnant with your sixth child. *That* would have been a lie."

"And so just saying that I have a boyfriend is… pre-emptive?" Nadia asked, doubtfully.

"Yup. Anticipatory. A little ahead of yourself." Holly smiled helpfully.

"More like *way* ahead of myself."

"Hey, it's Friday night! If you want a boyfriend so badly, let's hit the High Street and find you some idiot in a rugby shirt with a popped collar that you can change for the better."

Nadia sighed. "I've added some stuff to the Netflix list I thought you might like. We could crack on with some of that."

Holly shot her a disparaging look. "I was thinking more along the lines of something where we break up the love affair that is your arse and our couch. Come on. We're going out."

"Ah, Hols, you know I'm broke!" Nadia sighed, flopping

3

dramatically onto said couch. The Home Office had taken away her working visa and her passport nine months ago and she had been existing on a combination of savings, overdrafts and waning parental generosity ever since. "I wouldn't say no to sharing a bottle of wine from Budgens, though. I think I've got a few quid somewhere."

Holly cocked her head to one side and looked at her friend with exaggerated pity. "Oh, stop it, you're breaking my heart," she said, sarcastically. "Go and put some slap on, already. I've been cooped up in that office all week; I'm definitely up to stretching to a few drinks tonight."

Nadia laughed, easily persuaded. "Okay, sounds good. But I will still go and spend my few precious pounds on that bottle; we can drink it while we're getting ready."

"Sounds good. But I think I'm on the Mojitos later. I just really fancy a Mojito. Must be the weather."

"Okay, but please, let's not wind up in that dive bar again, drinking double-strength Mojitos at four in the morning. You know I had to throw away that top after last time? I loved that top!"

"I make no promises!" Holly laughed. "At four in the morning the liver wants what the liver wants."

"I guess it wouldn't do to mess with tradition," Nadia said thoughtfully; "especially as I am 'constantly mindful and respectful of historic and cultural traditions'," she laughed, quoting her recent visa application essay. Holly herself had come up with that particular piece of crap.

"Agreed. A night where we hit Clapham High Street and didn't over-indulge just wouldn't be the same. Right! Do you think I'll be way too hot in my skinny jeans?" The cheap Ikea bureau in her bedroom groaned as Holly yanked open one of the drawers.

And Nadia thought it, but didn't say it: this could be one of the last nights that she and Holly ever drank Mojitos together.

4

Alex

Alex had never had much of a life plan. He had an average grade in a broad subject, which – if anything – opened up too much choice, but the Home Office recruitment booth, decked out in Union Jack bunting, had immediately drawn his attention at that first careers fair. Seduced by aspirations of martinis – shaken, not stirred, naturally – and daydreams of parkouring across Middle Eastern rooftops after bad guys, Alex immediately signed up for their fast-track graduate scheme. Of course, it was just a desk job, the same as any other, and – with the recession double-dipping away – one that turned out to have no career progression, bonuses or benefits. Every year staff were reminded that their relatively low salary should be bolstered by a sense of accomplishment in knowing that they were working for the good of their country, which in the case of Alex's role seemed to primarily consist of preventing people's access to it.

Monday morning meant a whole new batch of applications. Almost all of them would be the usual – EU citizens looking for student, or sometimes spousal, visas. All Alex had to do at this point was read through them, making sure the applicant had ticked the right boxes – both literally and figuratively – before sending those who'd got everything right up the management chain.

It was all achingly repetitive – the insincere protestations of patriotism, the stiff Google-translated English, the bored-sounding formal references from companies who'd had the person in for an internship years ago…

"One time, Nadia and I were watching University Challenge; *the round was politics and she got every question but one absolutely right. How many natural British citizens do you think know that much about their country?"*

Alex blinked and re-read the opening line of the letter he'd just picked up. He felt his mouth twitch into a smile; it was a fair point. He skimmed through the rest of the wonderfully effusive letter, particularly affectionate sentences jumping out from the long, rambling paragraphs.

"*Nadia knows and excels at all the dance moves to Steps'* 'Tragedy' *and* '5-6-7-8'. *Her* 'Macarena' *isn't great, though.*"

"*She ran a half-marathon dressed in a hot pink bra with me to raise money for breast cancer after my aunt died of it.*"

"*I honestly think that were Prince Harry to meet Nadia, he'd probably want to marry her. How can you deny a potential future princess of this great nation the leave to remain in it?*"

"*If Nadia is removed from the country, you will be breaking up an epic pub quiz team. We win the Bellevue's quiz almost every week and would have serious trouble finding a replacement with Nadia's niche knowledge.*"

Alex felt his smile grow wider as he read on; this was mildly insane.

The concluding paragraph was neat and controlled and out of place in the general sprawl of the letter as a whole – as if the writer had belatedly remembered that she was writing a formal letter to the government.

"*You will know 'Nadezhda Osipova' from all your forms, papers and records. I hope, however, that I have been able to introduce you to 'Nadia' – the very best person I will ever know. I hope this slightly irreverent – but heartfelt! – letter has gone some way towards convincing you that she should have the right to remain in the UK on the grounds that she has an established private life due to her long residency here. Losing her would be like losing an arm. Please grant Nadia Osipova Indefinite Leave to Remain.*"

Alex lingered on the last sentence, his smile fading, awkwardness returning. Like it was that easy! Especially not for Russian nationals. He flicked back to the personal details form on the front of the application pack and took a more interested look. The twenty-six-year-old Nadezhda Osipova had been resident in the UK since she was eleven, when she'd enrolled in a prestigious boarding school just outside London. After graduating she'd clung on to her residency here by jumping from one temporary visa to another. But that particular cat was now out of lives.

Nadezhda 'Nadia' Osipova's immigration history was an absolute headache. Each year when her school had closed for the summer break she'd been shunted back across to her parents in Russia. She'd gone budget backpacking during her student years, taken typical beach holidays with mates, skied in the spring, returned to her family each Christmas. He wondered what the girl's immigration lawyer was thinking. There was no way she was going to get Indefinite Leave to Remain with all of these random, elongated absences from the country.

Feeling a little heavy, he read the rest of Nadezhda's supporting letters, which were all focusing on the same theme. He returned to the first and re-read it. It had got to be one of the stupidest letters he'd seen in his long years at the Home Office – and this made it strangely fascinating. He couldn't deny it had hit its mark, though, because he found that he really was seeing *Nadia*, the charity-marathon running, pub quiz-winning, cheesy-dancing friend, rather than Nadezhda, the foreign national, who he knew wasn't going to make the cut.

And so that's probably why, despite knowing that his manager would most likely toss the application out, Alex wished Nadezhda Osipova well and passed her up the chain.

Nadia
Ten weeks after her work visa had been taken away from her, Nadia had finished reading every book in the flat and given it two spring-cleans. Ledge had kindly given her access to his Netflix account and she'd racked up hundreds of hours of watching questionable American drama. She wandered up and down the high street, window-shopping for things she couldn't have afforded even before she lost her salary. She was bored, bored, *bored*.

So the three-days-a-week volunteer position at the local Oxfam shop was a godsend. It didn't pay her, so it didn't contravene the conditions of her immigration status, but it kept her busy and out of her own head, where these days she did almost nothing but obsess. Unfortunately, people weren't really knocking down the door lately – to donate or to buy – and so Nadia spent a large proportion of each day needlessly rearranging the musty stock, or picking a book off the shelf to leaf through as she perched on the wobbly stool behind the ancient till.

On Tuesdays, though, Caro had no classes and usually came into the shop for an hour or two's chat. It was, she cheerfully admitted, the only time in her life she ever contemplated setting foot in a charity shop.

"This is cute," she said, holding out a pink, fluffy jumper with a white kitten on the front of it. Nadia glanced up from where she was optimistically filling out Gift Aid labels.

"Then buy it," she suggested. "It's what, all of four pounds?"

"Oh, no," Caro laughed lightly, putting the hanger back on the rail but continuing to leaf through the jumble of items with her manicured fingers. It was hard to be mad at her; Caro's family probably gave more to charity every year than this tiny little back-street Oxfam made per annum.

Because Caro was rich; double-barrelled surname rich. Her family business was something dreadfully unglamorous, but dreadfully lucrative, which allowed Caro and her brother to officially Do Nothing. The brother had disappeared from Heathrow with a backpack and a credit card as soon as he graduated from his mandatory university degree. Caro was more of a home bird, and so had decided she'd rather remain the eternal student. She was currently halfway through Masters degree number two and starting to give serious consideration to which of her many qualifications she was going to take through to a gratuitous PhD afterwards. Considering that this was probably the biggest concern that Caro had, it was lucky she was genuinely sweet and a wonderful friend, or else Nadia would have long since strangled her with a charitably donated knitted scarf.

"So, I assume you haven't heard?" Caro asked, finishing with the jumpers and moving on to the rail arm of skirts.

8

"From the Home Office? No. I'm meant to by the end of the week."

"Still hopeful?"

"Yeah," Nadia lied. She wasn't exactly hopeful. But it was important that she pretended to the others that she was; it made things easier for them, especially for Caro, who was still smarting after having her generosity snubbed. She'd tried to insist on using Daddy's credit card to hire a proper immigration lawyer for her friend, but Nadia had just as insistently refused, assuring her that she and her family could handle the cost on their own. That was a lie too. The closest Nadia had gotten to a lawyer was a Google search for helpful blog posts on immigration law.

"Good." Caro smiled. "Me too." She pulled out a panelled tartan skirt. "I saw a lush skirt just like this in Bottega Veneta last month!" She laughed. "And that one was £845."

Nadia rolled her eyes. "So buy it!" Caro laughed again, as though Nadia had just made the funniest joke ever, and continued her blasé browsing.

Alex

Lila's thighs were clammy. Alex knew this because Lila kept mentioning it, as if it was absolutely no big deal to discuss the condition of her naked skin as she squeezed past him over and over again as they both tried to cook simultaneously in the poky kitchen.

Her pasta bake finally assembled and in the oven, Lila sat down on one of the kitchen's two foldaway chairs and crossed one (apparently clammy) leg over the other.

"It does feel sort of sordid having bare legs in the office and on the Tube," she confessed as she reached for her glass of water. "But even clear skin-coloured tights are just unbearable in this weather, you know?"

Alex snorted. "Imagine having to wear a suit and tie to the office and on the Tube!" he mocked. "You don't exactly have my sympathy, Lils."

Lila waved her hand dismissively. "Suit trousers aren't skin-tight," she argued. "It's not the same. Besides, you could always buy a pair of those city shorts?"

Alex gave her a withering look. "Lils, have you actually ever seen anyone wearing those shorts?" he asked her.

"Yes!"

"I mean, like on the Tube, not in a magazine!"

"Then no," Lila admitted, laughing.

"That's because they're a myth. Because men know that if they wear them, it will appear as if they have simply forgotten the bottom third of their suit."

"You said men wearing Ugg boots was a myth," Lila argued. "And then David Beckham wore them."

"David Beckham is a celebrity, not a 'man'!" Alex immediately countered, turning his attention briefly to his bubbling saucepan.

"Oh, he's a man all right," Lila joked. "And what a man!"

They both turned, distracted by the jingling of keys in the front-door lock. Lila hopped to her feet expectantly and moved out into the hallway to greet Rory as he arrived home, looking rumpled and sweat-stained, his tie already removed and three of his shirt buttons undone.

"S'bloody hot out there," he informed them, as if they somehow weren't aware of the fact.

"Was the Tube a nightmare?" Lila asked, sympathetically, going up on her tiptoes for a peck on the lips.

"Yeah. Central Line. Hottest line on the Underground, apparently."

"I don't understand how they can manage to give us WiFi underground, but not bloody air-conditioning!" Lila complained.

Alex stood awkwardly, half-in and half-out of the kitchen. Right on cue, that old third-wheel feeling had started up, making him feel like a horrible, pointless person. He'd mentioned it to Lila once, one night, after too many beers, and she'd just laughed, totally not getting it. She never got it.

"Third wheel?" she'd echoed. "Don't be silly. What if we're more like a tricycle, you, me and Ror?" But that was just her being sweet, of course, and it didn't change the fact that Alex was well and truly a sad little unicycle, all on his own.

On the face of it, it should all have been so different. Lila was *his* friend, or she had been, back at university, anyway. Sure, they may have fallen out of touch for a couple of years, but fate had intervened in the end. It was one of those "six degrees of separation" things; she was in a house-share with someone who was casually dating a mate of Rory's from work. If that mate hadn't thrown a house party at exactly that point in time, in a city of eight million people, Lila Palmer may just have remained an obscure Facebook Friend. And Rory – Alex's taller, darker, richer and generally more attractive flatmate – would never have met her. But meet they did, and within two weeks she was sitting sheepishly across the breakfast table from Alex wearing Rory's dressing gown and exchanging awkward small talk about how life had been to them since graduation. And within six weeks, Alex was painfully certain he was in love with her.

Alex remained stupidly paused in the doorframe as Lila followed her boyfriend into his bedroom, chattering away brightly as she'd just been doing in the kitchen with him; the bedroom door was kicked closed, almost like an afterthought. He guessed he wouldn't be getting to hear what else Lila thought about David Beckham, not that night anyway.

Alex jumped as his saucepan of veg finally boiled dry on the hob, hissing loudly as if it was as pissed off with Alex as he was with himself.

Nadia

Nadia was home from her shift at the shop a little later than usual for a Thursday evening; she'd stopped off at Tesco to buy herself a cheap (but probably not that nutritious) dinner of value-brand instant noodles (supposedly "chicken flavour" but ominously suitable for vegans). Holly was already home when she got there, sitting awkwardly on the very edge of the sofa cushions, knees and ankles together, shoes still on. An impossibly crisp white envelope sat on the coffee table in front of her.

"It came, then?" Nadia asked, in a ridiculously calm voice.

"It came," Holly confirmed, pressing her palms to her knees, as if she was physically stopping herself ripping open the letter herself.

"Hmmm." Instead of pouncing on the piece of paper that pronounced her future, Nadia walked into the kitchen and began methodically unpacking her shopping into the cupboards. Holly came to stand in the doorway.

"Well, aren't you going to open it?" she asked, incredulously.

"In a minute," Nadia replied.

"How can you wait?"

Nadia turned and rested her hands behind her on the kitchen counter. "I just need a minute, Hol, okay?"

"But…"

"That letter quite possibly tells me that I need to pack up and leave everything I know." Nadia tried for a light tone but failed miserably. "Let me just have a few more minutes in blissful ignorance, please."

"Oh, hun." Holly crossed the kitchen and pulled her friend into a hug. "You haven't been thinking that, have you? They're not going to deport you. You've lived here since you were a little kid. You've paid taxes here. You probably speak better English than me – and definitely better English than Ledge!" Nadia gave a weak little smile. "Everything's going to be fine," Holly promised. "Let's open the letter."

Nadia could barely open the envelope, her finger clumsily sticking as she used it to try and rip the seal. She shook the contents into her lap. A shiny folded booklet fell out first: a multi-ethnic group of people smiling out at her from under dark turbans and brightly coloured hijabs. It was followed by one piece of A4 paper, just one. Nadia tried to read every word at once; the print just swam before her eyes. She swallowed and cleared her throat, focusing on the familiarity of her name at the head of the letter and slowly fragments started to make sense.

Dear Miss Osipova... regret to inform you... application has been denied on the grounds that you have spent more than 450 days out of the country during your residency here... vacate the country within three months...

Nadia couldn't read any further. She let the piece of paper fall to her lap on top of the leaflet and pressed the hands that had been holding it against her temples. Vacate the country. In three months she would be back living with her parents, something she hadn't done since before she was a teenager. She'd have to go and live in a country that she barely knew. She may not have ever been totally accepted as British – her surname and her international school accent and her constant visa issues had never allowed for that – but it was even worse when she was back in Russia.

She spoke the language perfectly, of course – she had to, as neither of her parents spoke English – but she never managed to be quite au fait with things like the current slang or the latest fad, always earmarking her out as a foreigner in the country of her birth. She may never have fully belonged in England, but then she'd never quite felt as though she'd ever belonged in Russia, either. And at least here she had her flat, her friends – and a collection of close-to-useless degrees and qualifications sitting atop a mountain of student debt, none of which had mattered to the Home Office, or were any bloody good to her now. She felt sick to her core.

It took Nadia a moment to realise that Holly was speaking.

"We'll all be behind you, Nads; it'll come off. You'll see," she was finishing, her face hopeful. She'd taken the discarded letter from Nadia's knees and was holding it against her own.

"What'll come off?"

"The appeal." Nadia stared at her friend vacantly. "The appeal they're suggesting you do?" When Nadia continued to look blank Holly began to read aloud from the paragraph Nadia had given up before getting to.

"'However, we do accept that you may exhibit appropriate grounds for claiming 'private life' here in the UK under the Article 8 Law. You have not been a UK resident for the 20 years that is required in your case, but – due to your comparatively young age – a Court of Appeals judge may be able to arbitrate on this further. Please find enclosed a leaflet on how to progress your appeal should you not be satisfied with our decision to deny you Indefinite Leave to Remain in the United Kingdom. Please note, however, that there will only be scope for one appeal and that the decision of which is final and binding. Costs will not be awarded'."

Wordlessly Nadia took the letter back from Holly and read the concluding paragraph for herself.

"This is good news," Holly beamed, getting to her feet. "Let's celebrate."

By the time Holly returned from the kitchen with two gently steaming mugs of milky tea, Nadia had re-read the entire letter three times and still wasn't sure how she felt about it.

"Do you want to get a takeaway in tonight?" Holly asked, setting the drink down in front of her silent flatmate. "The cupboards are a bit bare for a celebratory meal."

"Oh, Hols. Thanks. I'm just… not so sure that we should be celebrating as such, at least not yet," Nadia admitted, her eyes drawn back to the letter again.

"What do you mean? Okay, I know it's not exactly what we were hoping, but at least it's not a 'no'."

Nadia stared at her. "It is a no. It's quite clearly a no."

"I think it's a strong 'maybe'," Holly argued. "They wouldn't bother suggesting that you appeal if they didn't think you had a good chance."

"I know, I know. It's just…" Nadia sighed. "It's just who knows how much longer I won't know where I stand, you know? How much longer am I going to be driving my parents into debt in order to get my rent paid?" She considered the letter closely again. "I reckon it might just be stall tactics; they're hoping I give up and leave the country of my own accord."

"Nadia, it's just typical government red tape, not some sort of plot against you personally," Holly frowned. "I think they're being quite decent, actually, flagging up that you have the right of appeal rather than burying it in the small print."

"You're right. I just thought – either way – that this would all be sorted out today. I hate the not knowing."

"Isn't it better that you're still in the dark, but still here?" Holly asked, quietly. "Rather than having to turn on your laptop to book a plane ticket right now?"

"Of course it is." Nadia looked at her friend. They'd been inseparable since their school days. She noticed how white Holly's fingers were as she held her mug of tea and remembered how pale her face had looked before the letter had been opened. She forgot sometimes that the not knowing was hard on her friends, too.

"I think I want… Chinese for dinner, then," Nadia grinned, folding up the Home Office letter and slipping it safely back into its envelope, along with the appeals leaflet.

"I could go for some Chinese," Holly agreed, thoughtfully. "The usual?"

"Of course."

"Right, well I'll get the order in. You" – Holly pointed mock-seriously at Nadia – "Go and call your parents and tell them the *good* news, right now."

Alex

Thursday was Alex's weekly "keeping up appearances" session at the gym. When he got home Rory was sitting on the sofa with a PlayStation controller in hand, besocked-feet up on the coffee table next to the remnants of a ready-meal curry, the neon-bright sauce already congealing on the white plate.

"No Lila this evening, then?" Alex asked, as he dropped his satchel onto a nearby chair.

Rory called up the menu to pause the game. "Nah. Good day? Kill any terrorists?"

Alex was never sure if this was just a long-running joke or if there was a part of Rory that genuinely believed his flatmate might be the British Jack Bauer. "No, not today."

"You need to step up your game," Rory told him matter-of-factly, starting up his own again. Alex sat down heavily on the sofa next to him, pulling the shoe off one of his feet with the other, relaxed in a way he never quite could be when he knew Lila was in the flat. He watched Rory progress through the level with a critical eye.

"No, you need to go up to the top of the general store. There's a weapons' cache up there. And a window with a great vantage point for shooting from," he ordered.

Rory shot him a quick look whilst continuing what he was doing. "You really do know this game like the back of your hand, don't you?" Alex shrugged. "You need to get out more," Rory frowned, only half-joking.

Alex just shrugged again. "You have a girl, I have a game," he replied with a sigh, also only half-joking. They sat in a comfortable silence punctuated only by the repetitive gunfire emanating from the television's speakers.

"Do you want to maybe pub it tomorrow night?" Rory asked, casually. "We can hit Clapham High Street, you know that's where all the totty is."

Alex rolled his eyes. "Thanks, but no thanks, at least on the totty front. Pub sounds good, though."

Rory continued, undeterred. "This guy at work says there's an epic pub quiz in one of the places by the Tube, loads of film-based questions and stuff, apparently. And people stay on in the place afterwards because they do a tray of Jagerbombs for, like, a tenner."

"A tray?" Alex echoed.

"A tray," Rory assured him.

"A tray of shots sounds a little heavy for a Friday night…" Alex said, tilting his head back against the sofa. Rory rolled his eyes and paused the video game once again.

"Look, I'm going to make this easy for you, okay? Go to Clapham Common Tube after work tomorrow. I'll find out the name of this pub from the girl at work and text it to you. You and I will then drink beer, astound everyone present with our fantastic general knowledge, win some cash, then spend it on trays of shots. You got it?"

Alex couldn't really argue with that. "Okay, sounds good," he smiled, getting to his feet to go and forage in the kitchen cupboards for something for dinner.

"Cool," Rory said, starting his game up again. "I'll tell Lila to get there early and make sure we get a good table."

Alex raised his eyes to the ceiling, pleading for patience. Of course Lila was going to be there. Of bloody course.

Nadia

Nadia was just trying to have one evening where she didn't have to think or talk about her immigration status. Unfortunately, nobody seemed to have got the memo.

"I really wish you'd let me get you some legal representation," Caro said, frowning, using one finger to delicately scroll on her iPad. "The information on the Home Office website makes the whole process seem very obtuse."

"Yeah, but the information in this leaflet makes the whole thing look like a piece of piss," Ledge argued, waving said leaflet for emphasis. "Don't worry, Nads. You turn up to court, you give 'em a big smile, you present your case and then the judge goes, cool, I see that you totally should be allowed to stay in Britain, sorry for the inconvenience love, bosh, done."

Holly rolled her eyes over her cousin's head and silenced herself with a substantial gulp of wine.

"Do you think that you could get one of the managers from your old company to be there in the court with you?" Caro continued, ignoring Ledge. "If this whole thing is hinging on how much of a 'private life' you have in the UK, the wider range of people we can get to show their face on your behalf, the better."

"I don't know. Maybe. I'll email them when I've got the court date," Nadia replied, reaching for the wine bottle and topping up her glass, even though it was still half full. So much for having a nice night in to distract her from her visa woes.

"Hope you get it confirmed sooner rather than later," Holly said. "It'll definitely be a weekday, won't it? And it's an absolute bitch for me to get time off work at the moment." Holly worked for a charity HQ, but her managers were the most hard-nosed, hard-arsed businessmen anyone could ever come across.

"Well, I'll be there!" Caro said, giving Nadia a clumsy one-armed hug, causing both of their glasses to slop wine.

"Well, it's not like you have to worry about getting your annual leave approved," Holly remarked, her tone sweetly polite. Caro just screwed up her nose and stuck out her tongue in eloquent response before releasing Nadia and turning her attention back to her iPad. Holly and Caro had a strange relationship; they were both close to Nadia and so spent an inordinate amount of time together, but Nadia sometimes wondered if the two girls would even bother keeping in touch were she to be deported back to Russia...

Deported back to Russia. Nadia sighed and topped up her wine glass some more.

"And I'll be there too," Ledge said, hefting himself to his feet and shuffling towards the kitchen. At the door, he turned back. "Hey, what are you planning to do about your 'boyfriend'?" he asked, genuinely curious.

Nadia jolted, her brimming glass of wine halfway to her mouth, sloshing chilled Pinot against her collarbones. She stared up at Ledge in horror.

"Her boyfriend?" Caro echoed, confused, looking from one to

the other. "What boyfriend?"

"The one she mentions on her application form," Ledge replied. "You know? The one I 'play football' with?" he clarified, with air-quotes to belie the lie he gave in his letter of support to Nadia's application.

"Oh." Caro settled back uncomfortably against the legs of the sofa. "*That* boyfriend…"

"Don't worry about it," Holly said immediately. "They wouldn't necessarily be expecting him in court, and even if they are, you can always just say you two just… broke up…"

"But that doesn't reflect that well on Nadia," Caro said, alarmed, sitting forward once again. "Besides, having a British boyfriend has got to be a massive box-tick for these people. You can't get much more of a private life than that!"

"Guys!" Nadia pleaded, dabbing her neck with the drier part of her top.

"Ledge, how do you feel about telling the government that you're seeing Nadia?" Holly asked her cousin, her 'business' expression firmly in place.

"Hols," Nadia tried again.

"I don't think that would work," Ledge replied slowly. "Didn't I say in my letter that me and her were really good mates, and that I play football with her boyfriend? Matthew, did we call him, in the end? Yeah, we used your dad's name, didn't we? It'll be too suspicious if we change the story now."

"We should have thought this through," Caro said, crossly. "We should have said that Ledge was the boyfriend from the start."

"Come on, guys! It's the government! They must get these sort of lies every day." Nadia rolled her eyes. "We wouldn't get away with it."

"Well, we won't get away with it now," Caro grumbled, glaring at Ledge as if it was his own personal failing that they as a group hadn't contrived to swindle the British government at an earlier stage. "We need to think of something."

"Why don't we just advertise me as a Russian bride to some sad old man on the internet?" Nadia suggested, sarcastically. "He'll save money on the shipping, because I'm already here!"

"Well," Caro said, winking as she reached for her wine glass. "Okay, it's not the *best* idea, but *in theory…*"

"Seems to me we just need to find some guy called Matthew and make him fall in love with Nads," Ledge proposed, returning to the living room with a cold beer.

Nadia spluttered again. "I'm sorry, I'm not quite sure if you guys are joking or not?"

"At the very least, we should all keep our eyes out for any eligible British citizens called Matthew," Holly argued, ignoring Nadia's protests. "There's no harm in that!"

"Yeah," Ledge agreed. "There must be thousands of guys called Matthew hanging around South London."

"Well, at least *a handful* of them anyway," Caro granted.

Chapter 2

Alex

When Alex got to the pub it was already heaving, people sitting hunched around tiny tables, in some places doubled-up to a chair. Lila must have been there for a while. She was sitting meekly, trying not to make eye contact with her fellow patrons, who were all looking quite squashed and annoyed that this slip of a thing was hogging a table for four all to herself.

Lila raised her eyes as Alex reached her and pulled the chair opposite out from underneath the table. "Hey!"

"Hey," he replied, with a smile. "Wow, it's busy in here!" he said, before cursing himself for his usual inanity in pointing out the obvious. "Do you want a drink?" he offered, by way of trying to recover, despite the fact that Lila had a full glass in front of her. Two, in fact.

"No, thanks," Lila answered. "In fact, you might as well have Rory's beer." She nodded towards the second drink on the table. "He just texted me to say he's going to be stuck at work."

"Oh." Alex realised he was still standing and hurriedly dropped down on the chair. "How late?"

Lila thumbed the condensation off of the swell of her wine glass. "Late," she answered, flatly.

"Oh." Alex reached for the beer. "Well, do you still wanna…?"

Lila shrugged. "Yeah. Well, I mean, I've already paid entry for a team. We might have a bit of an uphill struggle, though, a team of two against all these teams of six." She gestured around them at all the small groups of clearly quiz-hardened folk.

"We can do it," Alex smiled at her. "I have faith." Lila smiled back and took a sip of her wine.

They had made a good start on their second round of drinks by the time the quiz master came around with blank answer sheets and a selection of lidless biros. "Just the two of you?" he asked.

Alex looked up, mildly annoyed; he'd forgotten that the actual quiz part of the pub quiz evening would eventually crop up and spoil his alone-time conversation with Lila. "Yeah."

The quiz master looked awkward. "Well, we say that the teams should have a minimum of three members and a maximum of six…" He pointed to where this was helpfully stated in the small print on the bottom of the answer sheets, which of course they were only just seeing for the first time.

Lila sighed. "Really?"

"Well, we are waiting for a third, but we're not sure when he'll get here…" Alex added obligingly. The quiz master looked sceptical.

"Do you mind if I put you with another loose two in the meantime?" he asked. "They came in a team of eight." He gestured across the bar to where a large, loud group of people were crowded around a small circular table on an assortment of chairs and stools.

Lila looked across at Alex for him to make the decision. Alex sighed. "Yeah, sure. Okay."

"Great!" the quiz master beamed. "I'll send two of them over. Thanks guys!" He left them a mildly chewed pen and moved off in the direction of the large group.

"Well, we've just doubled our chance of winning, at least!" Lila said optimistically.

"And halved the potential prize money," Alex pointed out. Lila laughed.

"Who knows? Think positive. They might be rocket scientists."

"Brain surgeons, actually," the brunette who'd appeared at the side of their table cheerfully interjected as she set down a half-empty bottle of red wine; a blonde carrying their two wine glasses brought up the rear.

Alex laughed awkwardly. "Hi." He really wasn't that great with strangers.

"Hi," echoed the brunette. "Cheers for letting us cramp your quizzing style. We'll earn our keep, I promise."

"Does anyone want any wine?" offered the blonde. She had the slightest burr of a European accent, soft against her vowels.

"No thanks, I'm on the white," Lila declined politely, indicating her own glass. Alex watched her size up the newcomers, although the smile never wavered on her face. "I'm Lila."

"Alex."

"Holly and Nadia," introduced the blonde, indicating first her friend and then herself.

Nadia
Nadia tried not to take offense that she and Holly had been jettisoned from their team by immediate collective consensus. But it did make it important that – even if this new team couldn't win outright – they at least needed to place higher than Caro and her merry band of fellow art students. It was a matter of pride.

Trying to sound suitably competitive, but a couple of shades under scary, Nadia explained the situation to the other half of the dream team. The guy was nice and full of shy smiles, with reddish brown hair, attractive in a preppy way with his square-framed glasses and slim-fit suit. His girlfriend was pretty, honey-blonde, with dark eyes and eyebrows. She was also ever-so-slightly abrasive, but – then again – Nadia guessed that the girl had just had her date crashed, so she should probably cut her some slack.

"Nadia, your accent." The Lila girl tilted her head to one side like a curious bird. "It's cute. Is it Welsh or something?"

Holly guffawed with laughter. Nadia dipped her head slightly, hoping that her wine glass would conceal her own bad-mannered smirk. "Not quite!" she managed, after a moment.

"That's a new one!" Holly laughed. "Usually she gets French. Or Polish."

"I come from a city called Perm," Nadia explained. Holly snorted again; the name of Nadia's hometown was always a point of great amusement for her. Lila continued to look blank. Nadia sighed. "Russian," she clarified. "I'm Russian."

The guy, Alex, came to an immediate pause, his beer held halfway to his mouth. "Russian?" he repeated, as if it was a nationality he'd never ever heard of. "Russian?"

Nadia and Holly exchanged a look. "Yup. Rrrrrussian." Nadia drew her rolling R out in the standard Bond villain accent, rolling her eyes to match.

"She's lived here like, her entire life, though," Holly jumped in, immediately defensive. "She should be getting her British citizenship soon."

"Citizenship?" Lila echoed.

"It's not citizenship, not exactly. Not yet." Nadia shot Holly a look; that girl had no filter and a tendency to massively exaggerate. "It's technically called your 'Indefinite Leave to Remain'. You know, as in you can remain in the country." She shrugged her shoulders depreciatively in a "you know how it is" gesture; not that any of them would know how it was.

Across the table, Alex placed his pint glass back squarely on the table; he hadn't taken a drink from it.

Alex
A Russian girl, called Nadia, living around Clapham, with a slightly eccentric-seeming friend called Holly, midway through an application for her Indefinite Leave to Remain. This was – let's be honest, more than likely – THE Nadezhda Osipova come to life in front of him, casually drinking red wine; for a city of several million people, London sure was a bitch for this type of thing.

As the girls steered the conversation towards what their team name should be called, Alex surreptitiously tilted his head to better remind himself of the name of the pub he was in by reading the header of the bar snack menu. The Bellevue. *"If Nadia is removed from the country, you will be breaking up an epic pub quiz team. We win the Bellevue's quiz almost every week and would have serious trouble finding a replacement with Nadia's niche knowledge."* Hmm. For such an epic pub quizzer she sure had been palmed off by her team pretty bloody quickly!

As anticipated, his boss, Donnelly, had taken one look at Nadia's immigration history and rejected her. If there was such a thing as a huge Home Office rubber stamp that stamped a big red ink DENIED onto paper applications, Alex was pretty sure he would have used that. But Nadia Osipova had somehow struggled on. Her application was reviewed as part of the quality control system by Donnelly's own line manager. Although you wouldn't know it from that woman's fierce face and aggressively clacking high heels, she obviously had a heart, and had – like Alex – seen the potential that this particular claimant under Article 8, pointing her towards the Border Agency appeals procedure.

"Okay guys," called the quiz master through a crackling microphone, "we're going to make a start with Round One, General Knowledge. Question one…"

The three girls fell immediately silent, dipping their heads together close to the answer sheet, competitiveness kicking in. Alex tried to study Nadia, but her hair was loose and fell across her profile like a veil. There definitely was a touch of the exotic about her that had nothing to do with the slightly blurred accent. She was pale, but the sort of pale that would be classed as "pale and interesting", rather than a pale that suggested nausea, with light-blue eyes and natural ash-blonde hair like a fairytale princess. Lila – whose blondeness required an expensive six-weekly maintenance programme – was no doubt massively jealous. Holly gave a jokey answer to question two and Nadia laughed, reaching to tuck the fall of hair behind her ear. How weird that she was a real person. It suddenly felt a little seedy that he knew so many intimate details about this complete stranger; Alex decided he wanted some more of his beer after all.

Nadia

The quiz master announced a twenty-minute break between rounds three and four, allowing people to pop to the toilets or – more commercially concerning – top up their drinks at the bar. Nadia scanned back over the answers they'd so far come up with and nodded to herself, pretty impressed. They weren't doing too badly at all, she reckoned. Hopefully better than Caro and crew, anyway, and the geography round – Holly's time to shine – was yet to come.

Lila had thawed towards them, if her trip to the bar to bring them another bottle of red wine was any indication anyway. Nadia thanked her profusely, ignoring the now-customary burn of annoyance that this sort of charity meant so much to her these days; she was sure that Lila was doing it because the conversation had wound round to the fact that couldn't currently earn a wage and how tight everything had become as a result.

"I think it's disgraceful," Lila said, as she poured her two new friends liberally large glasses of wine. "I mean, it's not like you're here and you can't speak a word of English. Or you're fresh off the back of a lorry from Calais. Or you're a benefit cheat. Or a health tourist come to take advantage of the NHS. I mean," she looked Nadia up and down, "you are pretty much *English*." She said it like it was the best compliment she could give; maybe it was. Lila turned to Alex who was rather quieter – and soberer – than she. "Can't you do something about this?" she asked him.

Alex's eyes flashed up, wary. "Me? What could I do?"

"Well, I don't know, you could speak to the Home Secretary, or something," Lila wheedled.

Alex laughed. "Lils, you have a very high opinion of me and

my job if you think I'm desk buddies with the Home Secretary."

"But you work for the Home Office, don't you?" Lila insisted. Holly immediately sat up and surveyed Alex with interest. Nadia cringed. Typical! She'd been sitting here bad-mouthing her lot under the British Government in front of one of its civil servants. Fantastic.

"You work for the Home Office?" Holly asked Alex. "Wow! So, come on, spill! What's the inside track with this Indefinite Leave to Remain stuff, then? What does she have to do?"

Alex visibly squirmed. "I – I don't really know anything about immigration. I'm just an administrator."

"Holly, leave him alone," Nadia scolded. "The guy came to play a quiz, not be interrogated by randomers." She shot Alex an apologetic smile.

"Two minutes 'til round four, guys," called the quiz master.

"Come on, guys, let's kill it," cheered Holly, suitably distracted. "We can do it!"

"Yeah!" Lila agreed. "That first prize money has our name on it."

"It's only twenty-five quid each," Alex pointed out, with a smile. "I wouldn't put in your yacht order just yet."

"Well, to me," Nadia said quietly, "that £25 is a couple of days' worth of food money I don't have to scrounge from Holly or my parents." She laughed awkwardly to defuse the pity her words had stirred. Alex turned to look at her, softly sympathetic.

"I am so, so sorry guys," the tall stranger blustered as he rushed up to the table. Nadia and Holly watched, bemused, as he dipped his head to meet the lips that Lila had offered up to him. Nadia looked at Alex, confused; he was already looking back at her, amusement on his face, obviously well aware that she had thought he and Lila were a couple. The new guy cast around himself for a spare chair, but the pub was still absolutely packed. Seeing his predicament, Lila hopped up, exchanging her own chair for his knees.

Alex leaned forwards. "Nadia, Holly, this is Rory," he introduced, courteously.

"He got caught up at work," Lila clarified from his lap.

"Hey, I was only a few hours late!" Rory defended himself amiably. "But I see you've replaced me." He shot Alex a wide grin.

"Round four, question one," the quiz master called, before Alex could respond to the tease.

Alex

Maybe it was the addition of Rory's cache of general knowledge. Maybe everyone pushed the boat out a tiny bit more in order to get Nadia her food money. Or maybe they were always on track to win. Either way, win they did, and Rory – all flourishing generosity – declined his fifth of the pot and ordered another round to boot. Holly and Nadia might have been keen to get back to their mates now the necessity of the quiz was over, but the fresh bottle of red kept them anchored where they were, even though Rory immediately started boring them to death after they'd politely asked what it was that he did that had kept him in the office so late on a Friday night.

"But the Home Office," Nadia said, turning to smile at Alex, leaving Holly to fend for herself in the tedious conversation with Rory and Lila about the dizzying pressures of trainee law. "That must be exciting?"

Alex smiled back. "More exciting than law, anyway," he threw over his shoulder loudly at Rory, who ignored him. "What did you do, before…?" He trailed off, unsure how to finish the sentence; "*before the organisation I work for took away your livelihood and began aggressively vetting you like you're some sort of terrorist threat?*"

Nadia sighed. "Oh God! I've been jumping from work visa to student visa and back to work visa for so long, my CV is a total headache. I feel like I really have done it all. From working at an accountancy firm to working in a chippie…"

"A chippie? Did you just try for a really British-sounding job to look good on your application?" Alex teased.

"No, that would be the time I worked at the box office in the Royal Albert Hall," Nadia laughed. "And anyway, now I volunteer in the Clapham Oxfam." She shrugged. "I don't get paid, but at least I don't come home smelling like vinegar. Mothballs instead."

"There's always a silver lining, huh?"

"I like to think so." The pair smiled at one another again. And Alex felt the thought as it arrived – this was the right moment to let Nadia know that he'd been a part of her application process.

"You know, it's really weird, but…"

"Hey, we're moving on," interrupted a dark-haired someone, placing her palms on the table between them, angling her body towards Nadia and Holly and ignoring Alex; she already had her handbag on her shoulder, ready to go.

Holly looked up at her friend. "Where are you going?" she asked.

"Not sure. We were just going to walk down the high street and take a look at what's going on," the newcomer answered. "Maybe Bison?"

"Hey, do you guys fancy coming to Bison & Bird?" Nadia asked the table.

Lila beamed. "I *love* their cocktails," she answered, eagerly. "They've got one that tastes like Love Hearts." Holly and Nadia's friend gave Nadia a sideways look.

"Caro, this is Lila – and her boyfriend, Rory – and her, er, Alex," Nadia introduced on cue.

"Nice to meet you," Caro said, politely but dismissively. "Good quizzing," she congratulated, before turning back to Nadia. "Are you coming?"

In response Nadia looked at Alex, expectantly; she really did want them to come, he realised. And why shouldn't he go? It wasn't as if he had big plans for this evening. Besides, it felt very much as though the universe was telling him that he and Nadia Osipova were meant to be friends. He opened his mouth to accept.

"Another time maybe, girls?" Rory answered before he could. "We haven't partaken of a tray of shots yet. Apparently it's only a tenner here!" Nadia looked back at Alex, as if he might countermand Rory.

"Yeah, another time," he echoed.

"Okay." Nadia rose to her feet, her expression slightly disappointed. "I suppose an eight-quid cocktail can't compete with a tray of discount shots," she granted.

Holly stood too, seeing off the last dregs of her glass of wine as she did. "Great meeting you guys." She smiled at them, teeth extra white against her red wine-stained lips. "Thanks for being excellent quiz-team companions."

"We should do it again," Nadia said, sincerely, as she zipped up her bag, still looking at Alex as if she was expecting him to say something.

"See you around," Rory said cheerfully. And then, just as quickly and randomly as she'd entered his life, Nadia waved at him and left it.

Chapter 3

Alex

The fourth Jagerbomb was sitting rather sourly in Alex's stomach. Across the table, Rory had his face pressed into the space between Lila's neck and shoulder, making her giggle and squirm against him. The PDA between them always got worse when they'd been drinking; Alex looked away.

The chair that Nadia had been sitting on had long been pinched by an opportunistic bar patron, dragged off to another table, but the empty space there remained, looming large between him and his friends, who – quite frankly – wouldn't exactly be missing him if he *had* gone to Bison & Bird after all. As if to illustrate this point, Lila drew her body slightly back from Rory's and murmured something meant only for him to hear, her bottom lip grazing his earlobe – not that Alex could have heard her over the noise of the bar anyway. Rory listened to his girlfriend patiently, smiled and moved his head to kiss her again as she finished speaking. Alex had watched Lila be kissed like that so many times by now he almost fancied he knew exactly how it felt.

Distracting himself from that maddening chain of thought, Alex pulled his mobile from his pocket and swiped the touch screen with his thumb to wake it. He tapped his fingers against its frame. Surely some of his old mates would be out doing something, somewhere in this great wide city? He scrolled through his contacts list – past old uni friends and colleagues and people whose surnames he only knew because they were linked through his Facebook app – looking for someone suitable to text. Nobody jumped out at him. He guessed he'd spent a lot of time hanging around with just Rory and Lila over the past year, and as a result he'd sort of dropped out of general circulation. Going through his phone was highlighting this rather painfully, and Alex suddenly wasn't entirely sure whether watching Lila get kissed had been worth giving up the remnants of his social life for. He had to get the hell out of here.

The last two Jagerbombs sat between them on their sticky plastic tray, Lila having abstained, meaning he and Rory had been left with five each. Alex stood and reached for one; Rory and Lila didn't budge from one another's faces as he downed it purposefully, the combination of alcohol and energy drink streaming stupidity down through his body. He reached for the last one; *that* got Rory's attention.

"Hey," he protested, still half-pressed to Lila's throat. "S'mine." Alex did the final shot even faster than he'd done the one before and brought the empty doubles glass back down to the table top with a satisfying clatter.

"I'm off," he said, without preamble.

Rory's eyebrows creased together. "You're off?" he repeated.

"Hang on a minute and we'll come home with you, then," offered Lila, reaching underneath the table with her foot for her handbag.

"Oh no, I'm not going home. I'm just going to meet up with some mates." Alex waved his mobile phone as if to give the impression that it was crammed full of texts from exciting people inviting him exciting places. "Catch up with you guys tomorrow," he said, before Rory and Lila could invite themselves along to his fictitious evening. "Have a good rest of the night."

"Alex," Rory called after him. Alex didn't turn back, but somehow he could still picture his friends' incredulous expressions.

When he arrived outside on the pavement, the fresh air immediately washed some of the Jagerbomb impulsivity away; Alex swore under his breath. Now what? He couldn't go home for a while after what he'd just said. There probably were friends in his phone book who'd be pleased (if a little nonplussed) to see him, but latching himself on to them just felt a little too much like that same old third-wheel lie.

Moving carefully around the groups of drunken merrymakers, the queues at the bus stops and snaking out of small fried-chicken shops, Alex steadfastly picked his way down the high street in the opposite direction from the bus stop to his flat. He slowed as he saw the neon sign for the Bison & Bird cocktail bar glowing in the distance like the answer that he was searching for. It had been about an hour. Surely they'd have moved on by now? Maybe it was worth checking it out. Or was he being a tad stalkery?

But he couldn't shake that sliding-doors feeling. Nadia had been so friendly. And nice. And really rather pretty. And wasn't life meant to be about taking chances – or something like that?

Being a lone guy, he had to queue for a couple of minutes whilst the bouncer waved small groups of half-dressed women in ahead of him. Then he was ID-ed for good measure. Finally, feeling markedly insignificant, he was waved through to the darkness of the bar beyond.

Bison was a long and narrow space, all done in dark, shiny wood with rows upon rows of bottles and optics gleaming on their backlit shelves behind the bar, harried-looking bartenders rushing between them. Alex looked for the paleness of Nadia's hair in the darkness, but the open space in front of him had become an impromptu dance floor and he couldn't see beyond the mass of whirling people. Doggedly he pushed through the dancers to reach the booths at the back of the room. A brunette in a red dress grabbed his hand and made him spin her around as she laughed, startling a laugh out of him too. Released by his impromptu partner, Alex moved into the clearer space beyond the

33

dancers, still smiling. The energy drink and the bass from the DJ's speakers felt as if it was drumming in his blood, making him feel as though he could do anything, be anyone, and as if, for once, he was meant to be exactly where he was.

He clocked Nadia almost immediately, standing out in the gloom with her blonde hair and sky-blue dress. She opened her mouth and he could almost hear her laugh over the boom of the music track. The guy she was with was tall – taller even than Rory – and fair-haired, with the sort of artful stubble that would make Alex look as if he was homeless. The guy bent and spoke leisurely into Nadia's ear, touching one of his hands to her hip in a proprietary way. And just like that, the evening's buzz left his veins, and Alex was just the third wheel once again.

Nadia
The guy's Russian was so appalling, Nadia couldn't help but laugh.

"*Zdravstvyite*," she sounded-out the word for him.

"Zurdraztevee," he repeated into her ear, causing her to laugh again.

"How long ago did you say this holiday to St Petersburg was?" she teased.

"A while ago," he admitted with a smile. "So, how would I ask you if I could buy you a drink in Russian, then?"

Nadia shot him an amused look. "*Mozhno tebia ugostit*?" she answered obediently. "But *net, spasibo!*" she declined, nodding at her half-full cocktail. "I've already got one."

"Well, when that one's finished, then," the guy grinned, undeterred. "Consider it as payment for the Russian lesson."

Nadia laughed. "Well, when you put it that way. I'm Nadia, by the way!"

"Matt."

Nadia blinked. "Matt?" she echoed. "Seriously? Matt? MATT?"

"Er, yeah."

"Your name is Matt?" she repeated again. "Genuinely? Matt?"

She looked around herself suspiciously. "Has Caro put you up to this?" she asked him. Seriously, what were the odds?

"Er, no…" Matt looked at her a little less appreciatively and a little more as though she might be mental. "My name is seriously, genuinely Matt. Why? What's wrong?"

Knowing that explaining about her fake visa boyfriend would just confirm any suspicions that she was crazy, Nadia just laughed again. "It's a long story," she brushed him off. "Nice to meet you. Matt." She looked at him a little closer, mentally ticking off boxes as she noted his tallness, blondness, handsomeness… *And he was called Matt*. Finally, the universe seemed to be giving back; here was karma, wearing a Lacoste polo neck and drinking bottled lager. Delivery for Nadia, one boyfriend, please sign here.

"Hey!" Holly barrelled into her, grinning, sloshing cold drops of water onto Nadia's bare arm from the melted ice in her empty cocktail glass.

Nadia glared at her friend, using her free hand to steady her arm, noting with interest that Matt had very gentlemanly done the same. "Hols," she said warningly into her flatmate's ear, raising her eyebrows meaningfully, "this is *Matt*."

Holly ignored her, speaking over her to boot. "Look who I bumped into," she laughed, pulling Alex from the Bellevue quiz out from behind her with a flourish, like a magician pulling something from a hat.

Alex

Time apparently flies when you're forced into awkward proximity with strangers you've semi-stalked to a bar. It was getting late and the crowds were thinning out, most leaving to either make the last Tube or to join the queue for the nearby nightclub before it reached pointless proportions. Caro and one of her fawning tagalongs had usefully commandeered one of the larger booths. Alex rested his head against the clammy leather, feeling the bass from the DJ's speakers travelling through it to fizz against the back of his neck.

The longer he spent in Nadia's company, the more he liked her. She laughed without covering her mouth, danced so energetically that her makeup smudged into the creases of her eyes and her hair stuck to her forehead. He'd danced with her for twenty minutes straight, in the thrum of the dance floor, only copying her movements at first and then simply just letting go and moving however he wanted to. He'd danced in a circle with Holly and Caro and the others, complete strangers, accepting the sips of various cocktails from proffered straws, the crash of the liquor and the sugar keeping him going until he was out of breath from all the shouting over the music and dancing and laughing.

Nadia was over by the rear bar, queuing in formation with Caro and Holly, hoping that surely one of them would reach service soon. Glancing over her shoulder, she must have noticed that Alex was looking over because she shot him a smile.

"So, how do you know them?" asked Matt, nodding towards the girls. Alex felt inexplicably annoyed by the question.

"Met doing a pub quiz," he answered shortly, not feeling that there was any need to specify that the said pub quiz had taken place that very same evening.

"Ah, cool, cool." Matt drummed his hands nervously against his thighs. Alex wasn't even sure why this guy was still hanging around. His friends had left ages ago. "So." Matt dipped his head conspiratorially. "What's the deal here, with you and Nadia?"

"Deal?" Alex echoed, confused.

"You know," Matt urged, glancing across at the bar, where the girls were still waiting to be served. "Am I stepping on any toes here? If I ask Nadia for her number and take her out, I mean."

"Oh. The deal." Alex blinked. "Don't worry about it. There's no deal."

"It's just you guys seem like you're close," Matt explained, visibly relieved. "And she's a really cool girl, I thought for sure there'd be someone cockblocking me, you know?"

Alex blinked again. "No. No cockblocking here." He laughed to himself. "I get enough of that at home," he confessed, loose-lipped from excessive cocktail consumption.

"You what?"

"My flatmate," Alex clarified. "Cockblocker of the highest order. There's this girl, right? The girl of my dreams. We lost contact and then met up again." He lifted his hands expansively. "A year later and most nights I can hear him having sex with her."

Matt winced. "Man, that sucks."

Alex sighed, his good mood evaporating like the sweat off his skin now that he'd stopped dancing. "Yup," was all he said.

Nadia

A Facebook Friend Request notification slid unceremoniously onto Nadia's mobile. She hadn't been wholly convinced she'd even receive one. When Alex had suddenly announced he was leaving Bison last night she'd asked him for his surname so that she'd be able to find him on Facebook. He'd smiled and said that he'd add her instead; she'd be easier to find, her surname being much less common than his. Matt's Friend Request had arrived before she and Holly had even reached home that night. She'd been waiting on Alex's all day.

Accepting the request, Nadia scrolled with interest through Alex's profile. There wasn't all that much to see, unlike her own borderline-embarrassing page, full of selfies and check-ins. Alex was just as big an enigma to her now as he had been when she'd sat down at his table at the Bellevue. But still, there was something there, something drawing her in in the turn of his mouth as he laughed, or in the brittle sort of shyness he wore like a bad coat. She'd liked him.

After Alex had gone, Matt had taken Nadia out onto the dance floor for the final ten or so songs. It wasn't the same as dancing with Alex had been. Matt held her by the hips, trying to make her move in time with what he was doing, whereas with Alex it had all been free and easy and they'd danced in careless synchronicity, even though their bodies rarely touched. And then he'd kissed her, for the entire second half of Nickelback's 'Rockstar', which was nice, but also a little annoying, as it was one of her favourite songs.

Holly had been jubilant during their short walk home. "I can't believe it," she'd kept repeating, tipping her head back and shouting it up at the stars as if they were in on it. "I can't bloody believe it! How much is this *meant to be*?"

Nadia had just laughed. "It's just a coincidence. You've been watching too many bad films."

"But WHAT a coincidence," Holly had insisted. "Of all the names Ledge could have pulled out of his arse. And here he is! Your future husband! Conveniently British and conveniently called Matthew and conveniently *well into you*!"

"Hols," Nadia had protested, laughing and pushing her friend on the arm. But her good humour was infectious.

"So when you guys kissed, did he taste like crumpets and cricket and cream teas? Or just like a visa?" Holly had asked, mock-serious.

"Holly!" Nadia had glanced behind them just to double-check that Matt wasn't somehow within earshot. "I don't know what's going to happen between me and Matt, but if he overhears you saying shit like that, I've got a pretty good guess that the answer will be 'sod all'!"

"No, it's meant to be. This is it, Nads – it's what you deserve. Everything's going to be alright now," she'd insisted, earnest with relief. And Nadia had felt her eyes go hot. She gave her best friend a clumsy, one-armed hug and kissed her on the cheek.

"What a good night," Holly had summarised after a moment. "Did you get Alex's number too?"

"No, but he's going to add me on Facebook."

"Okay." Holly had dropped her voice conspiratorially. "I think he might fancy me or something," she'd admitted.

Nadia had laughed. "What makes you think that?"

"Well, he ditched his friends and full-on stalked us to Bison."

"We'd invited him!" Nadia had protested. But maybe, on

reflection…

"Has Alex added you yet?" Nadia was pulled back to the present and looked up to where Holly was leaning through the doorway part-way into her bedroom.

"What's it matter to you? I thought you weren't interested," Nadia teased.

Holly rolled her eyes. "Please, I'm not. You know me. I like a bad boy!" That was the understatement of the century. "And Alex is hardly a bad boy." But that was another one.

"Hey, he's quite sexy in a suit-and-tie sort of way," Nadia shrugged. "And he's got gorgeous eyes."

"I hadn't even noticed," Holly admitted. "And I don't know why you did, when you had Matt's, your future husband, eyes there to be looking into."

Nadia rolled her eyes. "Okay, I guess Matt's eyes were alright too."

"I wonder if your kids will have his colouring or yours?"

"Hols, please." Nadia gestured at her laptop. "He hasn't even poked me on Facebook yet. Children aren't exactly imminent."

Holly squinted at the laptop screen. "Who actually still pokes on Facebook?" she asked, incredulous.

"I think it's been so long that it's actually acceptable again now, it's retro or something," Nadia told her, authoritatively. "Maybe I should poke Alex," she decided.

Holly laughed. "Okay. I'll see you when you get back from 2006." She saluted dismissively as she slipped back into the hallway.

Alex

This was the first summer Alex was really spending time with Lila. Sure, there'd been parties and beach days and road trips in the warm weather throughout the three years they'd been in the same group of friends at university, but it wasn't quite the same thing. He'd had Alice back then, and that had blocked him from ever getting around to thinking about Lila in the way he did now. And last year, her relationship with Rory was too new, but this summer everything was much more comfortable. Including her attire.

"God." Lila exhaled heavily and rolled her tank top another inch up her stomach. "It's so hot." She sank down further into the sofa cushions. "Are there any windows left that we can open?"

"Nope, we've got them all," Alex told her apologetically, staring anywhere than at Lila, who seemed to consist of an impossible amount of naked arms and legs, bare creamy skin from all angles. He took a distracted sip from his glass of coke, which had hit room temperature in the space of five minutes. It was the very last from Rory's litre bottle, but, well, you snooze you lose – literally.

Lila blew strands of hair from her face listlessly. "I wish Rory would just get up. It can't be any hotter outside."

"Well, if he really drank another tray of those shots after I left, I doubt we're going to be seeing him this side of three o'clock, to be honest."

Lila made a cross noise. "I might just go home, you know. What's the point of me just hanging around here?" Alex must have allowed his hurt to flash on his face as Lila's expression immediately softened. "Aside from obviously getting to hang out with you. But you know what I mean." She smiled sadly. "Sometimes I feel like it's you and me who are the couple."

She did this, sometimes – he could swear it was on purpose. She created little openings by saying things like that, looked at him through her eyelashes as if she was expecting something. He wished he could work out what it was that she wanted from him. It was too much to hope it would be the same thing that he wanted from her. There'd been once or twice at uni where he'd gotten the feeling she was interested in him. But maybe that was just the arrogant sort of guy he'd been back then.

"Come on." Alex got to his feet. "If we're going to just doss around and waste our Saturday we might as well do it in the sun on the Common. Grab your flipflops."

Nadia

Matt appeared to be wearing the same Lacoste polo shirt he'd been wearing the night they'd met in Bison. Of course, it was entirely possible that he owned more than the one – did they come in double packs as standard, she wondered?

Realising belatedly that Matt had asked her a question and was waiting attentively for her response, Nadia stalled for time by taking a large drink from her wine glass.

"Oh, totally," she decided to go with, relieved when Matt just nodded enthusiastically.

"I know, right?"

As far as first dates went, it was a smidgeon underwhelming; it was mostly down to her to be fair. Not wanting to just assume that Matt would be bankrolling the refreshments – but unable to afford anything much – Nadia had suggested the Bankside All Bar One, where she knew you could always get a voucher for a sharing platter and a bottle of plonk for under eleven quid. The so-called Sauvignon was acidic and warm as bath water against her teeth – her own fault for ordering the house white and not insisting on an ice bucket. She swilled down another mouthful. She had a bit of drink envy. Matt was drinking a nice-smelling fruit cider from a slim-necked, fat-bottomed vintage bottle. Ironically, he'd said that he thought men drinking wine was effeminate.

What was she doing here? This was hardly the right time to start dating somebody, even if they were tall, gorgeous and conveniently named…

Her thoughts had wandered again; she forced them back to what Matt was saying just a moment too late.

"So what about you?" he asked with a wide smile. Shit! There was no fudging around that one. Sighing she put her wine glass down.

"I'm sorry, I just got totally distracted. What was the last thing you said?"

Matt's smile grew wider. "Only the very last thing?"

"I'm sorry," Nadia repeated. "It's so loud in here." Lie. Maybe if you were half-deaf. Matt's smile grew all the wider.

"Here, let's do this, then." He stood and dragged his chair from opposite her to next to her, reaching back to scoot his pretty cider bottle closer along the table. The scraping of the chair legs across the floor tiles drew attention from several tables over. Nadia saw a glossy city type in a fluffy pussy-bow blouse appraise Matt before dipping her head in closer towards her two friends to comment. They all then proceeded to stare across at them over the rims of their wine glasses.

Whereas she was normally pretty comfortable in herself, at that moment Nadia felt exceedingly rumpled next to Matt's Lacoste-clad glory. She wasn't sure how people who lived in year-round hot climates managed it, but the minute it got above twenty-four degrees she turned into a limp-haired, flush-faced state. She had agonised over the fact that the only clothing she could bear to put on her in this heat were linen sun-dresses, scantily short and pretty much see-through in the right light (which she very much hoped the bar didn't have). Still, Matt had greeted her with an appreciative look, told her she looked nice, and had kept his eyes politely on her face all night, ignoring the temptations of her loose spaghetti straps or mid-thigh hemline with aplomb.

Pussy-bow and her friends continued to look over shamelessly. Nadia very much hoped they were just fascinated by the gorgeous, perfect-looking couple and not wondering what the hell a godly stud like him was doing with a minger like her. *My hair's not actually greasy; I did wash it,* she wanted to rush over and assure them. *It was just really hot and sweaty on the Tube getting here…*

"Nadia?"

Matt had been talking to her again. Oh shit!

"I'm sorry," she babbled as she cast around for an explanation for her offensive inattention. "I, er, I think I know that girl. I was just trying to work out where from."

"Which girl?" Matt turned fully in his chair to look behind him. "Her?" He pointed straight at Pussy-bow, who panicked that she'd been caught staring and busied herself topping up her already full wine glass. Nadia cringed a little against her seat.

"Er, yeah, but actually I don't think I do know her, after all."

"Oh." Matt swivelled back to front in his seat and picked up his drink again. "Nadia, are you okay? You seem a little... nervous."

"Nervous?" Nadia echoed.

"Yeah." Matt smiled. "It's cute."

Bless him. He thought that she was just flustered and overwhelmed about being on a date with him, rather than just highly distractible that evening. To be honest, that's probably what he was used to, if Pussy-bow and co's reaction to him was anything to go by. Come on, Nadia, she told herself sternly. You have in front of you an absolutely drop-dead gorgeous guy who seems to be really into you and magically has the same name as your Fake Visa Boyfriend. The universe is throwing you a bone here. Take it, take it!

"So are you up for it?" Matt was saying as she tuned back in.

Fuck!

Chapter 4

Alex

He'd been trying to get through *The Girl With the Dragon Tattoo* since he'd been given it for Christmas, but he usually only managed about three paragraphs before he glazed over. The tatty paperback limp against his knees, he stared beyond the pages to the Tube carriage floor and wondered how many more evenings he'd have to work overtime before Donnelly noticed and put him forward for that promotion.

"I really enjoyed this series," someone said. It was the person who'd just got on at the last stop and sat in the seat next to him. "The film was absolute crap, though," she continued. Alex tensed. Only lunatics spoke to people on the Underground. Was he going to have to change carriages at the next stop? The girl laughed. "Don't you remember me?" And yes, he recognised the voice as he turned.

"Nadia, hey!" Alex greeted her, relieved and more than a little pleased. Nadia sat twisted towards him, smiling in the next seat, her bare legs stretched out in front of them, cork-heeled wedges almost touching the seats on the other side of the carriage, her hair in a pale, braided rope over one shoulder. "Wow, fancy bumping into you here! Small world."

"More like, small Northern Line," Nadia grinned. She took in his rather rumpled suit. "Are you just on your way home? It's late."

Alex scratched at the back of his neck, uncomfortably; it probably wasn't the best idea to talk about work with Nadia. "Oh, you know how it is. I'm gunning for promotion." He gave a self-depreciating smile. "Something a little less soul-numbing for a little more money."

"I don't think I could ever do a job like yours," Nadia told him, matter-of-factly. Alex refrained from pedantically pointing out that foreign nationals can't get jobs at the British Home Office. "Oh? Why's that?"

"Ah, it's like a big, grown-up, important job. I mean, you affect people's *lives*."

Alex scratched uncomfortably again. "I really don't do anything. I told you, I'm just the admin monkey. So," he hurried on, eager to change the subject, "what would your dream job be? I mean, if you could do anything."

"You mean, if I had a visa allowing me to work?" Nadia teased. She tilted her head, giving his question some thought. "I know you're meant to answer these questions with things like, soap star, prime minister, astronaut but..." She looked down at her hands against her thighs. "Lately I've been thinking I'd like to get involved in immigration issues..."

"I thought you said you couldn't deal with an important job?" Alex teased.

"No, I mean, I'd like to have a job where I could help people in my position. Going through the immigration ringer!" She rolled her eyes. "Give them advice, help them with their applications and appeals, that sort of thing. I mean, I don't know if I could actually ever become like, a full-on lawyer, but I could certainly work in translation to start with. Maybe teach Russian, or English to Russians!" She shrugged. "That sort of thing."

Alex, who would have probably genuinely answered that sort of question with "astronaut", felt rather silly and humbled.

"That sounds like a really good idea," he told her, sincerely. "And very worthy." He was rewarded by a full-on beam from Nadia.

"Ah, that's good to hear. You're the first person I've mentioned it to, so." The Tube slowed as it entered Stockwell station, the carriage almost emptying out as passengers changed onto the Victoria Line. "Anyway, I hope you've got a good dinner waiting for you when you get home. I trust Rory is being a good little housewife and cooking for his overtime-trodden flatmate?"

Alex pictured Rory wearing a ruffled pinny and fretfully stirring multiple pots on the hob and snorted. "I very much doubt that. My dinner plans consist of nipping into one of the many fine Middle Eastern takeaway dining establishments that Tooting boasts on my walk home."

Nadia crinkled her nose. "By 'Middle Eastern dining' do you mean a kebab shop?"

Alex nodded solemnly. "I do." He shrugged. "I don't even know if Rory's going to be in, to be honest! He might be round Lila's."

Nadia regarded him thoughtfully as she felt around in her bag for her Oyster card as the Tube sped up again, with the next stop her own. "Well, I've already eaten," she told him. "But I was going to hit Starbucks en route home and, to be honest, even a Starbucks toastie is going to be better for you than a kebab from Tooting High Street."

"You Clapham snob!" Alex pretended to be affronted. Nadia rolled her eyes, getting to her feet as the tube began to noticeably slow, swinging her bag onto her shoulder.

"Are you coming?" she asked him, with her hand on her hip and a small smile on her face. Alex closed his book decisively. Why not? It wasn't like he had anything in particular to go home to.

Nadia

"I hope you're not one of those 'I want a super-massimo soy latte, extra hot, extra foam, extra soy, extra latte, extra cup-holder please' people," Alex teased her, as they pushed open the glass door and entered the blessedly cool air-conditioned café beyond.

Nadia glared at him. "No, but there's nothing wrong with people knowing what they like. Besides," she sniffed, "'Massimo' is a Costa sizing and this is a Starbucks." Alex laughed and rolled his eyes at her. Across the tiled floor a harried barista in a long green apron looked over at them from where she was stacking chairs.

"We're closing in five minutes," she told them, accusingly, as if she suspected they were there to bed down for the night.

"Guess there will be no super-nutritious panini for me," Alex signed, gesturing to where the food shelves were already emptied. It was almost eight o' clock at night, of course Starbucks was closing.

Nadia winced. "Sorry. My bad. But to be honest, just air is still better for you than a takeaway kebab. Can we still get some drinks?" she asked the barista who looked towards the ceiling as if she was the most put-upon creature on the earth and mutely moved back behind the counter.

"Actually, it's still a bit too hot for coffee," she told Alex. "Could I have a Lime Refresher, please?" she asked the barista, taking care to be super-polite.

"Refresher? Isn't that a sweet?" Alex asked.

"Oh, it's a drink from their summer range. It's sort of like iced tea."

"It's made with real fruit and green coffee extract for a low-calorie boost of natural energy you can enjoy anywhere," the barista intoned in the most bored-sounding voice known to man, clearly reciting from her training script. Alex blinked at her.

"Er, sounds... great. Make that two of those thingies, then."

After a reasonably awkward exchange, where both tried to pay for the other, they each just paid for their own and left the miserable barista to her evening. Outside, the evening was still hot and sticky. Nadia sipped her drink through its straw.

"Well, go on then," she gestured at Alex's drink. "What do you think?"

Alex took a tentative sip, then a larger one. The fat ice cubes rattled inside the transparent plastic cup. "Hmm. Well, it's certainly 'refreshing'," was his blunt assessment.

Nadia laughed. "So you're not enjoying a boost of low-calorie natural energy right now?"

"Ask me again when I'm about halfway finished."

"Anyway, I'm sorry I dragged you away from your dinner plans for a drink that's a bit shit," Nadia apologised.

"I know, and it's not even an alcoholic one," Alex agreed solemnly.

"And we couldn't even sit in to drink them," said Nadia, gesturing behind them to where the barista had continued stacking up the chairs beyond the glass.

"So whereabouts do you live?" Alex asked her. Nadia blanched. She was enjoying his company and all – and she *had* been the one to drag him off the Tube three stops early – but she could imagine Holly's face if she suddenly arrived home with Alex in tow. Their flat was usually just on the embarrassing side of messy and there was more than the off-chance in this weather that Holly might be sitting on the sofa wearing only a vest top and knickers.

"Er." She gestured vaguely to the south-east.

"I can't bear the thought of getting back in that sauna of a Tube, even with my oh-so-refreshing drink," Alex explained. "I was going to walk towards Tooting over the Common. If that's on your way, I can walk you partway home."

Nadia felt stupid. Of course this very proper gentleman wasn't just inviting himself back to her digs.

"That sounds like a pretty great idea," she told him, turning on her heel in the direction of home. "A walk on Clapham Common of a summer's evening. Lovely!"

"Cool," Alex smiled, turning and falling into step beside Nadia as they moved off towards the green expanse ahead of them. "But I'm not going to lie to you, Nadia. When I reach Tooting, I am going to have the biggest, most disgusting kebab going."

Alex

"Oh, hang on." Nadia said, suddenly breaking off their conversation.

"I've just *got to*." She handed him her half-finished drink along with her little handbag and moved purposefully towards a small children's play area.

"I think it's locked up," Alex warned her, immediately noticing the shiny, large padlock holding the area's gate firmly in place. Nadia shot him a look over her shoulder as she reached with her foot for the top of the fencing. Alex glanced away politely as the hem of Nadia's dress rode up her leg, and by the time he looked back she was standing inside the small play park grinning at him.

"Well? Are you coming?"

Alex moved towards the fencing, dubiously. "Are we likely to get in trouble for this?" he asked.

Nadia shrugged, reaching over the fence and taking both drinks and her bag out of his hands. "I never have before."

"Before?" Alex studied the – admittedly very low – fencing carefully, testing its strength by putting his weight on it briefly. "Do you make a habit of breaking into playgrounds?"

"Just this one," Nadia told him solemnly. "Now stop being a baby, come on."

"I imagine it's locked up for a reason," Alex insisted, as he nervously swung one leg into place.

"Yes, to keep out dogs and teenagers," Nadia assured him, watching as he clumsily vaulted the barrier. "And we are neither." Alex surreptitiously checked his suit trousers for snags and rips as he pretended to dust them down. When he straightened, Nadia was looking at him with a little smile on her face. Without comment she handed him back his drink.

"Would you care for a seat?" she asked him, gesturing behind them as she dropped her handbag to the grass.

"More of a swing, really," Alex pointed out. Nadia ignored him, and sat down on the left-most swing, scudding her wedge heels through the tight-packed wood chipping that lay beneath them as she started swinging back and forth. Alex set his drink down to one side before settling on the second swing, holding on to both chains. Nadia wasn't even holding onto one; she smiled at him as she brought her drink up to her mouth.

"What's the matter?" she asked him. "Don't you know how to swing?"

"That sounds like a chat-up line from the seventies," Alex retorted. "But of course I know how to swing." Nadia raised an eyebrow at him and kicked off the ground a little harder, making Alex's stomach go all nervy about the fact that she still wasn't holding on.

"I always wanted to go over the bar when I was a kid," Nadia told him, looking wistfully up at the pole above them.

"That can't actually happen," Alex scoffed.

"Yes it can!" Nadia insisted. "I've seen it on YouTube."

"It defies the laws of physics," Alex argued.

"God!" Nadia laughed. She finally submitted to her perilous height by looping the arm that held her almost-finished drink around one of the swing chains. "Let's just put it this way. I sure hope my kids are the sort of kids that want to go over the bar, rather than automatically believe it's impossible."

"Are you saying that all of humanity splits into those who want to go over the bar and those who don't?" Alex teased. "That's deep, man!"

"No," Nadia shook her head emphatically. "But maybe I'm saying that humanity splits into those who dream about going over the bar and those that are too scared to try for it."

"Well." Alex laughed shortly. "That's a pretty damning assessment of my personality. And we've only just met!"

Nadia laughed too, looking sideways at him as she pushed herself higher and higher yet. "Okay, so that's a little black and white. But, it's true. I do think you could benefit from living life on the edge a little more, if you don't mind me saying."

"On the edge? Look at me. I'm trespassing, drinking some weird drink I've never even heard of before today, sitting on a swing and – okay, I'll admit it – I haven't been on a swing for at least ten years..."

"Really?" Nadia genuinely sounded surprised. "God, Alex! What do you do with your time?"

And Alex didn't answer, because he found he didn't really have one. They swung for a few moments in silence before Nadia broke the stalemate by dropping her now-empty plastic cup to the ground; the remaining ice clattered inside it.

"You know, Holly and I thought that Lila was your girlfriend, at first," she told him.

"I know," was all Alex replied.

"But, looking back, you didn't seem like a proper couple," Nadia continued. Alex flinched.

"Why's that?" he couldn't help but ask. "Do you think Lila is one of the 'over the bar'-type people, or something?"

Nadia laughed. "No, it's not that. But it didn't seem like..." She paused to choose her words carefully. "Like you were particularly comfortable, you know?"

Yup, Alex knew. He kicked off the ground a little harder, swinging completely forward for the first time, the soles of his shoes reaching free from the chipping. Ahead of him the sky was coral and pink as it chased the setting sun, all but disappeared into the west, sending their shadows yawning outwards behind them. It was still a tad too light for any stars to be visible, but it was getting late all the same. I must go home in a minute Alex told himself sternly. Instead:

"If you'd have told me when I first graduated and moved to London that I'd be doing all this overtime, I would have laughed in your face," Alex found himself admitting.

"Why?" Nadia asked, curious.

"Well, for a start, the Home Office was just meant to be CV filler, a good-looking first job, you know? I was meant to be doing something else by now."

"Like what?"

"I don't know. Something else." He couldn't seem to stop himself

51

talking all of a sudden. "I used to live with a whole bunch of guys," he continued. "It was a five-room house-share." Alex laughed at Nadia's exaggerated wince. "It wasn't that bad. It was a laugh. But one by one they all either moved out of London or shacked up with girlfriends – that sort of thing, you know. One got made redundant and had to move back in with his parents in Devon. Poor guy's still there. It's been almost three years."

Nadia winced again. "Poor guy," she agreed.

"Anyway, by that time we'd downsized to a two-bed so I was on my lonesome. And I met Rory by advertising on Spare Room dot com." Alex smiled. "He took said spare room, although first he bollocked me for advertising the flat as being in Balham when it is clearly in Tooting. And we get on great and all, don't get me wrong but... since he met Lila, I guess I'm sort of waiting for him to move on too. And he and Lila are sort of the only people I spend all that much time with at the moment, so, that's, well... it's going to suck."

Nadia had slowed her swinging to listen to him. She had her head rested against one of the swing chains as she looked at him sympathetically. He hated being looked at like that. Why was he even talking about this stuff anyway? And to somebody he barely even knew. Alex dragged his feet through the wood chipping to slow his swing down.

"What a pair we are," Nadia said suddenly. "You, scared of being left by people; me, scared of being made to leave."

"Oh, ignore me," Alex told her, growing more and more self-conscious by the minute. Why was it so stupidly easy to run your mouth off whilst on children's play equipment? "I'm just moaning. Sorry for all this 'I've got nobody to play with, boohoo' shit. Don't mind me. I've just got the London Blues."

"Oh no, you can't blame London," Nadia told him firmly. "None of this is London's fault!"

"It's much harder to be lonely in close-knit towns and villages," Alex retorted, immediately regretting his choice of words when he saw Nadia's face soften when he said "lonely". "Although, to be honest, my most fulfilling relationship would probably still be the one with my PlayStation, no matter where I lived!" he joked, trying to get the conversation back on a more even keel.

Nadia responded by finally taking hold of both of the swing chains and using them to propel herself even higher. And for a brief moment, he did actually believe she might be able to go over the bar.

"Well, I have a proposition for you," she said from high above him.

"What sort of a proposition?" Alex asked suspiciously, curious despite himself.

"I'm sorry, I can't hear you properly," Nadia called out cheerfully. "You're going to have to come up here."

Alex, by now pretty much stationary, looked up where Nadia was reaching the apex of her swing, what seemed like miles above him. "Ha. Funny," he dead-panned. "What's this proposition?"

"Can't, hear, you," Nadia sang, as she pushed herself higher and higher. Alex continued to stare at her, incredulous. Finally he sighed.

"Fine." He kicked off from the ground and started swinging again. "So...?"

Nadia looked down at him and laughed. "That's pathetic. Higher!" she ordered. Alex sighed again and pulled the swing chains backwards in order to push on higher. Although he was still nowhere near Nadia's dizzying heights, she seemed to appreciate his effort and take pity on him.

Nadia

"I'm going to help you – sort of like a life guru," she told him, matter-of-factly.

After a moment's pause, Alex spat out a laugh; whatever he'd been expecting her to say, it clearly wasn't that.

"No, I'm serious!" Nadia insisted.

"I bet you are!" Alex laughed. "Thanks, but no thanks."

"No, really. Once, Caro had me make all of her decisions for a month, just to test it out. We saw it on an episode of 'Friends'."

"You want to make all my decisions for me?" Alex asked her, clearly amused. "How will that work?"

"No, in this instance I'm just going to force you to live a little. Try new things, have new experiences, meet new people."

"Well, you're off to a good start; I've hit all three since the moment I met you," Alex muttered. He didn't even seem to notice that he was swinging higher than he ever had before, which Nadia decided to take as a good sign.

"I just think you need showing that the world outside is much bigger than the world inside your PlayStation," she insisted.

Alex scoffed. "Coming from someone who has clearly never played Skyrim."

"You're really just emphasising my point, you know."

"Okay, so, what is it you are really suggesting?" Alex asked scathingly. "You're going to take me on a tour of all the playgrounds of London? Let me sample the great swings of the capital? Expand my park horizons?"

"Okay, forget it!" Nadia sighed. Even she wasn't all that sure what she was getting at any more. She just felt sorry for this guy; the word "lonely" always made her feel so desperately sad. And it wasn't that she hadn't enjoyed spending time with Alex that evening, but the idea that this was likely to be the highlight of his social calendar was a little heart-breaking.

"Sorry," Alex apologised, obviously realising he was being a little ungracious.

Nadia laughed. "You're so British. Apologising all the time." She looked across at him; his body moved in and out of her peripherals as she continued to swing. "I love this city," she found herself telling the darkening sky. "You should make the most of it." Alex didn't respond, so Nadia continued. "I've been thinking, recently, that I should probably be hedging my bets a bit."

"Hedging what bets?"

"You know. In case I… can't stay." She always used phrases like "can't stay" rather than "have to leave"; they seemed less aggressive.

"Ah, Nadia," Alex said awkwardly.

She continued before he could say anything pitiful. "I just mean that I should be making memories. Reliving old ones. Whilst I still have the time. I've got a list on my phone of all my favourite things I need to make sure I do one last time and all the things I never got round to doing." She turned to face him, her swinging slowing, losing her height. "You always think you have enough time. But you don't," she told Alex, willing him to understand what she was trying to get across without having to resort to that old favourite: 'life's too short'.

Alex regarded her solemnly and she saw that he got what she was driving at. Even in the darkness of the dusk his eyes were expressive, straight and frank as they looked into hers. Nadia remembered how she'd told Holly how much she liked Alex's eyes.

The first slightly cool breeze that London had felt in three weeks rose up and teased past her. Nadia closed her eyes and tilted her face into it. Maybe the heatwave was finally breaking. Please don't let this be my final summer here, she begged the universe. Please, please.

"So what I think we have here is your basic two birds, one stone deal," Alex said suddenly, startling her out of her reverie.

"Huh?" Nadia turned round to Alex again; the wind had whispered away and the heat of the evening pressed down on them again as if it had never happened.

"Well, if you let me piggyback on some of this list of yours," he said, "I'm living a little, like you suggest, and having new experiences and you are…" he trailed off.

Nadia smiled, "Having old experiences?"

"Something like that. I mean, you don't have to have me tag along to absolutely everything, or anything you'd rather not," Alex clarified hurriedly. "But, you know, if you're short on company for something in particular that you want to do… you can just send me a message. I'm usually free!" he laughed depreciatingly at himself. She liked that about him.

"Okay. Sure." Possible entries on her "to do" list were already presenting themselves in her mind. Did Alex like Mexican food, she wondered? If not, there was always Bodeans. "How about Thursday evening?"

Alex baulked slightly. "Thursday?" he repeated, as if he hadn't actually been expecting her to take him up on the idea after all.

Nadia smiled all the more widely. "Thursday. How do you feel about doing a Mexican eating challenge where the food is so spicy I fully believe the restaurant when they claim it has hospitalised some people?"

Alex theatrically gulped. "Not wonderfully, if I'm honest."

"Then how about a rack of ribs so large, my friend Ledge theorises they come from a dinosaur?"

"Oh, the dinosaur ribs, definitely. They sound yummy."

Nadia laughed, finally starting to come to a stop, dragging the side of her wedges through the wood chip below the swing set. There was a low burn in her biceps from pushing against the chains and when she stood up from the rubber seat, her legs felt a little weak and peculiar. She reached for her handbag and pulled out her mobile phone from the front pocket.

"Here," she said, holding it out to Alex, who slowed to a stop himself, looking up at her. "Put your number in my phone."

"Okay." Alex took it and tapped in his eleven-digit mobile number carefully before handing it back. Nadia saved the number.

"I'm sorry," Alex said, already retreating backwards, already losing confidence. "I have just totally hijacked you and forced you to—"

"I told you already tonight, you apologise too much," Nadia said, sliding her phone back into her bag. "I will meet you at seven on Thursday, outside Clapham Common Tube station. But for now, I'd better get off home."

"Okay," Alex said, uncertainly, as he too got to his feet. "At seven on Thursday." He smiled at her. "Thank you for the drink. And for bringing swinging back into my life. And for the life-coaching session, or whatever the hell that was."

Nadia laughed. "You're welcome! To be continued on Thursday."

Chapter 5

Alex

He'd spent most of the week thinking it was all some sort of elaborate joke that he wasn't quite getting. He fully expected she'd cancel or, worse, he'd be stood up, left standing hopefully underneath the clock by Clapham Common Tube station like so many other losers before him. He'd gone to text her on Monday night (after deciding to plump for a McDonalds over the promised filthy kebab) before realising that he had never actually got her mobile number in return for his. And – let's be honest - a Facebook message just to tell someone about a burger seemed creepy…

Alex arrived at the station at an embarrassingly early seventeen minutes to seven. In an attempt to kill time he queued up at an ATM for cash he didn't need before slipping into Starbucks for a drink he didn't want – different barista, equally surly – and picked Nadia up a Lime Refresher whilst he was at it (despite the fact that this would just make him feel even more stupid if she didn't turn up). When he saw her appear from the Underground, blinking as her eyes acclimatised to the bright sunshine, the relief was a tangible rush. She clocked him almost immediately and her face broke out into a genuine smile as she made her way over to him.

"Are you, by any chance, in need of refreshment?" Alex asked, holding the transparent plastic cup out to Nadia as she reached him. She gave a startled laugh.

"Oh, my God! Thank you," she said as she took it. "None for you?" she asked teasingly as she noticed the hot drink takeaway cup in Alex's other hand.

"I think I'll stick to the natural energy boost that is a double shot of espresso," he told her with a wry smile, tilting his coffee towards her in a salute.

"Fair enough! So, are you hungry?"

"I'm ravenous," he answered her.

"Really? That's good."

"I actively did not eat lunch today in preparation for this," he admitted. "These ribs had better be as colossal as you led me to believe."

"Oh, they are!" Nadia assured him, dipping her head towards the nearby pelican crossing to indicate that they needed to cross the road. "I swear, you imbibe calories just by breathing the air in this place."

"Goodie!" Alex hurried to keep up as Nadia set off purposefully. "So did you skip lunch too?"

"Me? No! I'm probably just going to have a salad or a jacket potato!" she waved him off.

Alex snorted as he hurried to keep up. "Like hell you are!"

Nadia
Nadia knew her hair always smelt like barbecue sauce after a meal in this particular place, but couldn't quite bring herself to care. Alex's expression as he watched the waiter bring a plate – or, rather, a tray – of the so-called Jacob's Ladder ribs to a nearby table was too priceless.

"You weren't kidding," he told her, unable to take his eyes off the food. "Seriously! What animal *is* that?"

Nadia shrugged. "We always thought that as it actively doesn't specify on the menu, we probably didn't want to know."

"I think it's a bit rude to eat an animal and not even know

what it is. I might have to ask."

Nadia jokingly clapped her hands over her ears. "If you do, don't tell me!"

"It's probably buffalo or something..." Alex continued, teasingly. Nadia squealed in protest. "A buffalo that's been fed steroids all its life..."

"Can I get you guys some drinks to start with?" the waitress interrupted, with superb timing.

"He'll have a Cowboy Martini," Nadia interjected, just as Alex opened his mouth, presumably to order something less vodka-based. He frowned at her.

"What's that?"

"Obligatory," Nadia answered, airily.

"Fine then. Same for the lady, then," he told the waitress. "And the drinks are my treat," he said quickly, cutting Nadia off as she opened her mouth to argue. She didn't want him thinking this was a date, but then again, she was spending pretty much her entire week's food budget to eat out tonight.

"Two Cowboy Martinis," the waitress repeated, scribbling something intelligible on her dog-eared notepad. "Are you ready to order food?"

"Yeah, I think I am going to go for the Jacob's Ladder ribs," Alex said.

"Yes, I heard," said the waitress, arching her eyebrow. "And, by the way, it's just bog-standard beef. Nothing exotic. And no steroids."

Alex eyed the mountain of ribs that the people on the nearby table were barely managing to make a dent in. "No kidding."

"Okay, a full rack of the Jacob's Ladder ribs, then, please, with the standard sides," Nadia ordered with a smile.

"Each?" asked the waitress, her pen poised over the paper. Alex snorted.

"I think we're okay to share," Nadia laughed.

"Ease me in gently, and all that," Alex informed the waitress solemnly.

"You'd better prep the doggy bag," Nadia said in a stage whisper.

"Two Cowboy Martinis, one Jacob's Ladder to share," the waitress ignored them, good-naturedly, slipping her pen into her apron pocket. "Your drinks will be over in a few minutes, guys, okay?"

"I think that's the first time I've ever had my entire restaurant order done for me," Alex said, leaning over the table, closer to Nadia, as the waitress moved on. "Is this your idea of me living my own life? Not even getting a choice of food?"

Nadia crinkled her nose in response to his teasing. "Tonight isn't about the living-your-own-life thingy. Tonight is about a new experience."

Alex arched his eyebrow as he slid the laminated drinks menu back into its slot in the condiment holder, out of their way.

"Beef for dinner," he said, in a serious tone. "It's a brave new world..." Nadia laughed.

It was funny. She'd almost texted him to cancel yesterday. In the cold light of day – without swings and sunsets and Starbucks making things seem special – it was a bit of a mad idea. She was all for spontaneity usually, but this was a little over the top, even for her. She had enough on her plate at the moment, so she wasn't quite sure why she seemed to be trying to adopt a socially inept twenty-something stranger. Besides, Matt had texted her a careful three days after date number one, to arrange date number two, with Thursday as one of the evenings he was free. She could have taken him to Bodeans after all.

But this wasn't really a date place; this was a friend place. It smelt like meat and vinegar, had ugly orange lighting and the leather of the booths was scratched and faded pale where thousands of arses had rubbed before hers. Alex seemed to have noticed the shabby state of the booths, too, and rubbed his palm over the seat.

"Okay, so we know the meat isn't anything exotic... but what do you think the leather is? Moose hide?" Alex clamped his mouth shut guiltily as the smirking waitress returned to their table holding

61

a Martini glass in each hand, the rims dusted in fat white crystals of sugar. Nadia didn't even wait for the drink to be put down on the table; she took it straight from the waitress as she thanked her. She bloody loved these cocktails.

Alex looked a little more dubious. "Okay, so this is what, now?"

"A Martini. Muddled with mint leaves. So, I guess it's sort of a cross between a Martini and a Mojito."

"Okay. And what exactly makes a cross between a Martini and a Mojito Cowboy-y?"

Nadia shrugged, taking a generous sip of the sharp liquid. "What exactly are you looking for here, spurs on the glass stem? Just drink it."

Alex laughed and took a small gulp. "Hmmm." He swallowed and exaggeratedly pretended to consider the taste. "Not bad, actually. Still, I could do without the girly glass." He gently flicked the slender stem of the Martini glass with the back of his finger.

"Hey, if it's manly enough for James Bond," Nadia pointed out. "Besides, you could hardly drink it from a pint glass…"

"Wanna bet?" Alex grinned, taking a slightly larger mouthful; he clearly secretly liked it. Nadia studied his face in the pause as he drank. He was already growing familiar to her, good-looking in a preppy way, boyish and as carefully clean-shaven as the men in razor adverts. His hair was equally tidy, and a rich brown, although she knew it shone auburn in the sunshine. Tonight was the first time she'd seen him out of a suit and without his glasses – he must have gone home after work to change. He seemed bigger and more immediate with his biceps bare where they appeared from underneath the sleeves of his shapeless t-shirt.

"So," Nadia said, templing her fingers on the tabletop between them. "Go on, then. Tell me about yourself."

Alex had been about to put his glass back down, but instead re-routed it back to his mouth. He raised one eyebrow. "Has anyone ever told you that being with you is a little exhausting?"

Nadia made an affronted little noise in her throat. "How so?"

"I wasn't expecting my 'new experience' to be a job interview in a rib joint."

Nadia laughed. "It's just that I realised I don't really know tons about you."

"So?"

"What do you mean, so? It's just a bit weird."

Alex's eyebrow arched even higher. "Have you never been on a blind date? Or out with someone you met online?"

"Yeah," Nadia admitted, "a couple of times."

"Then how is this any weirder? Besides – you know where I work, whereabouts I live, who I live with…" He raised his hands expansively, as if to say: what more do you need to know? The hems on the arms of his t-shirt rode up towards his shoulders, momentarily revealing an enigmatic black smudge that looked as if it might possibly be part of a tattoo. Now that was a surprise! Nadia surreptitiously tilted her head for a better look, but the fabric had already dropped back down into place.

"You don't need to worry about small talk, you know," Alex continued. "This isn't speed-dating."

"Yes, apparently it's more like a job interview!" Nadia reminded him, pretending to be offended. "Although I don't know what's wrong with asking a few interested questions in *any* situation…"

"Nobody expects the Spanish Inquisition," Alex quoted with a grin.

Nadia rolled her eyes. "Did you seriously just quote *Monty Python* at me? Seriously?"

"Why, does the girl who breaks into playgrounds think that's a bit childish?" Alex mocked.

Nadia played along. "Seriously, if I'd known you were *this* lame, I don't think I would have invited you to dinner…"

Alex tilted his head. "Really? I thought it was because of exactly that – you felt sorry for me wallowing in my epic lameness and wanted to get me out and about."

"That's true," Nadia said, mock-thoughtful. "Okay, then. But you start quoting *Star Wars* and I'm out of here."

Alex

Nadia was looking at him strangely, as if he'd unexpectedly changed colour or something. Okay, he knew he was babbling a bit – okay, a lot – but his social interaction hadn't amounted to much over recent years and apparently his ability to small-talk had gone to pot as a result. He couldn't quite work out if she was looking at him oddly because he was talking too much, or because he was talking too little. Or maybe she just plain thought he was odd. Although, he comforted himself, this whole thing *was* her idea; she was the odd one.

Cheered by that realisation, Alex took another sip of his Martini.

"So," he began conversationally. "Part of this was you teaching me to love my city, wasn't it? Well, this cocktail is quite nice, but I don't think we can credit that to London. Isn't this an American chain?"

"I think so," Nadia laughed. "I think the 'cowboy' part of the 'Cowboy Martini' gives it away."

"And the American football," Alex added, gesturing at the suspended television screens that were broadcasting the unfathomable sport.

"Caro went out with an American guy once," Nadia remembered, shaking her head. "He used to call proper football 'soccer' and it drove everyone up the wall."

"So what's the deal with Caro?" Alex asked. "Granted, I've been in her presence all of thirty seconds, but she seems a little scary." Nadia looked flustered by the question and Alex fumbled to redeem himself. "I don't mean that in a bad way," he stressed. "Just you and Holly seem a bit more chilled out..."

"Caro always has a lot of stuff on her plate," Nadia granted, her tone carefully nonchalant as she fiddled with the stem of her Martini glass and Alex knew to leave the subject alone.

Nadia obviously wanted to change the topic too. "I went out

with that Matt guy last week."

Oh yes, broad, blond, Belgian-lager-drinking Matt; him out with the pretty, platinum-haired Nadia probably looked like Nazi Aryan porn.

"Oh yeah? Did you enjoy over-sized meat with him too?" Alex barely stopped himself from wincing as he belatedly realised the crude innuendo. Nadia blinked once, then gamely carried on with the conversation.

"No, we just went for drinks. You know, you're not meant to arrange an actual dinner on a first date."

"Why not?"

"In case you don't like them. In case they're boring. In case they, oh, I don't know; make wet noises when they chew, talk incessantly about their ex-girlfriend, order the gourmet steak and six sides because they think you are paying, or cry. A whole dinner is a long time to suffer a guy like that. The length of time it takes to drink a glass of wine is more manageable; especially with the speed with which I've been known to drink a glass of wine."

Alex laughed, ever-so-slightly aghast. "Wow, Matt did all that?!" he teased.

Nadia laughed too. "No, not Matt. But sadly I am speaking from personal experience of each of those date disasters."

"Christ! It's enough to make you give up!"

"Maybe, but not yet," Nadia said with a small smile.

"Ah, a hopeless romantic, eh?"

"You only have to meet The One the once," Nadia pointed out.

Alex felt a momentary strain in his chest and in the smile on his face. He just couldn't let himself believe that. First Alice. Now Lila. Both had been The One for him, in so far as one could ever be The One, when it was unrequited. He shook it off.

"And so is Matt 'The One'?" he asked, taking yet another drink, bringing his glass dangerously close to empty already.

Nadia gave a little embarrassed laugh. "Who knows? He might be!" She shrugged. "He's got the right name, anyway."

"The right name?" Alex repeated curiously.

The bridge of Nadia's nose flushed a pretty shade of pink. "Ah, just a stupid, inside joke," she blagged, seeing off her own drink too.

Alex gestured lightly towards her empty glass. "Same again? Or are there other spirit-based delights on the menu I should be sampling?"

"Oh no, don't worry," Nadia said immediately. "I'm okay."

"No, you don't worry," Alex insisted gently. "It was really nice of you to invite me out to dinner. You're a really cool girl," *Cool girl?* Christ, Alex. It just gets better and better from you. Poor thing was going to start thinking she was trapped in an American sitcom from the nineties. Shortly she'd begin eyeing up the door and running through her litany of excuses as if he was a bad date who'd eaten an expensive steak and cried about his ex-girlfriend, or whatever the nightmare was.

But instead, Nadia leaned a little closer to him across the table and briefly squeezed the knuckles of the hand he had lying on the tabletop between them.

"And you're a really cool guy," she told him, sincerely, before releasing his hand and reaching for the laminated leaflet that was the drinks menu. "If you insist, there's always that one cocktail that tastes like an apple pie…"

Chapter 6

Alex

"Okay." Alex clasped his hands thoughtfully behind his back and shifted his centre of gravity back on his heels to better embody the cliché of man-looking-at-art. A foot or so to their left a bored tourist was fiddling with his iPod, the tinny tsch tsch tsch of his music audible from his over-sized headphones. "So, which Henry is this?"

Nadia smacked him across the chest impatiently with the rolled-up programme. "Hey, this is your heritage here! Show some respect, or at least some interest!"

"I am interested!" Alex protested, whipping the glossy booklet out of Nadia's loose grip before she could do more damage with it. "I asked which Henry it is."

"I think it's an Edward," Nadia said, tilting her head as she surveyed the grand old portrait taking up the majority of the wall in front of them.

"You think? I thought you were into this stuff."

"Me?" Nadia looked at him incredulously. "I don't have a bloody clue."

"I thought we were doing all your favourite things?"

"As well as all the stuff I never got around to doing," Nadia reminded him, snatching the souvenir booklet back. "I never could get anyone bothered to do the National Gallery with me…"

Alex arched his eyebrows. "No kidding."

"Caro always said that you didn't need to go to the Gallery because all of the most famous portraits are reproduced on the Tube platform walls at Charing Cross."

"Caro seems like a resourceful woman."

"Hmm. And she'd probably know which bloody king this is. I'm pretty sure one of her degrees is a history one. I think, maybe."

"It's got to be a Henry. I mean, sheer probability, there have been more Henrys than any other name, right?"

"I'm pretty sure there's been just as many Edwards."

"Honestly, Miss Osipova, I don't know how you expect to get citizenship if you can't recognise every British monarch of the past thousand years…" Nadia thwacked him with the guide again.

The pencil-skirted gallery guard shifted from her position on a nearby stool, finally goaded into movement by the inanity of their conversation and the new, violent direction it was now taking. She gave them a pinched, suspicious look.

"This is a portrait of Henry II," she told them primly – Alex shot Nadia a triumphant look – "who reigned in the twelfth century. The portraits are all labelled," she sniffed, gesturing at the small, polished bronze plaque over to one side that Alex was suddenly very unsure how they'd missed. Nadia made a small squeak; Alex looked across at her and saw that she had her lips pinched together, desperately trying not to make things worse by giggling.

"Ahh," was all Alex could manage, laughter brewing in his own chest; his lips twitched.

The guard's narrow eyes narrowed even further. "If you would prefer a guided tour, they begin in the atrium at ten past and twenty to the hour," she said slowly. She flicked her eyes to a red-faced Nadia and then back to Alex. "You certainly seem like you could… use some guidance." Nadia made that small mouse-like squeaking again.

"Thank you, but I think we are okay," Alex announced politely, groping blindly behind him for Nadia's wrist. "Actually, we came here with the sole aim of seeing the Henry the Third, er, Second and so, er, I think we're done, right Nadia?"

Nadia squeaked again in response and allowed Alex to pull her with him as he slalomed through the pockets of tourists and art enthusiasts towards the exit.

A rush of city heat pressed against them as they left the air-conditioned gallery behind and escaped out onto the dirty white steps. Nadia immediately subsided into helpless laughter and Alex couldn't help but join in.

"Okay," Nadia managed finally. "So that wasn't so successful."

"To be fair, nothing is going to be as successful as those amazing ribs from the other day," Alex told her, gravely.

"Oh well! At least I can now say that I've been the loud, ignorant Londoner at a tourist attraction!" Nadia laughed, miming ticking a box in the air as she spoke.

"I think we were the first two Londoners to go to the National Portrait Gallery full stop, to be fair!"

Nadia nudged him playfully with her shoulder as she slipped the redundant rolled-up gallery guide into her handbag. "Ah well. I'm so sorry I got you to come all the way out to the centre of town on a Saturday afternoon for nothing." Nadia looked up at him, squinting slightly as the sun bounced off the whiteness of the building and created whorls of blurry heat haze. The days were still like a furnace, the city on its last nerve and smelling of baked dust.

"Don't worry about it. I had a great, er, ten minutes," Alex grinned. "That Henry II, eh?"

"Majestic!" Nadia agreed.

"So." Alex stuffed his hands into the pockets of his long cargo shorts. "What next?"

"Next?" Nadia echoed, confused.

Alex's mood immediately fell flat. "Oh. Unless you just want to head home…"

"No, no!" Nadia shook her head. "I thought you might want

to, though."

Alex shrugged widely. "Me? Pitiable loner with more friends on his PlayStation network than his Facebook, remember?"

"I assume you're exaggerating when you say things like that!" Nadia laughed. He was – but only a bit, worryingly; Alex decided not to specify.

"Well, we're in Trafalgar Square," he pointed out, nodding across past the stream of black taxis and bright-red buses to where Nelson's Column rose high against the cloudless sky, casting its long shadow across one of the large fountains nearby. "Do you want to keep playing tourist?"

Nadia

They walked cheerful circuits around Trafalgar Square, pigeons scattering lazily in their wake, until one of the benches became free, the back of it warm against their own as they sat. Nadia drew one leg up across the rest of her body as she turned ninety degrees to face Alex as they chatted companionably. He gestured across the square to where the old Saint Martin in the Fields church rose grandly in the east, looking like a transplant from some ancient Greek acropolis. She'd always loved that about London. Just as often as there was tradition, there was something unexpected, something that jarred against the outsider's preconceptions. Smiling, she watched a gaggle of over-enthusiastic Chinese tourists taking pictures over by one of the famous lion plinths. Even the tourists – as annoying as they were when you were stuck behind them when you were trying to get to work – were part of the magic of this ancient city; the old, and the new, and the now.

"Where's the best place you've ever been?" she asked Alex.

"Bodeans," he answered, without skipping a beat. Nadia rolled her eyes at him.

"You know very well I mean country, city, that sort of thing."

Alex rolled his shoulders back and looked up at Nelson atop his column. "I went to Majorca once, with my parents and my little brother," he answered, deadpan. "Me and Jason spent most of the week trying to find the nudist beach we were sure must be around somewhere."

"Oh, God! What were you? Ten?" Nadia asked, amused.

"Sixteen and fourteen," Alex admitted.

"Okay!" Nadia changed the subject. "Well, not to disparage the appeal of the Spanish islands, but Majorca is not an acceptable answer. Anywhere else?"

"Well, what is an acceptable answer, then? But if you start talking about 'finding yourself' at dawn on a Caribbean beach or building a well in Africa, I'm calling bullshit."

Nadia blanched; he was serious. "You've never been abroad?" she asked, slowly.

Alex frowned. "I told you, I've been to Majorca."

"I mean, abroad abroad. Somewhere where the local people don't all speak English and serve chips with every meal."

Alex looked uncomfortable. "I guess I'm not a travelling sort of person."

"You've never wanted to travel? Even a little bit?" Nadia couldn't believe it. "Where's your sense of…" She trailed off – "adventure" didn't quite cover it. She lapsed into Russian. "*Avantyura,*" she finished, gesturing vaguely. "Have you never, I don't know, wanted to expand your horizons..?"

"If you *must* know, I was going to take a gap year and do some travelling after I left university," Alex admitted, looking more and more put upon. "But the person I was meant to go with pulled out at the last minute, so I never went."

"Why didn't you go on your own?" Nadia probed.

"There was a lot of stuff going on at the time, okay?" Alex barked, before looking faintly embarrassed at his tone. "It just… wasn't going to happen. And then I had to get a job, and – trust me – I am nowhere near important enough to ask for a sabbatical off work to go travelling!"

"What about just two weeks in the summer, like the rest of us?

One week, even!" Nadia insisted.

Alex kept his eyes trained on Nelson. "I don't know. It just never appealed to me." He finally turned to look Nadia in the face. "So, is the Spanish Inquisition over now?" he asked, teasingly.

He was lying, of that Nadia was sure; what she wasn't sure of was why.

"I couldn't not travel," she said, bluntly. And it was true; the fact that she hadn't been able to go anywhere since the Home Office had confiscated her passport was driving her nuts, flat-out itchy with wanderlust. "I've gone somewhere abroad like, twice a year, for as long as I can remember."

"And you wonder why your application for ILR was denied?" Alex muttered darkly.

Nadia pulled herself up short. "What did you say?"

Alex had looked uncomfortable before, but that was nothing compared to how he looked now. "Nothing, nothing," he insisted, immediately. He rubbed the back of his head so that his hair there mussed every which way; she was starting to notice he did that when he was nervous.

"You said something about my Indefinite Leave to Remain being rejected because I travel too much," Nadia pressed. "What makes you say that?"

Alex kept her eye contact, apologetic yet oddly defiant. "Well, obviously I'm just assuming. If you really have gone abroad that often. Don't you need continuous residency for a certain amount of time? I mean, I'm just going by something I think I heard..."

Nadia nodded slowly. "Yeah." She felt as deflated as her tone. Every so often, such as on days like today – with good weather, good company and her beloved London spread out at her feet like a personal secret – she'd let herself forget. But if even Alex was pointing out her appeal's shortcomings, what chance did she really have?

"Hey, hey," Alex said, reaching awkwardly to rub her upper arm. "None of that, now. It's going to be fine."

"I think that sometimes. I can't quite believe I'll actually go. But then I go and do this." Nadia asked, despondently. "My swan song," she clarified, doing sarcastic quotation marks with her index fingers. "Dragging a stranger to the National Portrait Gallery. Force-feeding him ribs."

Alex gave her a slow smile. "Well, I wasn't going to admit this, but I'm just jumping on this bandwagon for selfish reasons. I don't believe you're going to get deported in the slightest. I just wanted to see that portrait of Henry II so fucking much."

Nadia rolled her eyes, lips twitching into an unexpected smile. "Well, I'm glad my immigration problems have proved to be of assistance."

"I mean it. Don't worry about it," Alex insisted. "You'll have your day in court. And no sane judge in this country will be able to look at you, and listen to you, and know you and not agree that you belong here, with your friends."

Nadia felt an embarrassing little clench in her chest. She ducked her head as she felt a flush spread across her cheeks. "I guess I can only try my best, huh?"

"Do, or do not," Alex intoned solemnly. "There is no try."

"Alex!" Nadia slapped him playfully on the hand he still cupped to her shoulder. "I warned you about quoting *Star Wars*!"

Alex

They'd talked all day, sitting on that bench in Trafalgar Square, heedless as the sun moved clear across the sky, Alex careful to skirt around any mention of her visa after his earlier near miss. Eventually hunger drove them away from Nelson, and they'd eaten Vietnamese street food standing in the cobbled mews off the Strand, where they'd found the vendor. Finally, remembering their abortive attempt at the National Portrait Gallery, they'd headed down into the Underground to take a closer look at what they'd missed out on.

They'd shared what was left of their lukewarm bottle of mineral water and moved from one National Portrait Gallery reproduction to the next, Nadia snapping selfies with her phone of them blowing kisses at Mary I, looking shocked at Henry V, making tasteless neck-slicing gestures in front of Anne Boleyn, holding the mouth of the plastic water bottle helpfully up to Shakespeare's grey lips. They'd run laughing through the closing doors of the last Tube, almost missing it despite the fact they'd been on the platform for nearly an hour by then.

They'd parted reluctantly, both caught in the magic of a day that nobody else would ever understand. Nadia had lingered in the Tube seat next to him, even as the train began to slow in its approach to Clapham Common. She'd email him a link to where he could buy an entrance ticket to the next activity she'd promised him – and yes, this was definitely something she'd done before. When Alex had jokingly asked if there was a high probability of them being kicked out, Nadia had thrown her head back and laughed. They'd have to be very, very bad to get kicked out of this particular place, she'd assured him, an appropriately wicked glint in her eye.

It had gone half-twelve by the time Alex let himself in, the flat so still and quiet that he would have been convinced Rory was over at Lila's, were it not for the fact he'd noticed a low light glowing through the front-room window as he'd made his way up the street. Sure enough, the lamp was on in the main room. Lila was sitting on the sofa, her legs curled up underneath her; she readjusted her position as Alex entered the room, turning down a corner of the page of her book as she did so.

"Hey," she said quietly, "it's late."

Alex felt an irrational flare of annoyance. So what if he was coming in late? She wasn't his keeper. She wasn't even his girlfriend.

"Rory went to bed," Lila continued, in that same hushed, slightly accusatory, tone.

"Did you guys have a good evening?" Alex asked, at his normal volume, as he kicked off his shoes.

"I brought over that film you said you wanted to watch," Lila said, gesturing over to where a DVD in its case lay carelessly in front of the TV bench.

"Oh."

"I didn't know you were going to be out. All night," Lila continued, the accusation growing unmistakable.

"Oh," Alex repeated again, feeling stupid. "Sorry Lils?" He allowed the apology to come out like a question; he wanted her to know that he wasn't actually sorry.

Lila continued to stare at him, as if she suddenly wasn't quite sure who he was. "What did you get up to?" she asked, and Alex felt the frustration flare again. What was her problem? Was he seen as that much of a lapdog that he couldn't have one night away from her?

"Just out with a friend," he answered airily, as he moved into the kitchen to pour himself a pint of water. He wasn't all that surprised that Lila followed him, standing unsure and small in the open doorway between the kitchen and the main room.

"A friend?" she echoed.

Alex moved past her politely and out into the corridor. "Yup. Lunch with Admiral Nelson; drinks with Will Shakespeare," he said with a grin. "G'night."

Leaving Lila standing gratifyingly open-mouthed, Alex shut his bedroom door behind him.

Chapter 7

Nadia

"It's so inconsiderate," Holly moaned, stomping aimlessly around their living room. "Six *hundred* pounds. That's not a weekend away, that's my yearly *holiday*." Nadia stared at her friend balefully across the rim of her mug of tea. Holly continued ranting, heedless. "It's going to be chick peas for dinner from now until then. *Tesco Value chick peas…*"

Nadia, who had eaten value chick peas for dinner the previous night, and twice last week, lost her patience.

"Well, don't go then!" she snapped.

Holly stared at her. "You know I can't *not go*," she scoffed.

"Why not? I'm not going," Nadia countered.

"Yes, well, that's because you *can't go*." Holly let her sentence trail off as she realised what she'd said and looked across at her friend guiltily. "Sorry!"

Nadia exhaled with a sigh. "Don't worry. It's not your fault." Their friend from school was throwing a prohibitively expensive – yet no doubt epically fun – hen weekend skiing on the Swiss/ French border. Even if Nadia hadn't been as skint as she was, without her passport the closest she was going to get to skiing was the dry slope in Milton Keynes. "I'm just crabby because I'm jealous," she admitted. "You know how much I love skiing."

"I haven't been skiing since – when did we go to Bulgaria?"

Nadia squinted, counting back. "God. Like, three, four years ago?"

"Where has the time gone?" Holly asked, sadly, finally flopping down on the sofa next to Nadia and laying her head on her shoulder. "You should definitely schedule in a super-fun weekend while I'm away," she said, after a moment, with a suggestive grin and a waggle of her brows.

Nadia laughed. "Yes. We were thinking all-nighter movie marathon at the Prince Charles, actually. I hope the weather has cooled down enough that I can wear my onesie."

Holly looked at her curiously. "Wear your onesie? Why the hell would you wear your onesie?"

"We're talking, like, eight hours of cinema here," Nadia explained. "Comfort is of the essence."

"I don't agree with your onesie at the best of times," Holly countered, raising her head, "so I don't agree with it in public, and I most *certainly* do not agree with it being worn on a date!"

"A date? No, I don't mean I'm taking Matt to the Prince Charles cinema, I mean I'm taking Alex!"

"Oh." Holly arched one eyebrow. "I meant Matt..."

Alex

Alex was quite looking forward to whatever the third thing on Nadia's to-do list was. He hadn't seen her since their random day in Trafalgar Square, but they'd been in near-constant email contact making big plans ever since. A few days earlier he'd received an email that linked him to a ticket vendor site, urging him to buy entrance to something called "Candy at Closet" on Thursday night. The entrance was only £3 – the booking fee the same again – and apparently showing the confirmation number at the bar would entitle him to a free "Candy Cock Tail"; he wasn't quite sure if that was an innuendo or a typo.

Nadia met him straight after work in Piccadilly Circus. She

was immediately noticeable amongst the tourist throng, standing on the highest step around the Shaftesbury Memorial, bright and obvious in denim shorts and a flowy top the colour of pistachio ice-cream, her hair in a style he was learning she favoured, the loose side-plait almost white in the sun. She shaded her eyes with her palm when she caught sight of him, as if confirming it was him. Recognising that it was, she firmly but politely skipped her way through the throngs of people on the lower steps and met him on pavement level, the tides of commuters and tourists breaking around them as if they were standing on an island.

"Hey!" Nadia greeted him with a grin. "How's your week been?"

Alex skimmed through his week in his head: work, work, microwaveable meals, more hours than necessary playing *Call of Duty* online, Rory working late more and more evenings and Lila ghosting in and out, reprimanding and silent, giving him looks akin to those of a disappointed parent.

"Fine," he answered, with a shrug. "What about yours?"

Nadia wrinkled her nose. "We've got some sort of… infestation at the shop. Someone donated something with bed bugs or something on it and so we've had to call the pest people out. Quite a lot of the backroom stock has been ruined. It's taken ages moving everything and trying to save what we can. Weird to work for free and still be doing overtime! But, you know, it had to be done."

Immediately Alex felt like a bit of a shit. There he was – only not in his pyjamas by seven each evening because Lila was so often hanging around – doing sweet F.A. (aside from shooting bad guys, obviously). Maybe he should consider some sort of volunteer work?

"That sounds like the week of a girl who could use a drink. Now, where can one get a nice Cowboy Martini 'round here?" he joked. Nadia laughed and linked her arm with his, moving them north towards Golden Square.

"We're on the Candy Cock Tails tonight," she reminded him. "I hope you like rum."

They left the wider streets behind them and entered the network of mews, the capillaries of the city and – even with the temperature as high as it was – a chill fell over their exposed skin as they moved into the shade of old, damp buildings. Closet, it transpired, was one of those "secret" bars that Alex had only ever heard about; he felt a frisson of excitement. You'd totally miss it if you didn't know it was there. Just a stately black door behind equally stately black railings, as one mews turned a corner and became another, a heavy brass door knocker in the shape of a C the only hint that this was the place they were looking for. Nadia confidently banged the knocker, before turning around and nudging Alex when she noticed he didn't have his ticket confirmation print-out in hand, like she did.

The door pulled open, letting loose a blast of stale air and R&B music from within. The bouncer merely glanced at their print-outs and waved them on inside, down a dark staircase with slightly rickety bannisters and a threadbare carpet runner down the middle of its wooden steps. Nadia went first, turning back halfway down the descent to give him a grin; what sort of place was this anyway? It seemed pretty dingy, and dingy just didn't seem like Nadia's style. A short, equally shabby, corridor at the foot of the stairs led to a thick beaded curtain, concealing the room beyond, from which loud music and conversation pitched to be heard over it was emanating. With another smile at him over her shoulder, Nadia slipped through, sending the beads jerking and twisting in her wake.

The main bar was even darker than the staircase had been, lit at low levels with lamps with red bulbs and faux-chandelier shades. There were a few chairs here and there, but mainly seating seemed to be the beanbags and oversized cushions that were scattered across the floor. Slender silver poles were columns holding up a heavy, tasselled canopy over a spotlit stage directly across from the bar, the queue for which was already three people deep across its entire length.

Alex was startled out of his staring by Nadia deftly plucking his print-out from his limp grasp.

"I'll get the freebie cocktails," she told him. "I know the barman," she confessed, "so I'll get served quickly, and he'll make them extra strong! Why don't you grab a seat?"

"You mean, grab a cushion?" Alex asked, gesturing sarcastically around them. Nadia screwed up her nose at his crabbiness and whirled away to inveigle herself at the bar. Feeling immensely stupid, Alex wandered the open space until he picked out what he considered to be the plumpest floor pillow and awkwardly sat down on one side of it. The nearby red light cast a pinkness like sunburn onto his arms.

True to her word, Nadia was back almost immediately, carefully balancing two long cocktail glasses as she picked her way across the cluttered floor. She handed him both drinks so she could sit down before taking one back off him and chinking her glass against his with a smile.

"Cheers," Alex said as she did. "So, when does this 'show' start?"

"In about half an hour," Nadia answered. "Or whenever. It's kind of 'go with the flow' in here." She sipped at her drink through the straw and Alex followed suit, grimacing a bit at the creamy sweetness of it.

"I think I prefer the Cowboy Martini," he confessed. "And, you know, chairs."

Nadia stretched her legs out in front of them, easing her flip-flops off her feet and leaving them casually on the floor. "Oh, come on Alex!" She sunk down on the big cushion until she was lying completely on her back, knees bent to the ceiling and bare feet flat to the ratty carpet. "You asked me to help you live a little!"

"I asked you no such thing," Alex grumbled, feeling distinctly uncomfortable with the amount of lounging that was going on. The place was getting busier by the minute and the rest of the patrons seemed to have the same idea as Nadia, lolling haphazardly on their beanbags, drinks held aloft to prevent spillage. "But what exactly is tonight's new learning experience? How to get a bad back?"

Nadia simply sank all the deeper into the cushion. "Oh, I don't know. How to laugh..?"

Nadia

Nadia had been coming to see Candy at Closet since she was an undergraduate. One of her course mates had started getting hot and heavy with Closet's owner, a man thirty years his senior who went by the professional name of "Aslan". As it happened, the pair's working relationship went on much longer than their sexual one, as Sean was now Aslan's front-of-house manager and always, always good for an extra shot's worth of strength in a cocktail.

Alex was sitting ramrod straight as if he was on bare concrete rather than an over-stuffed velvet cushion. Okay, so it wasn't exactly a surprise that an underground gay bar wasn't exactly his "scene", but Candy always did a show the first Thursday of the month and Nadia never missed it. Besides, she liked pressing Alex's buttons; he was so English, so tight and scrunchy.

"So," she began, conversationally, turning her head to see Alex all the better. "Have you ever had any gay experiences?"

Alex went the same colour as his pina colada. "What?" he spluttered. "Why would you ask me that?"

"I just thought it was contextually appropriate."

"You what?"

"You know, because we're in a gay bar?" Alex looked around himself again, eyes widening in realisation. Nadia burst out laughing. "Come on, Alex! You knew this was a gay bar!"

"I did not!"

"Alex, it's called *Closet*."

Alex opened and closed his mouth like a goldfish; you could almost see the cogs whirring.

Nadia narrowed her eyes. "You don't have... a problem with this being a gay bar, do you?"

"No!" Alex insisted vehemently, still looking around as if he was seeing the place for the first time. "Not at all, it's not that. It's just... I was surprised. And I'm straight."

"So?" Nadia pressed, propping herself up a little on one elbow. "Me too."

Alex pitched his voice low. "So are we even allowed in here?"

Nadia laughed again. "Of course we're allowed in here, you idiot! Calm down. Here, sit back a bit, people are looking!"

Alex slunk back against the cushion, letting his legs spill over to the floor like Nadia's. "So, did you really think I was gay?" he asked her, taking a drink from his cocktail, sipping straight from the glass, forgoing the obviously far-too-phallic straw.

"No, not really, but you never know," Nadia shrugged. "And loads of people have had at least one, you know, *experience.*"

Alex looked directly at her, tilting his head on the swell of the cushion. "Oh yeah? How about you?"

"Okay, well, not me personally," Nadia granted. "But Caro is bisexual. She's had a full-blown girlfriend. They went out for, like, six months. And Holly had a snog with a girl at school, which I'm not certain counts, but she likes to roll it out to titillate men, nevertheless." She wasn't sure if Alex was titillated or not, but he took a very deep drink from his cocktail.

"I've never met anyone like you," he said to Nadia, after a minute. "You're really..."

"Great?" she supplied, with a sarcastic grin. "Wonderful? Fabulous?"

Alex pondered her face silently as he carefully considered his choice of words, and Nadia noticed – despite herself – that when he looked more intense like that he really was very handsome, and she felt her heart do its silly fast pitter-patter under the frills of her blouse.

"Artless," he supplied, eventually, and Nadia came crashing back to reality. She groaned aloud, unable to help it.

"Artless?" she echoed, in disbelief. "How flattering!"

"Hey, it's a compliment!" Alex insisted, a small smile on his face.

"I don't even know what you mean by it!"

"A compliment," Alex repeated, his smile growing wider. "You say and do what you want. You don't mind what people might think of you. You invite strangers into your life and you try and swing over the bar. You're just you and it's effortless – artless. You don't try to be someone else. And that's great. That's all I meant by it."

Alex fell into silence and sipped from his cocktail self-consciously. Nadia felt a warm little lump in her throat. "Artless" turned out to be much more of a compliment than "amazing" or even "beautiful".

"Well," she said, after a moment, having gotten herself back under control. "Thank you. But right now, I'd love to be someone else. Someone with a British passport!" Alex laughed a little too politely at her bad joke and suddenly things were weird and awkward where they hadn't been before.

Saved by the bell, Candy's entrance music crackled and popped from the ancient speakers and Alex's attention turned to the stage, where Candy himself – London's most beautiful drag queen – twirled onto the stage to rapturous applause in a cascade of sequins and light. Nadia saw Alex laugh in delight at the display and settle down a little more comfortably, the beanbag adjusting around them both.

Chapter 8

Nadia

It had taken up two courses of food and a good bottle and a half of wine, but Matt was still stuck on the same topic. Nadia honestly was happy that his dad had finally got a Tottenham season ticket after being on the waiting list for what sounded like most of his lifetime, but it really wasn't a subject that deserved two hours of discussion.

As Matt studied the dessert menu, Nadia studied him. This was their fifth date, a full-blown three-course affair in a restaurant that had proper candles, not tea-lights, and all on Matt's dime. He'd been sweet and attentive, and had even worn a shirt – not a polo one, a real one – with buttons all the way down. She knew how he was anticipating – if not flat-out expecting – the night to end and had given herself the time taken by the meal to decide if she agreed with him.

"Hey, random question…" she found herself asking. Matt looked across at her over his menu expectantly. "What's the best compliment you've ever given a girl?"

Despite the warning, her question was clearly more random than Matt had predicted; he blinked twice and a slight panic set in around his eyes as he rapidly racked his brain for the best way to answer.

"Forget it."

"No, no, I'm just thinking. Do you mean like, a chat-up line?" Matt asked. Nadia managed to keep her sigh contained inside. "Because," Matt laughed, "I had a great one at university. I used to use the old, 'I can make your bed rock!' He continued laughing at his own joke; Nadia just looked at him, nonplussed. "I er, studied geology at uni," Matt belatedly explained. "You know, bedrock? Bed rock?"

"Ahhh." I know what seats in White Hart Lane your father has a season ticket for, but I didn't know what your degree was in, Nadia caught herself thinking.

"My mate Joe, though, he was the worst for the bad lines," Matt continued, clearly not clocking Nadia's mood. "One time, he actually got a bird by going up to her at the student bar and saying, "Hey, girl, I'd like to wear you like I wear my sunglasses – one leg over each ear!" Can you believe it? I shit you not. They went out for like a year after that. Bizarre!"

"Yeah. Bizarre," Nadia echoed, not quite sure what else she was meant to say to information like that. "But I meant an actual compliment. You know. Something personal."

Matt gave her a sly grin, closing his menu and placing it flat on the table between them. "Aww, Nadia, are you fishing for a compliment?" He reached across the table for hers.

Nadia reared back slightly. "No. No, it's nothing like that. It's just that a friend and I were having a conversation about compliments…"

"Because I've already told you that you look beautiful tonight," Matt continued, still smiling. And he had, Nadia remembered belatedly; it hadn't really registered. But before she could answer, Matt half-stood and lent his entire body across their table-for-two, lifting her face up by the chin and kissing her soundly. Nadia felt as well as heard the immediate lull in conversation as nearby tables stopped to look across at the display.

Nadia felt herself relaxing into the kiss, her blood thrumming excitedly under her skin as her body responded to the proximity of his. Matt's conversation skills might leave a lot to be desired, which only meant he was bound to be all the better at the sort of thing that didn't need any words. As he finally pulled away, she noticed his eyes were as glazed over as she felt and she was a little gratified to see that he felt it too.

She guessed it was her way of pretending, pretending that nothing was going to happen, pretending she wasn't going anywhere. She should be thinking about decluttering her life, her parents had warned her. Thinking about closure. Of goodbyes. Definitely not hellos. Definitely not fledgling friendships, new relationships, first-time-sex all over again. She was sick of feeling the edge of loss already, as if she was a ticking bomb or a carton of milk whose expiration date was nearing. It felt good to be present. And it felt good to pretend.

Alex

Nadia was a little full-on for 10am on a Sunday morning. Well, Nadia was usually a little full-on, full stop, but that day she seemed to be on some sort of higher setting.

Alex considered her question, seriously. "I need more information. Presumably this necessitates the loss of the hands or feet alongside?" he asked her.

"Of course." Nadia rolled her eyes. She was doing that magic thing she could do, walking backwards through a crowd without bumping into anyone or anything, as if she had eyes in the back of her head. "You couldn't just have like, stumps at your shoulders and then random hands just sort of floating there, two feet below. Be serious." She walked on, sure-footed; the Southbank tourists parted for her without comment. Alex trailed in the wake.

"Do you have to do that? You're making me nervous."

Nadia laughed. "I'm hardly going to walk into the Thames."

"How do you know? You can't see where you're going."

"I like to be able to see your whole face when we talk." She shot him a grin. "Every eye roll, every pursed lip of disapproval," she teased.

Alex laughed. "I don't disapprove of you. But I do disapprove of walking backwards, as a rule. Mind out, I doubt he'll move out of the way for you!" Alex gestured at the street entertainer just a few feet away from them, a long-suffering living statue, staring glassily out across the Thames to where the heart of the city began its sprawl, apparently heedless of the small child attempting to climb up his trouser leg as her parents snapped photos on their iPhones.

"Fair enough." Nadia span on the ball of one foot and fell into step with him, leaving Alex with just her profile, and a better idea of what she meant by how it was nicer seeing someone's whole face. "So. Arms or legs? Pick one. No more stalling."

"I'm not stalling, I'm thinking," Alex protested. "It's a big decision. Look at these guys." He slowed, pulling Nadia out of the flow of people to lean against a railing, shadowed by the buildings above and pleasantly cool against his skin. In front of them a pocket of teenagers were making full use of the tiny skate park tucked underneath the overhang of the theatre, crouching low as they flew from one ramp to the next, hardly anything more than black blurs against the riot of colourful graffiti covering every surface. "*They* clearly need both."

"True," Nadia agreed. "And *he'd* be a pretty niche living statue if he lost half his limbs," she nodded at the nearby entertainer.

"And those guys," Alex pointed at the people who had paused in their walk along the Southbank to mill around the tables of used books set under the shade of the next bridge over. "Wandering from table to table." Alex patted his thigh. "Flipping through a nice paperback." He held his palms out and wiggled his fingers. "How could anyone choose?"

"We could always get you a Kindle," Nadia pointed out.

"Ah, but, how would I get it to change the page?" Alex asked, sagely.

Nadia laughed, hooking her arm into his and pulling him on.

"We'll set the text up really big and you can learn to operate it with your toes."

Nadia

Nadia's answer to the old "which would you rather lose?" conundrum changed depending on her mood, but that day she probably would have chosen to keep her legs. They walked until her shoulders and her collarbones pinked in the sun and the balls of her feet ached in her flimsy gladiator sandals. They stopped for lunch: over-stuffed and inauthentic burritos sold out of a van and ran for coveted free space on a river-facing bench, where they sat and ate in companionable silence before getting back up and walking some more.

She hadn't walked the South Bank for years; the snaking queue out from below the London Eye and the parade of chain restaurants usually depressed her. But it turned out not to be as bad as she'd remembered.

Alex was already so much more at ease with her, a building settling on its foundations, a favourite old tee loosening at the neck. His slightly awkward stop-start conversation had matured into an easy chatter. And it turned out that he was quick and he was funny (albeit in that terribly British sarcastic and self-deprecating way) and the way that he always laughed when he made her laugh made her laugh again in turn.

Nadia had always given her friendship cheaply. She sensed that Alex was the opposite, which made his unfettered acceptance of her all the more important. What a waste. Such a rare gift, the honest friendship of a guy like Alex Bradley. And she might be gone before winter arrived. Another little piece of herself that Nadia would have to wrench off and leave behind. Another friend to disappoint.

As if he sensed her sudden dip in mood, Alex paused.

"What are you doing later?" he asked her. "If you're free, maybe we can tackle some of those 'must-watch' films." They'd had a long conversation about how each couldn't believe the other had never seen particular films, Alex being particularly fond of cult 80s classics with terrible CGI and Nadia loving anything that had her crying by the end.

Nadia laughed. "Sounds like a plan. But we're going to my place, and we're starting with *The Notebook*."

Alex

Usually he remembered to take his phone out of his pocket before he sat on the floor, and for good reason. For once Rory was beating him, but Alex blamed this blip entirely on the fact that his mobile was pressed up against the back of his thigh, jauntily vibrating every twenty seconds, distracting him horribly from the gaming task at hand.

Round four finished and the weapon selection menu up, Rory took a long drink from his pint of Coke and turned to Alex with a triumphant grin.

"Last round. And how would you like your arse handed to you today, good sir? By hand? Or on a plate, as is traditional?" Alex ignored him, twisting so he could slip his offending phone out of his jeans pocket. "And what the hell's going on with your phone?"

"Facebook notifications," Alex mumbled, noticing the many, many little boxed F icons at the top of his phone's screen.

Rory raised his eyebrows. "Wow. In demand, much?"

"Apparently so." Alex swiped his thumb to see what exactly he was being notified about. *Nadia Osipova has tagged you in nineteen photos* his Facebook app informed him. He felt his face lift in a smile.

There were only thirty or so photos uploaded in the new album, a mash of images that would probably seem totally bewildering to an outsider. But for once, Alex wasn't an outsider – there he was, in over half the pictures. He was tucking his arm behind his back to emulate Nelson in front of the column; puckering up to blow the Queen Elizabeth I portrait in Charing Cross station a cheeky kiss; up onstage at Closet looking like a frightened rabbit as a statuesque drag queen wrapped a feather boa around his neck; looping his arms in a giant O above his head, mirroring the huge arch of the London Eye in the background; picture after picture of him, cycling through happy, embarrassed, mildly annoyed and back to happy, ones on his own and ones where Nadia too was squeezed into the frame, her arm stretching out of shot to snap the selfies.

Was it really only just a month ago that he'd glanced, uninterested, at Nadia's application form? Alex felt a stab of guilt at how easily he'd written her off. But then again, who could ever have foretold that in the space of a few weeks, a stranger would be fast becoming one of his best friends?

"Hey," Rory called, pulling Alex out of his thoughts. "You ready?" When Alex looked at him blankly, Rory gestured with the PlayStation controller.

"Er, hang on a second. I'm going to make a cup of tea," Alex said, as he lifted himself to his feet.

"Tea?" Rory's incredulous tone followed Alex out of the room. "Mate, it's a hundred degrees out there. Also not 1864, by the way."

Alex ignored him, moving into the kitchen and, once he'd checked the water level in the kettle, setting it to boil. He leant with the small of his back against the edge of the countertop and flicked through Nadia's pictures again. There was one he quite liked – a recent one – from one evening earlier that week when they'd gone to a grotty old man pub in Camberwell. He meant "old man pub" quite literally; every single other person in there, including the barman, must have had at least sixty years on them. Most of them brazenly ignored the smoking ban, one even puffing on an acrid-smelling pipe, their only deference to the summer heat rolling up their shirt sleeves to their elbows.

The reason Nadia had this pub on her list, it transpired, was that it boasted a collection of retro board games, which patrons were encouraged to play while they enjoyed a drink. Alex and Nadia had rifled through shelf upon shelf of mouldy, battered boxes, played hours and hours of Frustration and Scattergories and Tri-Ominos, eking out a single bottle of wine, until the ancient barman rang the bell for last orders and it was suddenly time to go home again.

That last picture was of Nadia and Alex sitting together on an upholstered bench; it wasn't a selfie, the barman had taken it – being surprisingly sure-fingered with a smartphone for someone of his age, Alex remembered – and, as a result, it was the only full-body picture of the pair of them yet taken. Nadia still had one hand on the board on the table to the side of them, loosely holding a few Tri-Ominos tiles. She'd been wearing pale-blossom pink – she always seemed to be wearing the colours of spring – and the curve of her body looped around Alex's, who was staring confidently into the camera with an easy smile on his face. Alex liked the picture. It didn't really look like him, but he liked it. It reminded him of pictures taken back during uni; pictures with Alice.

Before he fell into the trap of over-analysing it, Alex clicked the necessary options to make the photo his Facebook Profile Picture. The kettle came to the boil.

"Come ON in there, Mr Darcy," Rory shouted from the living room. "You're just delaying the inevitable!"

"Care for a spot of tea, Ror?" Alex called back sarcastically, and only got a loud scoff in response.

Nadia

"I know I'm running the risk of coming across as desperate here, but I've gotta ask. Do you have any hot, single, non-dickhead friends you could set me up with?"

Matt gave Holly an apologetic smile. "I'm afraid I think in the case of my friends, it would be a 'pick any two attributes' scenario."

Holly sighed dramatically, pulling her bare feet up underneath her on the sofa. "The rumours are true; there are no eligible single men left in London any more."

"Nope," Matt agreed with a grin, placing his arm proprietarily around Nadia's shoulders. "Guess I was the last one." Nadia and Holly groaned in unison at his bad joke.

"Come on, Hols, you know that we're just... in between windows right now," Nadia assured her.

"I guess," Holly agreed, morosely.

"Windows?" Matt echoed, confused.

"You know, windows of opportunity." Nadia turned slightly to face him to better explain. "There's always an abundance of single guys in their early twenties, because people have left university and, you know how it is, broken off student relationships that weren't going anywhere."

"And similarly there's always more single guys in, like, their mid-thirties, because that's the sort of age you either break up or get married," Holly added. "Unfortunately, I'm looking for a guy in his late twenties or early thirties, maybe; right in between the windows."

"And, just for future reference," Nadia continued, mischievously, "another window opens up around fifty."

"Bitter divorcees," Holly explained, laughing. "And then finally – of course – you have the final stage. Widowers!"

Thankfully, Matt laughed too. "Wow, you women really have all this figured out, don't you?" he teased.

"At least one of the genders has to," Nadia teased back.

"The literal survival of the human race depends on it," Holly pointed out.

"Okay, fair enough," Matt laughed, clapping his palms to his knees. "Time to leave you two old romantics to your own devices. Holly, nice to see you again," Matt continued as he started to make his exit.

"You too, Matt," Holly smiled. "I'm sure I'll be seeing you again soon!" she teased.

"I hope so!" Matt called as he moved out towards the flat door. At the last moment he spun on his heel and grabbed the trailing Nadia gently but purposefully by the back of her neck, his fingers digging into the curve of her messy fishtail plait as he kissed her goodbye.

"I had a really great weekend," Matt murmured as the kiss broke apart. "Thanks."

"You're welcome," Nadia replied automatically.

"Hey, do you want to go to the cinema this week? We could do *two-for-one*?"

"Sorry, I'm busy…"

"Doing what?"

"Seeing a friend." And she was really looking forward to it. It was one of her favourite things, and Alex was going to love it.

"Well, can't you see them on a day that isn't two-for-one day?" Matt beseeched.

Nadia looked at him. "Sorry, it's all arranged. Maybe next week?" Matt looked dejected – there was no other word for it – and Nadia suddenly felt like a giant bitch. She trailed her fingers up and through his hair at the curve of his ear, mirroring how he was still holding her, trying to recreate the intimacy of the previous night. "But how are you fixed for Tuesday? I could cook us dinner!"

Matt smiled and looked himself again, dropping his hands to take her at her waist. "Tuesday it is. But, just so you know," he winked, "I don't really like borscht."

Nadia huffed indignantly as she moved to close the door behind him. "I was actually going to make spaghetti bolognese."

Chapter 9

Alex

"You should know," Alex called out as he approached, "that I'm really not up for helping you move a body or anything like that!"

Nadia laughed as she turned from where she was sitting on the bottom of the steps leading down to the shoreline. "What are you on about?"

"This whole very dodgy and mysterious rendezvous," Alex teased as he descended the worn concrete steps. "Meet me underneath Blackfriars Bridge, 8pm. Dress down; wear comfortable shoes…" Alex imitated the content of Nadia's earlier text message using his creepiest voice, wriggling his fingers in a dastardly fashion for good measure. He came to a stop on the step in front of Nadia just as she had got to her feet. The steps were old and steep – it made Alex tower over Nadia, her face below his was close enough that Alex noticed the pale ghosts of freckles trailing across the top of her cheeks and the bridge of her nose underneath her makeup.

Nadia stepped back almost immediately, giving Alex the opportunity to join her on the stony "beach" of the Thames, which was flowing mulishly a few metres from his feet.

"We're just going for a walk!" Nadia assured him. "Besides," she teased, her eyes flashing, "I'm the sort of girl who could handle a dead body on her own – trust me!"

"Oh, I believe you!" Alex laughed. It was the coolest evening they'd had for weeks – Nadia was even wearing a cardigan – and the slowly purpling sky was traced across all over with the beginnings of rain clouds, heavy with promise. "So, a walk?"

"Yes, a walk!" Nadia repeated, turning on her heel and stepping carefully across the muddy, flinty bank. "So let's walk!"

"So, are we actually doing this whole tourist thing?" Alex asked, moving quickly to catch up. "Are we going to look at St Paul's Cathedral and take pictures of Tower Bridge?"

"Those are both in the other direction, genius," Nadia pointed out, cocking her thumb behind them where Alex could just about make out the pale curve of the roof of St Paul's at some distance across the river. "How long did you say you've lived in this city again?"

"Well, it's not like I've got a season pass for the Hop On, Hop Off London Bus Tour," Alex retorted, scathingly.

"I used to work on a tour bus, you know," Nadia said suddenly. "Got the job due to my 'language skills'," she said, complete with sarcastic air quotes.

"Well, no wonder you know all this stuff."

"It's only because an ex-boyfriend used to take me down here. He used to look for stuff washed up by the river. Mudlarking, it's called. You can't dig or mess about without a license or the Museum of London will come and get you, but if stuff is just lying there at low tide its fair game."

"Jesus. Sounds like the guy thought he was Indiana Jones," Alex scorned grumpily.

Nadia laughed. "Hardly. Once he accidentally picked up something that turned out to be a bone and he freaked out and flung it away from him and never went 'mudlarking' again."

Alex stopped walking. "A bone?" he echoed in horror.

"Oh, it was probably just a dog's. Don't you start!" Nadia mocked, continuing to steadily pick her way around the subtle curve of the riverbank. "I came back though. I liked it down here. It's quiet. It almost feels like the city is yours alone, rather than being stuffed in with eight million people, don't you think?" Alex knew exactly what she meant. There wasn't a single street in London where you weren't sharing space with countless others. But down here, as the sun disappeared behind the turn of the water and everything started to turn as grey as the rocks they walked upon, it really did feel as if they were the only two people in the world.

"You're right, it's really cool down here. Your ex sounds like a bit a weirdo, though," Alex said, taking Nadia's arm to steady her as she stepped up onto an old crumbling cinder block lying on its side in the mud. She was almost the same height as him now, but down at water level it was too shadowed and her freckles were invisible to him. They were like Nadia herself; so ridiculously open most of the time, but then again, sometimes so hard to read. "Speaking of boyfriends, I presume that things between you and that Matt guy are going well?"

Nadia made a non-committal noise, looking out across the Thames and back towards the red ironwork of Blackfriars Bridge. "Yeah, Matt's okay."

Alex tilted his head. "So when do you make the big announcement and go In A Relationship with him on Facebook, then?" He dropped his voice conspiratorially. "That's like the twenty-first-century equivalent of being married."

Nadia shot him a warning look. "Don't get ahead of yourself. I don't want to talk about Matt."

"Obviously, being as you never do. What's the deal there?"

"There's no 'deal'!"

"Don't get me wrong, because you know I love adventuring around London with you, or whatever it is that we're doing, but why aren't you sharing your special Thames walk with…"

"Alex!" Nadia's tone succeeded in pulling Alex up short. "I mean it. There's no 'deal'. Things are going great with Matt. It's all cool. Can we please drop the subject?"

As if to emphasise her point Nadia hopped down from her

vantage point on the cinder block and kept moving. A sleek Thames Clipper boat – weighed down low in the water with passengers –swept noisily through the middle of the river and it felt as if a spell had been broken.

"Sheesh. Okay," Alex muttered, wondering what nerve he'd had the misfortune to hit.

"Speaking of exes," Nadia said, breezily, as Alex caught up with her again. "Out of curiosity, what happened between you and that Alice Rhodes girl?"

Nadia

Nadia had been wondering about Alice all week; she was surprised she'd been able to keep it in as long as she had. Monday had been her day off from the shop and nobody had been around to play. So Nadia had just lain on the sofa and played with Holly's iPad all day long; she wasn't even sure why she bothered password-protecting the thing. Holly had had the same PIN for everything since they were fourteen, and Nadia had known it since they were about fourteen and a half.

And somehow aimless web-browsing had turned into a shamefully full-on Facebook stalk. To be brutally honest, there wasn't all that much of Alex to stalk. Clicking back beyond the photos of him that she'd recently uploaded, Alex's Facebook identity seemed to mainly consist of his head popping shyly out of occasional group photos. He hadn't been kidding. He barely did anything, or at least, whatever he was doing, the evidence of it wasn't turning up online. Back and back Nadia had gone, feeling the customary weirdness that came with looking at pictures of friends from before you ever met them.

And then, suddenly, there was an Alex explosion. He'd looked different – younger for sure – sporting a confident short haircut and a lazy fuzz of matching stubble on his face; but the real difference was everything else. He'd once been photographed running barefoot and bare-chested on a pebble beach; smiling broadly on a ratty sofa with his arms around the shoulders of two friends; photobombing a pair of posing, mini-skirted girls with both hands held aloft, making drunken peace signs. And here, there and everywhere had been a girl tagged Alice Rhodes...

"Alice?" Alex echoed, tone suspicious, as if he thought this was some sort of a trap. "What about Alice?"

"Well, I'm just assuming she's your ex," Nadia needled gently. "You're in like thirty thousand photos with her; even kissing in some! I mean I'm not exactly Sherlock Holmes, but..."

Alex visibly winced; Nadia wondered again where the boy in those old photos had gone.

"Yeah, we went out," he said, eventually. The pair walked on for a minute in weighted silence.

"Alex and Alice," Nadia said, after a while. "That must have been annoying."

"Yup," Alex answered shortly.

"University girlfriend, then?"

"Yup."

"Sheesh, I'm drowning in information over here!" Nadia cried out dramatically; Alex rolled his eyes. "Anyway, check you out, you dirty dog. She's absolutely gorgeous!" And it was true. The first thing Nadia had noticed about Alice was that she was an absolute stunner. Nadia would have killed to look anything like her: exotic and sexy with tanned skin and a riot of ink-black curls, the complete opposite of 'milk-and-water' Nadia...

"I suppose." Well, at least that was an improvement on 'yup'. Alex flashed Nadia a hard look. "You been all over my Facebook, then?"

Nadia shrugged lightly. "I was bored."

"You could have always just asked," Alex pointed out, not looking at her as they continued to walk, moving quickly past the unwelcome bustle of Gabriel's Wharf. "We're friends, aren't we?"

Nadia looked at him curiously. "Of course."

The great, grey behemoth that was Waterloo Bridge reared up ahead of them like a finish line. Alex slowed.

"Do you remember me telling you that I was due to take a gap year, but the other person pulled out?" he said, quietly. Nadia nodded slowly. "Well, that other person was Alice." Alex shrugged. "Everything arranged and paid for, down to the airport transfers either side. Four days to go."

"She… decided she didn't want to go travelling?" Nadia asked, confused.

"She decided she didn't want to go anywhere with me," Alex clarified ruefully. "Ever again. We'd been together for two and a half years. It was pretty harsh."

"Harsh" sounded like a bit of an understatement to Nadia, but she echoed it nevertheless. "Totally harsh…"

"She'd already cancelled her half of things without telling me," Alex blurted out. "Like, she didn't even give me a chance to change her mind, plead my case, you know? It was already too late before I even found out about it."

Nadia considered her words carefully before responding. "Well, I'm sure you wouldn't have wanted to patch things up with somebody who could be so… harsh – as you put it – would you? Much less travel around the world with them. Really, it was a blessing in disguise!"

"Oh yeah, I know that now, totally," Alex assured her, maybe a little too quickly. "But at the time, it felt like the end of the world. Hence I couldn't even pick myself up and go it alone."

"Oh, I know." Nadia rolled her eyes. "The devastation of first love gone awry and all that! When my high-school boyfriend stopped replying to my texts and started sitting at the back of the bus with Eloise Adams I cried for a week straight."

"It was a bit more than that." Alex gave a little self-deprecating laugh. "Because. Well, I was only going to ask her to marry me during the trip."

"Alex! What!"

"I know." Alex laughed again. "I'd gotten my grandmother's ring resized and everything. How utterly shite."

Nadia shook her head in disbelief. "Yes. Harsh. Shite. Absolutely, horrifically awful. All of the above?"

"It knocked me for six alright," Alex agreed, seemingly weirdly cheerful and relaxed for someone who had just confessed utter heartbreak.

"And nobody really since?"

"Nobody since," Alex confirmed. "Rory made me sign up for internet dating once, but either my face or my description was massively unappealing as I got zero bites."

"You?" Nadia was baffled. "You got NO dates?"

"Not one."

"But you're totally good-looking!" Nadia blurted out.

Alex grinned at her. "Must have been the wording, then."

"What the hell did it say? That you hate puppies and babies and chocolate and that you moonlight as a Jack the Ripper copycat serial killer?"

Alex threw his head back and laughed, loose and genuine again. "I think that would probably be quite successful, but I reckon it would attract a very niche type of girl."

"Ah, Alex, I don't understand it." Nadia shook her head. "I wish I could set you up with someone. You don't happen to fancy Holly by any chance, do you?"

"Nope, sorry. Not to disparage the lady. And now are you going to offer me Caro?"

"Why? Do you like her?" Nadia asked, giving him a hard look.

"No, I was just wondering why Holly was thrust into the fray and not Caro!"

"Caro is seeing someone," Nadia explained.

"Boy or girl?" Alex asked teasingly, obviously recalling their conversation about Caro's colourful sexual history.

Nadia laughed. "A guy," she confirmed, before swiftly changing the subject back. Had Alex ever considered speed dating? It could be a laugh...

Alex

He hadn't talked about Alice for ages and was pleased to find that it hadn't felt like it used to, that is: like somebody had gutted him navel to nose and taken a cheese grater to what they found inside. That was definitely progress. Of course, it helped that Nadia was the one he'd been talking to; she was probably the easiest person to talk to that he'd ever met. She put him at ease even in the most awkward of situations – hence he was here, walking the floodbanks of the Thames at dusk, he supposed.

She was relating some of the internet dating horror stories she'd heard and was all haloed in orange by the dying light of the day, making him laugh, putting him so expertly at that usual ease. For a moment he felt as if he should tell her about Lila, about how he felt as though she could be The One, about how a second chance at true love might have missed him by just one guy. Or about how Lila was looking at him recently: uncharacteristically silent, with a bruised little expression in her eyes and how his confusion over it all was keeping him lying awake at night.

But for whatever reasoning, he wasn't quite ready to make the biggest thing in his life into a Big Thing and he didn't really want to invite Lila down onto the shadowy beach with them, so instead he simply walked and chatted with Nadia – something that was fast becoming one of his most favourite things.

Chapter 10

Alex

"You know, when we talked about this, I didn't think it was going to be so… immediate," Alex murmured as they moved past the bored-looking attendant who had taken their money in exchange for a sheaf of paper and a numbered name badge and waved them on through to the function room beyond her desk.

"Hey, imminent deportation here," Nadia teased. "No time like the present, and all that."

Alex rolled his eyes. Nadia loved to get her way by playing the 'imminent deportation' card. She'd miss that once the appeal went through.

"And what is this?" he continued, waving the stapled bundle of paper incredulously.

Nadia skim-read the first page of her own. "Oh it's just a standard questionnaire. The agency just want to know stuff about you so they can invite you to the right kind of singles' events and stuff."

"Yeah; age, sex, location I get," Alex insisted. "But why do they need to know whether I prefer staycation UK breaks or going abroad?"

Nadia laughed. "Says a lot about your personality, your priorities? I don't know."

"Well then, what does my favourite sandwich filling say about my priorities?

"Oh, just answer any old thing. It's all just a bit of fun," Nadia advised him. "In fact, I'm going to take this opportunity for a little self-improvement. Tonight I feel like being an inventor of something. What could I have invented?"

"Does it matter?"

"Of course it matters!" Nadia insisted. "Come on. It has to be something well known, but not well known enough that it's obvious I didn't come up with it. And something I understand the basics of, in case they ask questions. How about some sort of app?"

"How about just being yourself?"

Nadia waved her hand dismissively. "'Myself' is boring."

Alex just laughed at her. "Nadia Osipova, 'yourself' is the most interesting person I've ever met."

Alex watched with pleasure as Nadia's cheeks flushed with a pleased pink. "You charmer," she teased, deflecting from her blush, looping her arm with his and pulling him on. "That's the way to impress the girls. Now come on. Let's claim our free class of cheap champagne and fill these suckers out."

Nadia

In true Alex-fashion, he had thoughtfully and truthfully answered each of the questions; it turned out his favourite sandwich filling was ham, cheese and red-onion chutney.

It wasn't Nadia's first spin at speed dating. She and Caro had gone twice before. Caro excelled at this hard-and-fast sort of flirting, where Nadia was more in it for the complimentary drink aspect. She'd thought Alex might chicken out or sit there like a startled rabbit while strangers filled the five minutes with desperate chatter. He'd certainly seemed incredibly unconvinced right up until the moment they separated for the start of the event. The men remained sitting at their little tables-for-two while the women rotated clockwise around the room, five minutes with each guy, that blonde one chasing an indefinable spark; that red-head for a man for her immediate needs; that brunette, something in between.

Nadia kept a weather eye on her friend, watching him smile politely as each girl settled herself opposite him, remembering how she'd received that same cautious greeting as she'd sat down at his table at the Bellevue quiz. It wasn't hard to imagine what these girls were thinking. Alex was looking his best, wearing a V-neck in a shade of green that brought out the redder warmth in his brown hair, paired with dark, well-fitting jeans and had allowed a little stubble grow in, all at Nadia's gentle direction. He'd followed up his glass of free champagne with a sophisticatedly dark-looking glass of red wine, every inch a gent.

"Well hello, number 12," he drawled as Nadia finally rotated his way; it was her favourite number and she'd requested it specially.

"Hello yourself, 19," she retorted as she scooted her chair closer to the table. "How's it going? Have you met Mrs Right yet?"

"No," Alex replied stoically, picking up his glass and cheering the air with it. "But the girl behind the bar pours a fair old measure."

"What more do you need?" Nadia agreed dryly. "True love."

"Is that what is meant to be accomplished here? I feel like I'm slowly boring the women of London to death in five-minute increments."

"Bloody hell, what are you talking about?" Nadia asked, alarmed. "You're not talking about work or football are you?"

"No, nothing like that. They're doing most of the talking. I seem to be basically just nodding in agreement. I feel like the Churchill dog."

"Well, that's no bad thing." Nadia relaxed. "Women like to talk about themselves!"

Alex eyed her. "You're not exactly talking about yourself, though, are you?"

Nadia waved her hand dismissively. "Semantics."

Alex lowered his voice. "I heard you tell that last guy you invented courgetti."

104

Nadia shrugged again. "Someone must have." She helped herself to a sip from Alex's glass of wine. "Anyway, stop complaining. I'm here for *you*."

"You're here for the free champagne," Alex immediately retorted.

"That too," Nadia agreed.

"I just think you should take a little of your own advice," Alex continued after a moment. "You never know when you're going to meet someone, and you should be open to it and all that. Remember all that? The lecture you gave me for the entire bus journey here?"

Nadia shifted uncomfortably in the thinly padded chair; that clock-countdown feeling ticking through her, little knocks to the heart. What good would it be to meet The One now?

Alex drew back slightly, mistaking the reason for her hesitancy. "Oh wait. I suppose I forget about you and Matt."

"Mmm, Matt," Nadia agreed; it was as good a reason as any, she supposed. The timer on the wall went off, making her jump. Their five minutes was up. To her right, number 20 was bidding a reasonably disinterested farewell to the departing number 11, already looking over at Nadia to see what the next offering was. "Well, catch you in the interval I guess, unless you meet Mrs Right in the meantime. Or want to hook up with that barmaid."

"Nadia, hold up." Alex had also got to his feet, taking his wine glass in one steady hand and Nadia's now-empty champagne flute in the other, pouring in some red for her to take onward.

Nadia squeezed his fingers gratefully as she took back her glass. "Good luck, soldier," she winked, before leaving her gent to the attentions of lucky number 13.

Chapter 11

Nadia

It was embarrassingly *When Harry Met Sally*, but lately things were starting to feel tense with Alex in a way she couldn't articulate. He'd been a bit like a kid brother (albeit older than her, fine), lost and sad, someone who appealed to the philanthropic side of her nature (as well as the side of her nature that liked to goad people until they snapped) – but she couldn't reconcile that Alex with the Alex she got glimpses of now and then; the Alex who'd once built illegal bonfires on Brighton Beach and sat around them with his smoking hot bitch of a girlfriend; the Alex who was starting to feel tall and important as he walked beside her; the Alex who bit down on his bottom lip in an impossibly suggestive way when he was trying not to laugh at her; the Alex that – okay, she'd admit it, but only to herself – she was starting to develop the smallest, tiniest crush on.

She'd so far been able to pass off the warmness, the excitement she felt at getting to see him as mere anticipation at getting to spend time with someone who'd become a good friend. But the night before she'd been in bed with Matt and caught herself thinking of Alex, over and over, again and again, and there really wasn't any misconstruing that...

Nadia jumped as a wadded-up takeaway leaflet hit her squarely on the forehead.

"Paging Nadia!" Ledge called from the doorway to the kitchen. "Are you receiving? Over!"

"What?"

"You've got a text message. I've told you, like, three times." Illustrating his point, Ledge waved the mobile that she'd left on the kitchen side at her.

"Oh. Sorry." Nadia cupped her hands in front of her and Ledge lightly tossed the phone into them. The text was from Alex. She felt a little quiver of embarrassment before wondering why he was texting her; he and his friends should be on their way over by now.

"Everything okay?" Holly asked, bending down to place a shallow bowl of plain Doritos on the coffee table.

"It's just going to be Alex and Lila tonight," Nadia explained as she digested the message. "His flatmate Rory has to work."

Holly raised an eyebrow. "On a Saturday evening?"

Nadia shrugged. "Some big client emergency, apparently."

"We're not going to be even-numbered for the games," Holly complained.

Nadia did some quick mental arithmetic. "Yes we are. There's six."

Holly gave her a hard look. "Nads. Have you not invited Matt?"

"No, why would I have invited Matt?"

"I thought things were going well between you two?"

Nadia shrugged. "Things are going fine. That doesn't mean he needs to become surgically attached to me."

"There's a world of difference between getting an invite to your girlfriend's game night and becoming a conjoined twin, sweetie."

"I don't really feel like I'm his girlfriend yet."

"Well considering the walls in this place are paper-thin – I can definitely confirm you *sound* like you're his girlfriend," Holly teased.

Nadia groaned. "Get out of the fifties. There is such a thing as sex without love."

"Heaven's above!" Caro cried mockingly as she entered the room to place a strong-looking pitcher of Pimms on the coffee table next to the tortilla chips. "Now who are we talking about here?"

"Her and Matt," Holly clarified, putting her hands on her hips.

"And who's the one that's coming this evening?"

"Alex," Nadia supplied.

"Okay. And which one is she dating again?" Caro asked Holly.

"Both!" Holly answered, raising her arms in a wide, sarcastic shrug.

"No! I'm seeing Matt – *casually*." Nadia shot Holly a warning look. "And Alex and I are just friends."

Alex

"I really feel like I'm intruding," Lila was saying for the third time as they got to street level at Clapham Common and began the short walk to Nadia and Holly's flat. "I mean, the invitation was initially for you and Rory. I was already just tagging along, and without Rory it's even more like I'm interloping…"

"Lils, don't worry about it," Alex reassured her – again, for the third time – as they moved through the muggy, still-bright streets. It had finally rained earlier that day, a short; sharp burst of a shower, with the heat evaporating the puddles off the pavements only minutes later. "Nadia is cool. She doesn't have it in her to make a guest feel uncomfortable, so don't stress."

Lila gave Alex a sideways look. Since Nadia began uploading photos from their random adventures onto Facebook she'd been questioning him regularly about exactly what was going on between them. She and Rory just couldn't get their heads around the fact that even though they were seeing each other three or four times a week now – sometimes for adventures, but sometimes just for a little stroll and chat in the evening cool – it was completely platonic.

"That Russian chick really is a stone-cold fox," had been Rory's verdict after he'd flicked through Nadia's Facebook album with interest. Alex had shrugged. "Oh come on! You can't tell me that you don't secretly want to pork her!"

Alex had just winced. "How poetic." He'd looked across at Rory, who was grinning suggestively. "Yes, she's a very pretty girl!" he accepted. "But we really are just friends. She's got a boyfriend."

"A boyfriend?" Rory had repeated, looking back at the Facebook photo album open on his laptop screen. "Well, I don't know when she finds the time to see him then, being as she's always with you. Not porking."

"I feel almost like I'm meeting a celebrity," Lila said airily as they moved through the quiet residential streets. "You talk about her all the time…"

Alex laughed. "You've met her before Lils. You met her when I did."

"I know. But it's you she decided to keep for a pet."

Alex slowed. Lila's tone was perfectly casual and carefree, but he didn't like the edge to it. That was the best word to describe how she'd been in recent weeks – 'edgy' in herself and full of edges when it came to him. He supposed he had to cut the girl some slack. Rory had been around less and less lately and sometimes at night Alex could hear the two of them arguing, voices pitched low and angry. And once again Rory had begged off at the last minute and Lila was embarrassed and floundering and alone.

Well, not alone. Alex reached to give Lila a consolatory shoulder-squeeze, which she returned with a half-hearted smile.

"It's here on this side," Alex said after a moment, gesturing at the three-storey townhouse conversion a little further down the road. "Number 14."

Alex rang the flat using the bulky silver intercom and was buzzed in immediately. He and Lila navigated past the piles of junk mail, bicycles and prams, a feature of communal hallways, and climbed the steps to the first floor. Nadia was waiting for them, lounging against the doorframe to Flat D. Her face lit up when she saw him and Alex felt his own lift in response.

"Hey," Alex grinned as he made his way up the final few steps to the landing. "I bring supplies!" he cheered, holding aloft the two plastic bags from the off licence that he'd been carrying. Nadia moved towards him and he went to hand her one of the bags on reflex, only to succeed in swinging it clear into her stomach – she hadn't gone to take one of the bags, she'd gone to kiss him hello. "Oh shit!"

Alex immediately dropped both bags to the floor and grabbed her hands with his. "Shit," he repeated, "Nadia, I'm so sorry!" Nadia just laughed and assured him that she was fine, waving him and Lila on into the bright flat behind her.

Alex was mildly mortified. And all he could suddenly think about was the fact that Nadia had never kissed him hello before, so how had he been expected to know…?

Nadia

It was funny, but if you'd asked her two months ago whether she thought her friends would get on with Alex, she wouldn't have been sure. Alex had been a little too hesitant, too vanilla, a certified background character; she would have thought that people like Ledge and Caro would have been impatient with him.

But tonight he was a different person than he'd been all those weeks ago at the Bellevue pub quiz. Everyone was charmed by this funny, cool guy who kept their glasses topped up and won most rounds of Cards Against Humanity hands down.

"You've worked a transformation," Holly told her as they hurriedly replenished the jug of Pimms together, grabbing handfuls of pre-cut fruit from the chopping board and throwing it in.

"You make it sound like he was made of wallpaper before," Nadia admonished, rolling her eyes.

"That first night, in the Bellevue, and Bison? It was like being trapped in a terrible Hugh Grant movie from the nineties. I stepped on his foot on the dance floor and *he* apologised to *me* – twice."

"You can't possibly moan that someone is too polite!" Nadia

defended Alex, ignoring the fact that she'd just been thinking about how awkward he used to seem.

"He was a drip," was Holly's blunt assessment. "But now he's a laugh. You've worked wonders with your weird Bucket List activity thing. You should patent it as some sort of lifestyle."

"Alex was always a laugh," Nadia said quietly, "he just doesn't always like to be." She didn't appreciate the truth in that sentence until she'd actually said it and found herself wondering just how many masks Alex had on, how many walls he'd put up, how many bad clichés she could apply here…

Holly arched an eyebrow. "Right. Because that's not at all creepy or weird." She moved across to the sink to rinse the stickiness of fruit juice from her palms.

"It's not creepy or weird," Nadia insisted, again slightly surprised by the force of her defensiveness. "He's just had some shitty times and known some shitty people."

Holly just rolled her eyes again as she shut off the tap. "Jeez, haven't we all?" And before Nadia could stick up for Alex again, Holly had hoisted the refilled pitcher off the kitchen side and moved back through into the living room.

Alex

Nadia was more relaxed here in her home environment; less gung ho and get up and go. She sat cross-legged on the floor wearing pyjama trousers that were so long they concealed her feet; laughed so much she got the hiccups; picked the chunks of fruit out of her Pimms to eat with her fingers; got tipsy and lay back on the carpet with her head on Holly's thigh; held her cards so carelessly it seemed she didn't give a shit that everybody could see what was in her hand.

Alex was revising his original opinion of Caro. Yes, she acted as if she owned the room and checked her mobile phone with irritating frequency, but she also had a wickedly sharp sense of humour and a no-nonsense attitude that appealed. 'Ledge' – as they called him – had been harder to read until his fifth or sixth pint, at which point the hackles that seemed to have risen at the introduction of another guy into this cosy social group were calmed. But Holly – who had been nice as figurative pie to him the night of the Bellevue quiz – was uncomfortably reserved and watchful. He hadn't expected disapproval from that corner.

With Lila being weird and quiet too, the night had a bit of a peculiar vibe. It fell far short of outright awkward, but there was a definite sense of agenda nonetheless. But Nadia was there, and it might be unfathomable and it might be stupid, but Alex was perfectly content; he just flat-out loved spending time with Nadia. It was the only time he really felt like himself.

Caro had already upped and gone, having made a rush for the last Tube hours before. Ledge and Lila were conversing out in the hallway as they put their shoes on, raring to go. Holly was in the kitchen, rinsing out the empty Pimms' pitcher, a klaxon that politely blared "It's 2 o' clock in the morning, will everybody please get out of my house?"

But somehow over the course of the past couple of hours, Nadia had shifted – or maybe it had been him – and now she was sitting so close, tucked into him as if he was a blanket over her shoulders. He could have leant only slightly forward and kissed the curve of her face; you know, if he wanted to... At first it had been a bit weird and he hadn't been entirely sure where to put his arms, but now it was insanely comfortable and he didn't really want to move.

Nadia was doing something with the pack of playing cards they'd been using earlier, laying them out on the carpet in front of them in nonsensical piles, counting under her breath as she did so, so obviously there was some sort of method behind what she was doing. Her hand stalled suddenly and she stiffened oh-so-slightly. It was almost imperceptible; he only noticed it at all because her shoulder blades were pressed against the plain of his chest.

"What?" he asked. "What are you doing?"

Nadia pulled her hand through the haphazard piles of cards

to pull them back into one messy deck again. "Trying to foretell my future," she sighed.

"Don't you need actual tarot cards for that?" Alex teased. "Or how about a crystal ball?"

"Hey, don't knock it!" Nadia chastised. "I went to a boarding school, remember? Girls in boarding schools have to make do. This method was created by girls generations ago and it was always good for predicting if you'd pass your exams, if you'd get a snog off one of the townie boys, things like that."

Alex laughed softly. "Okay, okay. So what are the cards telling you?"

"Not a lot."

Alex arched an eyebrow. "Not a lot?" he repeated. "Well they said *something* you didn't like."

Nadia sighed; Alex felt it more than heard it. "Oh, I just got lots of odd-numbered pairs."

"And that means...?"

There was a suspended moment, and all at once Nadia seemed to realise how she was sitting against him. She sat up, pulling her plait over her shoulder nervously and combing her fingers through its tail, flustered. Alex felt cold and exposed where she'd been touching him.

"It means," Nadia said, after another flustered moment had passed, "that I'm not going to get what I want..."

Chapter 12

Nadia

There really was no denying it any more. When she saw a message from him on her phone her stomach flipped over as if she was a teenager. When he smiled at her the skin on the nape of her neck tingled stupidly. She'd started to daydream, had fantasies where she'd slip her arms under one of Alex's t-shirts, before pulling it up and away, over his head and finally getting a good look at that tattoo she'd caught a glimpse of months before.

This wasn't meant to happen. It was already going to be too hard to leave behind so many people she loved in London; she didn't exactly want to add another to the roster. That boy on the swing in Clapham Common had felt safe; white bread down to his bones, boring and predictable, someone she could have fun with and have as a mate, for sure, but she'd sensed from the off that he'd never let her close and that had suited her just fine. It was bad enough that they'd become such close friends, let alone something more... she was damned if she did and damned if she didn't.

But then there was that *something* inside of her, hot and selfish, that kept on pointing out the entirely random way that Alex had fallen into her life, the entirely unprecedented way she was feeling, insisting, insisting that it might be *meant to be*; and who was she in the face of something like that?

The sound of Alex's name drew her attention. "Pardon?"

Matt just smiled indulgently; he was used to her- by now habitual - lapses in concentration. "I was just saying, that Alex guy. I met him, right? At Bison, the night we met?"

It seemed a lifetime ago. "Yeah, you did."

"I was thinking that you guys are such good friends and all – and you look like you have so much fun in all those photos I see – I was wondering if we should do a double-date or something?"

Nadia shifted uncomfortably. "He's not seeing anyone at the moment."

"Oh? I thought he was seeing that little blonde scrap that was in all the photos from that games night you had the other week?" Nadia tensed again.

"No, that's just Lila."

Matt raised an eyebrow inquisitively. "'Just Lila'?" he echoed.

"Yeah. She's his housemate's girlfriend."

Matt laughed suddenly. "Oh yeah, of course. The flatmate's girlfriend, I remember."

"No, you haven't met her, I don't think…"

"Oh no, I know. But I remember Alex talking about her when we were in Bison."

There was something in Matt's tone that made Nadia curious. "What was he saying?" she asked.

"Oh, I'm sure you know it all." He rolled his eyes. "The love-sick whining. 'The girl of my dreams is banging my flatmate' and all that. He needs to man up!" Matt laughed.

And Nadia's stomach flipped over again. And not in a good way.

Alex

It wasn't that late; it wasn't even full-dark yet, but still Alex had made to go after Lila when she'd come flying out of Rory's bedroom and straight out of the flat door, pausing just long enough to turn her sticky, tear-stained face in Alex's direction, breaking his heart.

After staring after her in mild shock for a beat or two, Alex turned to get a pair of shoes from his bedroom. He pulled up abruptly; Rory was standing in his doorway, rubbing the pads of his palms aggressively against his temples.

"Sorry about that," he said after a minute.

"Is she alright?" Alex asked, without preamble.

Rory exhaled dramatically. "Why do girls always do this? Why does there have to be a bad guy? Such martyrs, all of them."

Alex fixed his friend with a hard look. "And what exactly is it that you've done to 'martyr' Lila..?"

Rory returned his look. "Nothing. She's throwing a bitch-fit about the hours I'm working. Said I just don't want to spend time with her. And I said it wasn't that at all, but maybe it's not such a good time for me to be in a relationship at the moment, because I obviously can't give her what she wants and..." Rory trailed off and gestured eloquently towards the flat's front door. "And she apparently agreed."

Alex had to digest that for a moment or two. "You broke up with her?" he asked, incredulously. "You broke up with *Lila?*"

Rory groaned. "Stop it, will you mate? I already feel like I'm your dad come to tell you that your parents are getting a divorce or something."

Alex looked towards the door again. She'd probably already be on a bus off the high street by now; it was too late to follow. "She didn't even say goodbye..."

Rory gave a bark of a laugh. "It's not like you'll never, ever see her again."

"Oh, I hardly think she's going to be spending much time sitting on our sofa watching you and me play *Call of Duty* any more, Ror."

Rory shrugged dismissively. "Nah, she always liked you. You'll stay friends, I'm sure. But don't let her turn you against me. I didn't *want* to hurt her – you know – didn't want her upset; that's why I had to end it. It wasn't going anywhere any more, and she knew it." Rory's voice hitched slightly, so slightly, right at the end, and Alex belatedly realised that his friend was actually quite cut up about it after all.

"Okay," he agreed after a moment. "Right, so, how are we playing this? I've never been present during break-up aftermath before. Do I get you a cup of tea or do I get you a beer?"

Nadia
Alex was distracted, odd; or maybe it was her who was the one being weird, she couldn't tell. All Nadia knew is that suddenly there were elephants in the room where before it had been only them.

Because they'd agreed they needed proper sustenance to fuel an all-night movie marathon they'd decided to fit in a late dinner before the first showing. Nadia's cotton onesie was balled-up in a tote bag at her feet; she wasn't quite brave enough to wear it in a Soho restaurant, even though she'd had great fun convincing a horrified Holly she was going to do exactly that.

When she noticed that Alex was checking his phone more often than he was putting forkfuls of food into his mouth, Nadia snapped.

"What's up with you?" she asked, a little forcefully. "You're like an expectant father waiting for news or something."

Alex laughed. "Sorry. I'm just waiting on a text." Although Nadia clearly indicated for him to elaborate, he didn't, dropping his eyes to his plate and raking his fork prongs through his cooling jambalaya. He seemed startled to find Nadia still scrutinising him when he looked up again. "I promise I won't use my phone in the cinema, miss!" he joked, holding up his fork and fingers like a Boy Scout salute. "Scout's Honour." Nadia softened and allowed herself a smile.

She knew it was physically impossible, but lately Alex seemed to be filling out his clothes a lot better. She'd even wondered if he'd bought new things, but she was more or less certain she'd seen him wearing that evening's particular loose-fit t-shirt before. Maybe it was more in the way he sat. He always used to sit slightly forwards, with his shoulders pinched inwards towards one another. Now he sat back, open and expansive and comfortable in his own skin, in a way she would never have imagined him doing before. That night it was Nadia who was slightly hunched and closed-off.

Because she didn't know what was bothering her more; that the Alex she was falling for was in love with someone else, or the Alex who was one of her best friends had never told her about it. Both affronts stung her in different ways.

Alex quickly glanced at his phone again; it was almost as if he didn't realise he was doing it.

"I tell you what, I'm glad we're spending tonight watching films with lots of explosions," Alex said suddenly, shaking his head. "I couldn't sit through anything heavy. It's been a weird old week."

"How-so?"

Alex looked at Nadia for a beat before he answered. "Ah, Lils and Rory are having a spat. Well, actually I guess it's more than that. They've actually broken up."

Suddenly Nadia found that her mouthful of jerk chicken was stuck in her throat. She swallowed laboriously.

"They've broken up?" she echoed.

Alex shrugged. "Apparently. Well, they've both set their Facebook relationships to 'single' anyway, which is about as serious as these things can get," he laughed. "Anyway. Speaking of relationships, how are things with Matt? He didn't fancy getting in on nine straight hours of *Avengers* action then?"

Alex

Nadia seemed sad. She wasn't wearing any makeup – she said there was no point just sitting in a dark cinema all night – but even aside from that she seemed somewhat diluted. He'd wondered if she was just tired – asked her three times if she was sure she was still up for the epic superhero movie marathon that she had booked them in for – but she'd insisted she was fine. But whatever she said, her mouth still had a sad little tilt and her eyes were shadowed and for the first time since the moment he met her she felt far away.

He'd never seen her wearing a dark colour like this before – she was in a deep plum that made her look even paler than normal and made her blonde hair shine dully under the restaurant's dim lighting. Her hair was loose, threaded over with deep kinks where she'd previously had it plaited. She'd picked the braid apart with quick, nervous fingers shortly after their arrival, shaking the hair loose as she talked.

Alex was struck, not for the first time, about how emotive Nadia was. When she smiled, the whole world smiled with her. When she was down, well… He supposed it didn't help that he was already bummed out about Lila. He'd messaged her twice since Wednesday night but she hadn't replied. He hoped it was because the whole thing with Rory was still a little too raw and not that she was going to cut him out of her life completely now she wasn't going out with his flatmate any more.

Lila, single. For some reason it had never occurred to Alex that Rory and Lila might ever break up. He should be thrilled, jumping cartwheels; the girl he'd been pining for from not-even-that-afar was now available. But instead the situation was sitting heavy and queer inside of him, like way too much food, which probably explained why he had no appetite. Maybe it wouldn't be such a bad thing if Lila never got back in contact. She obviously would never feel the same way about him, so maybe this could be a golden opportunity to cut his losses and run. But then, equally, he could always grab the opportunity to confess his feelings; he had nothing left to lose, after all.

He sighed. "Do you think it's always right to fight for love?" he asked Nadia, having another half-hearted go at his rapidly-cooling jambalaya.

Her eyes narrowed. "It depends. You're not going to get all overly involved in this break-up and try and get Rory and Lila back together, are you..?"

"No. No, I think that ship might have sailed," said Alex ruefully.

"I'm thinking more… generally. You know I always wondered if things would have been different if I'd battled Alice – you know - when she broke things off with me. If I'd fought for our relationship rather than just lying down like a dog and taking it. Who knows how different my life would be? And I think I would have been able to convince her and save us, you know, if I'd had the balls to try…" He trailed off. He wasn't sure if he was really thinking about the Alice of years ago or the Lila that might be in his future.

After a moment, Nadia reached past her plate and their water glasses and squeezed his arm sympathetically.

"I'm glad you didn't," was all she said.

Nadia

It was so hard to be stand-offish with Alex when he could have absolutely no idea what he'd done wrong. In fact, that in itself was a total misnomer. It wasn't "wrong" of him to have feelings for someone. Nadia had no claim over his feelings and probably never would and she *really* had to start accepting that.

It was equally hard to stay mad at him whilst he was wearing pyjamas. His lounge pants were hysterical – navy and dark-green tartan – like something that her grandfather would wear. The constant rotation of big-budget superhero movies projected on the screen ahead of them also served nicely to remind her that there were bigger problems in the world than her bruised emotions and that the world needed saving more than her heart did.

It was somewhere around five hours in – mid *Iron Man 2* – that Alex fell asleep, his head lolling suddenly to the side as he lost the fight for consciousness. Nadia – a little more than half-asleep herself – smiled drowsily. They'd lasted longer than she had on her last all-night marathon at the Prince Charles. She allowed her head to tilt too, her cheek pressing into the curve of the slightly scratchy upholstery of the cinema flip-seat. Her face was so close to Alex's she could feel the warmth of his breath on her skin.

And because she was so far gone into sleep it all already felt like a dream, and because she'd been drinking warm acidic wine from plastic pint glasses for hours and hours, Nadia decided to lean forward those extra few inches and kiss him, just to see, keeping her lips as light upon him as his breath had been upon her.

And he didn't wake up, and the ceiling didn't cave in on top of them, and Nadia found that she didn't feel any better about things. She settled back in her seat and – as a still-rowdy group of boys towards the front of the screening room cheered a particularly large CGI explosion – fell asleep.

Chapter 13

Alex

Everything in his life seemed to have piss-poor timing.

After ignoring him for three days, Lila had suddenly reappeared on his phone saying she'd like to have lunch with him. Unfortunately, Lila's version of "Sunday lunch" wasn't a roast like everyone else's, but rather falafels from her favourite vegan café off Balham High Street, where the menus were all in Arabic and it smelt like his parents' damp garage. Even more unfortunately, Alex was hideously hung over, with a trapped nerve in his neck from the two hours of fitful sleep he'd got at the cinema.

After his first cinematic nap, Alex had woken with a start, at first just confused as to where he was, then secondly confused as to how he'd missed the second half of *Iron Man 2* and what appeared to have been a rather large chunk of *Thor*. Nadia had still been asleep, her mouth slightly open, her fist curled up loosely by her face and her whole body turned in the chair towards his, like a uninhibited toddler snoozing in her all-in-one pyjamas.

"Are you okay?" Lila asked, sharply. Alex realised he was smiling vacantly at his Arabic menu as he recalled the sleeping Nadia of just a few hours before.

"Yeah." He threw the dog-eared laminated menu down on the table top. "I don't know why I'm even trying to read that."

"Just get the falafels," Lila told him, right on cue. "They're lovely."

Not really having any other option, Alex agreed and waited patiently whilst Lila relayed their order to the café's one bedraggled waiter.

"So, Lils," he barrelled in as soon as the waiter had placed their pint glasses of tap water in front of them and disappeared into the kitchen. "What's up? How are things?"

Lila took a very careful sip from her water, tucking one side of her honey-blonde bob behind her ear with her free hand as she did. "Things are… okay," she said, after a moment. "It was a long time coming, actually. But you're sweet to be concerned." She flashed him one of her usual warm smiles, the kind that made him feel giddy and reckless.

Alex had seen Lila's text as a sign. Obviously she wanted to stay friends; but Alex wasn't sure that he could stay being "just friends" with Lila Palmer. He had to grow a pair – as he was sure Nadia would say – and tell the girl how he felt, right now, here, at this point where he had the least to lose.

He just wished he didn't have such a wicked hangover for what could turn out to be one of the defining moments of his life.

"I'm just looking forward to taking some time to myself, enjoying being single, reconnecting with Penny and my other friends," Lila was saying. "You know, it got pretty intense pretty quickly, me and Rory…" Alex nodded solemnly; he sure did know. "I'm actually not surprised it burnt out the way it did."

"It obviously wasn't meant to be…" Alex agreed, wondering how the hell he was going to subtly circle the conversation away from bloody Rory.

Lila hesitated, momentarily biting at her bottom lip. "Can I… Alex, can I ask you something?" She looked across at him nervously through her lowered eyelashes.

Alex blinked. This felt momentous. What if he'd had it wrong and Lila had always secretly had a thing for him? A thing she was now free to confess? There had certainly been *something* between them in recent weeks, since the shit had started to hit the fan with Rory, anyway. There had been deep, lingering looks that lacked context, barbed comments that made no sense, expressions that caused questions, questions…

"Sure," he managed, after a moment, straightening his feet under the café table, preparing himself both mentally and physically.

"Do you think that Rory might have been seeing someone else?"

Alex's visions abruptly deflated like a collapsed soufflé. "What?" he managed, fumbling through the mental wreckage of his hope.

"Like, an affair. Like, maybe he wasn't working late at all – he was seeing another girlfriend." Lila's bottom lip trembled and she clenched and unclenched her fists against the plastic tablecloth.

"Oh, Lils, no. I don't think so. Rory may be a pain in the arse, but I don't think he'd do that to you. He cares about you, I know he does. He's just genuinely… in a place with his work at the moment…"

"Oh, don't you start!" Lila barked, drawing both of her hands into her lap and out of sight. "I've already heard it. 'In a delicate place in his career' and all that bollocks," she said, mockingly. She exhaled shakily. "It might actually be better to be dumped for another woman than for his desk…"

The waiter chose that moment to interrupt, with two plates of slightly wilted-looking salad and falafel balls. Alex and Lila politely paused their tense conversation until he'd retired into the back once again.

"Lila," Alex started, trying to inject as much sincerity into his tone as possible. "You shouldn't take this at all personally. You were too good for Rory to start with! Even he agrees! The reason he's broken up with you is because he thinks you can do better, isn't it? So you can find a guy who's not quite so much of a douche about work and can give you all the time and attention in the world."

Lila gave a little, watery smile. "Do you really think that?"

"I know that. Come off it, Lila! You're gorgeous, you're funny, you're smart. You could have any guy you wanted. "

Lila looked at him curiously. "Do you really think that?"

"Totally. Any guy off the street!"

"No. About me being… pretty and stuff."

Alex's heart suddenly thumped in alarm. "Of course," he managed, after an agonising beat. "You're… great." And here it was – a golden opportunity on an equally golden platter. Time to stop being the loser that Alice Rhodes had turned him into all those years ago and just say it, spit it out; fight for love. Alex inhaled deeply, steeling himself. "In fact…" he choked out.

"Oh, Alex," Lila said at the same time. "You're great, too. I'd really, really like for us to stay good friends, despite Rory, you know?" She smiled at him as she picked up her knife and fork and cut energetically into the falafel ball, causing it to fall apart into a heap of processed crumbs.

Alex couldn't help but relate.

Nadia

Nadia planted her palms flat on her living room's crumbling sill and hoisted her entire upper body out of the sash window, straining her eyes to see as far down the road as she could. Caro was by now twenty-five minutes late. Caro was never, ever late.

Swinging back inside again, Nadia swiped her phone from the top of the coffee table, tapping the call button impatiently to re-dial the last number in her history. Once again, Caro's mobile rang out, proving only that she wasn't trapped underground on the Tube with no signal. Nadia dropped her mobile phone to the table top again, half concerned and half annoyed. Caro had promised she'd be round before one o'clock – and that she'd bring lunch – and that the two of them would do some work on the basics of Nadia's Indefinite Leave to Remain appeal. She was due to get her court date before too long and the whole thing was getting much harder to ignore.

Throwing herself down on the sofa with a sigh, Nadia pulled her laptop towards her. She might as well start reading the advice blogs without Caro, no point wasting any more time. But instead she found herself loading her Gmail and typing out a quick message to Alex.

She imagined him noticing the email notification sliding up in the corner of his screen and giving one of his unhurried smiles. She often amused herself by picturing him at his desk. He'd admitted the other day that he wore glasses at the office to reduce the strain on his eyes from the computer screen, which fitted in nicely with her whole Clark Kent/Superman opinion of the real Alex Bradley. At work he was the guy she'd met all those months ago; he probably had his hair super-tidy, his face cleanly shaven, glasses on, neat and prim in the sort of suit she now only saw him in if she was meeting him directly after work, a sensible half pint of chilled water from the cooler to the side of his keyboard…

Okay, so she knew she was picturing Alex's office like something out of the fifties and she knew that he'd told her not to email him at work that often in case he got in trouble for personal correspondence, though he couldn't be all that worried about it because he always immediately replied.

Nadia was so engrossed in their email conversation that she almost didn't realise her mobile was ringing until the call had almost rung out. Letting her laptop slide from her legs she reached to grab her phone; Caro was calling back, at last.

"Hello?" she said, allowing her annoyance to be evident in her tone. "Are you okay? Caro, I swear to God…" Nadia trailed off as she realised that Caro wasn't making excuses; in fact, Caro wasn't saying anything at all. "Are you okay?" Nadia repeated. "Where are you?"

"Lavender Hill," Caro admitted, in a small voice.

Realisation dawned. "Caro, are you with Monty?" Nadia asked, not really wanting to know the answer.

Caro sniffed, an altogether very un-Caro-like noise. "I was." She fell silent.

"And are you coming over?" Nadia asked impatiently after she felt the dramatic silence had gone on for too long.

"I left my Oyster card and my keys in his flat," Caro admitted, her voice even smaller than before.

Nadia's ears pricked up. "Have you guys had a fight, or something?" she asked, taking care not to sound too pleased at the prospect.

"We've had *the* fight," was all Caro said.

Nadia sighed. "Just get in a taxi."

Montgomery Fletcher had been a thorn in Nadia's side since the start of the previous academic year. Caro had come to the pub after her first day of classes for her new Masters' in Art History full of stories about the impossibly rakish lecturer who wore converses and skinny ties and seemed truly and honestly passionate about his subject. Within a month, Caro was hooked. Before the autumn term was over, she was in love. At the departmental Christmas drinks the pair had shared a drunken kiss and suddenly, by the time January came around, it had become a full-blown secret affair.

And while Caro was blissfully happy, Monty became increasingly paranoid. He was her tutor, after all; if the university found out about them he would lose his job and Caro would be kicked off the course. He'd probably never work in education again. But that wasn't the reason that Monty was so paranoid, why he refused to even smile at Caro in public, why he constructed overly elaborate reasons for her being in his office so often, why he took out another phone contract to conceal the fact that he was in always contact with her.

Monty was paranoid because he was married – with a two-year-old daughter – and because Monty had already been caught cheating twice during his marriage, he knew that he was truly on his final strike when it came to his long-suffering wife. Sally must never find out, he stressed to Caro, raising his voice at her as though somehow it was all her fault; *Sally must never find out*. And it was for that reason he shunted Caro in and out of his Battersea flat like a package whenever Sally was out of town with the baby, vacuuming the flat obsessively, over and over, even whilst she was still there, as if Sally would return home and immediately notice a rogue strand of hair in a brown two shades darker than her own and cry foul.

And despite the constant pleading from her friends to get out of it, this had been Caro's life for the past eight months. Because despite all evidence to the contrary, despite being told otherwise by absolutely everyone she knew and despite knowing somewhere deep in her own heart that she would never be the exception to the rule, Caro wanted to believe that one day Monty would leave his wife for her.

"He's never going to leave his wife for me," Caro wailed, wedging herself as small as possible into the corner of Nadia's sofa. She was the very embodiment of woe: ratty strands of dark hair sticking to her wet cheeks, a handful of already half-sodden tissues clenched in one fist.

Nadia placed a steaming mug of Caro's favourite extra-strong green tea on the coffee table in front of her.

"Of course he's not going to leave his wife," she said, not unkindly. "They never do."

"Sometimes they do," Caro insisted, despite herself.

Nadia launched into her usual script; they'd been having this same conversation for the last half a year. "And what if he did? What then? Could you ever have a proper relationship with him, ever trust him, knowing that he'd cheated on his wife like that?"

"I don't know," Caro admitted miserably. "But it's a moot point anyway because *he's not going to leave his wife.*"

"No," Nadia agreed, sadly, taking a sip of Caro's tea herself. "He's not."

Alex

Alex frowned slightly, opening the Outlook ribbon and clicking Send and Receive, just to check that there were no emails pending somewhere or other waiting to get in to his inbox. Right in the middle of a very animated conversation about films they thought were severely overrated Nadia had disappeared on him, leaving him alone with his exceedingly boring afternoon in the office.

Alex sighed and turned his attention to the pile of applications and forms he had to process and separate, as well as log onto their systems. It was the usual: student visa applications, extension requests, notifications about over-stayers; human beings reduced to the information you could fit onto one A4 piece of paper. And Alex couldn't help but wonder how much longer he could do this job.

He'd toyed with the idea of quitting on and off for years now; after all, the Home Office was only ever meant to be a stop-gap, a nice little entry to jumpstart his CV and to allow him to begin paying off his eye-watering student loan. But for whatever reason, he never actually seemed to get around to job-hunting. And now the promotion he'd been working overtime for all summer had gone to a girl who had only started working in his department the year before. He just didn't display the passion for it, was Donnelly's blunt feedback, as he'd scratched the paunch straining against his TM Lewin shirt in a bored fashion, like it didn't even matter. And the thing was, it actually didn't.

Not everyone could be passionate about their jobs, Alex used to think. Not everyone could have a calling: be a teacher or a doctor or something useful to society. Alex got up and went to work every day simply because otherwise he'd have no way of paying his rent, and that was that. And then he had met Nadia, somebody who had so much passion for everything she did that she was almost exhausting; she was passionate about London, passionate about her volunteer work, passionate about making him into a better person.

"Not a better person," she'd corrected him when he'd told her that, shaking her head empathically as she spoke. "Not *better*. Not a *different person*. Just more *you*."

Alex's thoughts wandered to his upper arm, remembering the buzz and sting of the tattooist's needle there all those years ago.

He'd been meaning to get an appointment and get all that sorted out for years; yet another entry on that mental to-do list that he was never going to get around to. Mainly because it was Nadia's to-do list was all-encompassing these days. Alex smiled at the thought, wondering what could possibly be next on her agenda.

But he didn't remember there being any rule that stated Nadia had to set *all* the activities.

Hey, you, he opened up a new email window to type. *I was thinking and I've realised that there's something that you've definitely not experienced before that I can help with. When do you next have a spare six hours?*

Nadia

Holly, bless her, had not stopped to ask questions when she'd come out of work to a voicemail from Nadia which perfunctorily instructed her to pick up several boxes of Party Rings biscuits and a large bottle of dark rum. She'd just done as she was told.

The rum had been polished off even quicker than the biscuits. After that, Holly had stepped up and pulled several dusty bottles of expensive red wine out from under her bed; her office had given her one every Christmas in lieu of a bonus for years. The empty bottles joined that of the rum in the plastic recycling box; all three girls' lips were stained purple in the corners.

The combination of sugar and alcohol had done the trick; Caro was no longer crying. Instead she was that sombre sort of silent, staring into the dark depths of her wine glass as if she could see her future in it if she just tried hard enough.

"You just need to cut him out of your life now," Nadia insisted. "See this as the opportunity it is. A kick up the arse."

"How can I avoid him? He's my fucking teacher," Caro moaned.

Holly and Nadia exchanged a look. "When is this course over?" Holly asked.

"January."

"Ahhh." Holly took a tactful sip from her wine glass rather than commenting further.

"You're going to have to see him tomorrow. He's got your house keys, for crying out loud," Nadia pointed out.

"I bet I'll find a manila envelope in my departmental pigeon-hole tomorrow with my stuff inside it," Caro sighed. "That seems more his style."

"His 'style' is being an absolute arsehole," Nadia retorted, the hours of heavy drinking making her tongue loose and her words harsh. "His 'style' is *having his cake and eating it too*, that's what his flipping 'style' is."

Holly's forehead creased in drunken confusion. "Wait, wait. Is Caro the 'cake' or the 'too' in this situation?"

"That's not the point!" Nadia declared, waving her wine glass dramatically in Caro's face as she did. "The point is, you shouldn't have to put up with it. Why you have for so long, *I don't know*."

"Because I love him," whined Caro, causing both Nadia and Holly to instantaneously roll their eyes.

"But *why?*" Holly pressed.

"I guess that's something that *I* don't know," Caro admitted, rolling her head back against the plush back of the sofa. "Love is an absolute shitter," she concluded, petulantly.

"You're sort of making me glad I'm a professional singleton," Holly sighed. "Come on, you girls are meant to give me hope in true love, not utterly destroy my faith in it." She turned to Nadia. "Please tell me how great things are going between you and Matt and how your future is full of marriage and babies and puppies before I slit my metaphorical wrists."

Nadia fidgeted awkwardly. "I keep telling you and telling you. Matt and I are just casual. In fact, I'm thinking of breaking it off…"

Caro gasped and sat forward, immediately distracted from her own woe. "Well, whatever you do, don't bloody do it before your court hearing."

"You see this, Hols?" Nadia pointed at Caro with the hand that was holding her glass, causing the wine within to slosh alarmingly.

"*This* is why romance is dead."

"This isn't about romance, this is about being practical," Caro retorted. "The perfect *British* boyfriend with the *exact* name fell into your lap at *precisely* the right time and has remained there ever since. The sod might as well have Golden Ticket stamped across his face."

"I hate myself a bit for it, but I agree with Caro, Nads…" Holly admitted.

"The universe saw you were in need and the stars aligned and sent him to you," Caro continued, characteristically theatrical.

"Okay, I don't agree with that…" Holly added quickly.

Caro sighed. "I used to think that the universe had brought Monty and I together…"

"I think there's something in all of that, you know," Nadia interjected quickly, half to distract and half to console Caro. "NOT about you and Monty," she frowned, "but the whole *people come into your life for a reason* thing. Think about it," she insisted, ignoring Holly's doubtful expression. "If your parents hadn't been going through that messy divorce, then you wouldn't have been sent to our school, right?"

Holly rolled her eyes. "Oh yeah, that's right. Bring up my painful childhood; unwanted by my parents! Shunted off to boarding school…"

"And if my grandfather hadn't died when he did, my parents wouldn't have had the money to send me to the UK for my education," Nadia continued, warming to her theme. "And we would *never have met*." Nadia took advantage of the dramatic pause to liberally top up everyone's wine glass.

"And then us two wouldn't have met at uni," Caro pointed out. "And I wouldn't be sitting here, far too drunk for a Tuesday…"

"Not knowing Nadia wouldn't mean you'd never meet Monty the Pervy Professor, I'm afraid," Holly pointed out. "You'd still be stuck with that. But you wouldn't have such attractive and accommodating drinking company, as well as access to several bottles of Châteauneuf-du-Pape." Holly and Nadia chinked their glasses together in a toast to themselves.

"But who's to say in this alternate universe Monty didn't leave his wife for me?" Caro pointed out, eyes gleaming. "Or – even better – was never married in the first place!"

Holly placed her glass down on the coffee table in exasperation. "Talk about a dog with a bone," she muttered under her breath.

"Isn't it scary? How easy it could be to be living a different life..? Sit next to a different girl at school when you're eleven; balls up a job interview at eighteen; marry the wrong guy at thirty." Nadia considered the depths of her wine glass. "Do you remember, Hols, how that night at the Bellevue quiz, we refused at first when they wanted us to be moved to that other team?"

Holly looked at her curiously. "Yeah."

"See what I mean? Such a simple thing. If two other people had gone over to Alex's table instead of us that evening, I'd never have met him."

"Nadia." Holly sat forward as she spoke; Nadia winced at the formality of her full name being used. "About Alex. Usual disclaimer: I'm only saying this because I love you. I think that it's this little Stockholm Syndrome crush you've got going on for him that's impacting on your relationship with Matt."

"Stockholm Syndrome?" Nadia echoed, incredulously. "He hasn't *kidnapped* me."

Holly gestured dismissively. "Either way round."

"Well, I haven't kidnapped him either!" Nadia immediately argued. "I dared him to come to a couple of random places with me. It's not like I locked him in my basement."

"Well, you live in a mansion block," Caro pointed out, gravely. Holly and Nadia looked confused. "As in, you don't have a basement," she clarified.

"Even if I happened to have a basement, kidnapping random men and locking them inside it wouldn't exactly be my first thought," Nadia pointed out, scathingly.

"Daddy keeps wine in his basement," Caro added brightly, following the mention by topping up everyone's drink once more, despite the fact that Nadia had just done so, and that she'd clearly already had enough.

"If there's wine in it, doesn't that make it a cellar?" queried Holly, picking up her glass to take another drink the moment that Caro had stopped pouring.

"Anyway," Nadia said, belatedly, "I don't have 'a crush' on Alex. I'm not fifteen." She scowled at Holly, who graciously ignored it.

"Nadia and Alex, sittin' in a tree," Caro sung to herself, delightedly. "K, I, S, S, I, N, G..."

"Nads. You forget how well I know you," Holly continued. "And I knew you when you were fifteen. You are crushing. Hard."

"I have to admit, I've picked up on this too. The chemistry between you two the other night. You are totally crushing," Caro declared, matter-of-factly.

"And it's alright to be, you know," Holly added. "I like Alex. He's grown on me."

"Yeah, I totally see it. He's quite hot. You know, in a geeky way," was Caro's opinion.

"It's not like that between us," Nadia insisted. "He's not interested in me, not in *that* way..."

"Probably because you have a boyfriend?" Holly pointed out bluntly. "And he's all super-gentlemanly and wouldn't want to, you know, get called to a duel by Matt because he's coveted his lady. Or whatever."

"Okay Hols, is Alex Hugh Grant from the '90s or a Victorian duke?" Nadia sighed, "because I don't think he can be both."

"Did Hugh Grant ever play a duke?" Caro asked, absently. "It seems like the sort of role he'd play..."

"Either way," Nadia interrupted impatiently, growing immensely tired of the meandering conversation. "He..." she hesitated, still not remotely comfortable with the idea. "He likes someone else. So that's that."

134

"Not more than he likes you, surely?" Caro scoffed immediately. "He's like, your biggest fan."

"He's always looking at you," Holly added.

Nadia blanched. "What do you mean, looking at me?" She had a flash of Alex with his face pressed up against the window leering at her and giggled at the image.

"You know, when he's talking to you. He looks at you."

Nadia raised her eyebrow. "Oh no," she intoned, sarcastically. "What a creep."

"No, no, I know what Holly means," Caro interjected, readjusting her position on the sofa so that her legs were underneath her; she bounced a little with excitement. "He *looks* at you," she paused dramatically, "like you *really matter.*"

Nadia couldn't help but snort with laughter. "That's sort of the least I'm looking for in a friend, guys," she giggled.

"You say that, but it's actually quite a big deal," Caro frowned. "Monty only really *looks* at me at all in the immediate seconds before climax." She rolled her eyes. "I bet Hugh Grant looks at women like they matter," she continued, half to herself, half to her drink as she brought it to her mouth again.

She still wasn't entirely sure what they were even talking about, but Nadia felt very in love with her stupid friends in that moment. And also, also, she felt her heart nudging inside of her chest when she thought about Alex and the way that he apparently looked at her.

Nadia stretched forward and poured the dregs of the final bottle out equally between their three glasses.

"That's it for the wine then, ladies," she announced. "And speaking of High Grant, anyone up for watching *Notting Hill*?"

Alex

Alex had been mentally checked-out since lunchtime; the compulsory Friday-afternoon team meeting had just about killed his already-meagre work ethic stone dead. For yet another week

135

running he watched the same faces all studiously staring at their laps to avoid making eye contact with Donnelly, listened to the same crap about budget cuts and productivity levels and missed targets and felt very much as though he wanted to scream.

After what felt like a million years, Alex's team were released back to their desks to see out the tail end of the working week. Boring afternoons at work had become a lot easier since Nadia had come into his life, although Alex seriously hoped his bosses weren't monitoring his personal email use. Although, if they were, he'd dare them not to get totally sucked into it; Nadia had a way of making the most stupid topics ever into amazing conversation. That morning they'd been earnestly discussing whether or not the world's governments were covering up proof of extra-terrestrial life. Nadia's arguments that they were seemed to mainly be based around a childhood of watching *The X Files*. She'd been in full flow, sending him jpegs of pixilated blurs in the night's sky that she swore were UFOs when he got called into the team meeting, so he was eager to see what inbox delights were awaiting him now he was out.

Most recent, appearing at the top, was a subjectless email from Lila Palmer; Alex felt an embarrassing little jerk in his stomach. Since their awkward falafel lunch the other week, he hadn't had any contact with her, save the fact that he hadn't been able to stop himself from "liking" all of her latest Facebook activity (he was only human). He'd gotten the distinct impression that, despite all her grand words about staying friends, he was being phased out. So why? Why this sudden email? He almost didn't want to open it, glanced wistfully at the one from Nadia, sitting a few lines below, before resolutely double-clicking on Lila's.

The message began innocuously enough.

Hiya! Are you good? Has your flat deteriorated into a total testosterone pig-sty by now??

Lila was forever peppering her texts and emails with little faces; this particular sentence was punctuated by a tongue-sticky-outy face to show she was only kidding. The flat was pretty much pristine actually, Alex thought, a little annoyed; neither he nor Rory were hardly ever in, these days.

I was just wondering if you're free tonight? the email continued, making Alex's heart soar. *I fancied going to the cinema. I know it's short notice, but Penny just bailed on me saying she's not feeling well.* Sad face. Alex pulled a matching grimace, feeling the rollercoaster dip of disappointment. A stood-up Lila had clearly just mentally scrolled through all her acquaintances and decided that he, out of all of them, was most likely to be free on a Friday night. Charming.

Let me know if you're up for it! Lila had concluded, smiley face.

Lila had already been waiting for a response for over twenty minutes, but for some reason Alex didn't feel inclined to reply straight away. He minimised Lila's email and opened Nadia's. It was, as he'd expected, far more cheering. Much like Lila's little emoticon quirk, Nadia's habit was to over-exclaim; even the most humdrum sentences seemed to merit at least two exclamation marks.

Look at this!!! Nadia demanded, underneath where she had pasted the link to a conspiracy theory blog. *How can you say that nothing was going on in the fifties!?!?*

Nads, seriously, Alex replied immediately, grinning to himself. *I'm currently in a government building! I really can't be clicking on links to anti-establishment nut-job websites!* He rolled his eyes. *Anyway, changing the subject here before I get fired/arrested/ sectioned. Do you fancy the cinema tonight, if you're not busy? If you let me pick the flick, then the tickets are on me…*

Nadia shot back a response almost immediately. *Okay. Not another American gross-out comedy this time, please!!! I'll get the popcorn.*

Smiling to himself again, Alex revisited Lila's email. *Sorry Lils…* he typed, already almost regretting his impulsive decision; but was it too much to hope that he could ever be more than a last resort to the woman he loved? *I've already got plans tonight. Another time, yeah?*

Alex couldn't hold back an audible laugh as another email from Nadia shot into the corner of his screen: *There's a film about an alien invasion on at 7pm at the Picture House!! Book it! Quick!!!*

Chapter 14

Alex

The summer seemed as if it was set to last for ever. Every single one of the flat windows was wide open, but the breeze running through the rooms was barely more than a breath.

Nadia was kneeling in front of his shelving unit, her bare knees digging into the living-room carpet. She was wearing those denim shorts he'd become accustomed to, so old and faded that in places they were closer to white than blue. Her hair was pulled up in a messy, gravity-defying knot on the top of her head. She seemed so entirely of this time, this summer; he couldn't imagine what she looked like in winter, all bundled up.

She glanced up at him. "I really, honestly don't have a preference."

"Are you happy for me to choose, then?" Alex asked with a smile. "Because there are a couple of titles in particular that I'm leaning towards…"

Nadia eased herself to her feet. "Knock yourself out. You definitely know better than me."

"Okay, then." Alex knew she'd make him pick, which is why he'd already got one in mind. She didn't look wildly enthused about the day's activity, but she was nothing if not a good sport, and had headed dutifully for Tooting once her Saturday-morning shift volunteering at the charity shop was over.

"Just nothing with guns, okay?" Nadia frowned, settling herself gingerly on the sofa. "And I don't want to have to wear a headset thing like in the adverts."

"I wasn't thinking anything like that," Alex assured her. "I was thinking of an RPG." Nadia looked at him blankly. Alex sighed. "It will have characters and a proper story," he clarified. "And, you know, things like… magic." He wiggled his fingers dramatically to indicate said magic. Nadia looked supremely unimpressed. Alex sighed again. "Look, just go with me on this one," he appealed, bending down to feed the video game disc into his PlayStation.

An hour later, Nadia was no longer walking her avatar into walls and had stopped flinging the controller at Alex with a squeal of alarm every time she was attacked by an enemy. By hour two she was shushing him when he tried to chat over story sequences and it wasn't long after that before she started trying to pump Alex for more information on the back story of the game's characters.

"I don't agree with spoilers," Alex laughed. "Just stick at it. There's probably only about, oh, eighty-odd hours of play before you get to the end. If you rush through and don't bother with any side quests, that is."

Nadia looked amazed. "I didn't realise these games were so *in-depth*."

Alex laughed again. "You've always teased me for wasting so much time playing video games," he pointed out. "So surely it can't be that much of a surprise?"

It was gone five o'clock by the time Rory arrived home, rumpled from the gym and toting a plastic Tesco bag with his work clothes stuffed inside; he'd spent another day doing overtime at the office. He surveyed the scene without comment: Alex looking up at him with amusement, Nadia so intent on the boss she was battling that she couldn't even acknowledge him. Rory shook his head. He disappeared briefly into the kitchen.

"So," he said, reappearing with a handful of glossy takeaway leaflets. "What shall we order in?"

Nadia

Holly was trying so hard to keep her face straight, but she was failing miserably.

"His PlayStation," she repeated, for the fourth time. "His *PlayStation*."

"Yes, his PlayStation," Nadia echoed, rolling her eyes as she tried to focus on what new armour was best to equip onto her White Mage. "This way I can play when I have those lonely days off from the shop with nothing to do."

"Does he have another one, or something?" Ledge asked cautiously, from where he was sitting on the chair in front of Nadia's dressing table.

"No, I don't think so," Nadia answered, distractedly, button-mashing as she spoke.

"So basically, he's given you his favourite thing in the world," Holly pointed out, smirking.

"Not given it to me. Lent it to me." Nadia defended, feeling her face flush. "And besides, it's his stupid fault I'm addicted to this game anyway. I would have been quite happy finishing my life having never played a video game, and now I'm hooked. And there's like TWELVE other games in this franchise, with a new one every year! I'm never going to catch up!" she moaned.

"Cor," Ledge murmured, as Nadia finished up by changing the boots equipped to her Thief; they covered more skin than anything else the character was shown to be wearing. "It's so weird that the women characters in these games are designed to look like absolute sluts."

"I know, like where's the logic there?" Holly laughed. "It's hardly defensive to have your tits and ass hanging out."

"Maybe it's intended for distraction purposes?" Ledge sniggered.

"You guys, please!" Nadia wailed. "I'm trying to concentrate here!"

Alex

"Your PlayStation!" Rory moaned, and not for the first time. "I can't believe you gave her your PlayStation."

"Stop whining," Alex frowned. "We've still got your Xbox to play games on."

"But we only own the PlayStation version of *Call of Duty*," Rory complained.

"Look, if I hadn't given it to her, then she'd be here every night playing *Final Fantasy* in our living room, on our TV," Alex pointed out, "and surely that would have annoyed you more?"

Rory made a sullen noise of agreement and returned to flicking grumpily through the television channels; Alex turned back to replying to Nadia's text message.

"Hey, Ror," he said, after a moment. "Are you up for coming with me to a house party in Brixton next Saturday?"

"That entirely depends," retorted Rory, leaning to one side so he could slide his mobile phone from his rear pocket. "Whose house party? I don't know anyone who lives in Brixton. Is it the dodgy end?"

"Both ends of Brixton are dodgy ends," Alex quipped. "And I don't know them, actually. Friend of Nadia's."

Rory's eyebrows raised. "A friend of Nadia's? Can I assume this is also a blonde Eastern European stunner? If so, I'm there with bells on."

Alex frowned. "Rory, you've been broken up with Lila for like, five minutes."

"Exactly. *Broken up* with. As in, I'm single. So I should mingle." Rory laughed heartily at his own bad joke.

"You broke up with Lils because you didn't want a girlfriend," Alex pointed out. "So I'm just surprised you want another one so soon – Eastern European and stunning or not."

"I never said anything about having a girlfriend, mate," Rory grinned wickedly. "I just said I wanted to... 'mingle'. He waggled his eyebrows suggestively.

Alex coughed back a laugh. "Well, I doubt you'll want to mingle with this house party's host," he said, contritely. "Being as it is Nadia's boyfriend's housemate and his name is Jeremy."

Nadia

Somehow this was the first time Nadia was meeting the infamous Jez, Matt's "complete lad" of a housemate. Whilst Jez had featured heavily in almost all of Matt's stories and anecdotes, he'd not been at home on any of the few occasions Nadia had been over, and so she'd never had the pleasure. Either way, when Matt cheerfully informed her they were throwing a house party for Jez's birthday – and that she should bring people and turn up around eight – Nadia's first inclination was to decline. She was trying to break things off with the guy: being introduced to his friends en masse seemed somewhat counter-productive.

But Caro had insisted that she needed the distraction from her troubles with Monty, and Holly had pointed out that quite frankly she could use the access to a new pool of single men, and so Nadia had agreed to go. But that, she told herself sternly, was it. Since realising she might have real feelings for Alex she hadn't been able to bring herself to spend much time with Matt, let alone sleep with him again, and things were getting awkward. Even the innocuous touch of their hands brushing together by accident set her skin to a guilty crawling. So she'd been avoiding him. And he'd noticed. This was going to be the first time she'd even seen him for almost three weeks now.

At least Alex would be there alongside her, she told herself, in an attempt to buoy her spirits as she tiredly applied her makeup. It was one of those days where no matter what she did, no matter how much slap she applied, no matter how she fluffed her hair, she just felt a bit meh. The mascara she was trying to artfully smear on her bottom lashes just left sad little clumps. Nadia sighed and reached for a makeup wipe so she could start over again. This would be the first large-scale social event she and Alex had been at together. She bet he played a mean drinking game; he was so quick and clever, even after a few too many.

She wondered if he'd get drunk tonight. If he did, would he let his manners and the boundaries between them blur? Would he look at her across that room full of strangers and feel the same pleasurable little jolt she felt when she glanced at him? Would he appreciate the new dress she was wearing – short and the colour of blushes – that she'd have to go without food next week to be able to afford?

Finally satisfied that her eyes were as artfully smoky as they were going to get, Nadia stood up straight and stepped back from her mirror, before reaching into her cosmetics bag once again. She pulled her lips into an exaggerated pout to slick some pale-pink gloss over them. She never wore anything on her lips – not really – but tonight she wanted to look different and she wanted Alex to notice. This evening felt important. Nadia felt as if she'd been walking a precipice for weeks now; the time had come to either be rescued from the edge or to let herself fall over.

She just wasn't sure if Alex was the cliff or the precipice. Maybe he was both. Or maybe Matt was? Or maybe Matt was nothing at all in this cliché scenario – and that was, of course, the biggest problem of all.

Nadia was distracted by the familiar sound of Holly bickering with the newly arrived Caro.

"Seriously, it's not far. We were thinking of walking it."

"Walking it?" Caro echoed, sounding as dubious as if Holly had just said that she'd been planning on can-canning all the way to Brixton. "These shoes really aren't meant for walking," she continued as Nadia wandered into the front room to join them. Sure enough, Caro was sporting a pair of impressively vertiginous white stiletto sandals that looked as if she should be on a podium with a pole in Ibiza rather than attending a casual house party in South London.

"Or we can jump on the 322," Holly continued from the kitchen, over the tinkling sound of wine glasses against the imitation-slate counter. "It will take us practically the whole way there."

"The bus?" Caro grimaced. She whipped out her sunshine yellow-coloured iPhone from her clutch bag. "Don't worry, ladies, Uber has got this," she announced grandly as she busily consulted her taxi booking app.

Holly exchanged an amused look with Nadia as she re-entered the living room holding two over-full glasses of white wine. The mere mention of having to travel by bus and suddenly Caro was always happy to pay for a taxi.

"Thank you, you're a star," Nadia said with great sincerity as she took one of the drinks from Holly's grasp. Whilst sensibly hooker-shoe free, Holly had also obviously made an effort for tonight, having chosen to wear a flirty denim mini skirt and having tackled her usually fluffy hair into sleek submission with the use of her GHD straighteners. Holly put the second glass of wine down on the coffee table near the preoccupied Caro and returned to the kitchen to grab her own.

"You look gorgeous, by the way, Nads," Holly told her when she returned, drink in hand. "I love that colour on you."

Caro glanced up from her phone. "Fit!" was her appraisal. "I love the hair!" Nadia put a hand to the back of her head self-consciously. She'd borrowed a set of complicated-looking heated rollers from her colleague at the Oxfam shop and had had them in her hair for most of the day, resulting in thick, soft waves that made her look a bit like an old-fashioned Hollywood movie star.

"You don't think it's a bit much for just a house party?" she asked, worried. Holly cast a meaningful glance down at Caro's towering heels

"You look amazing," Caro insisted. "Alex's jaw is going to be on the floor." She laughed as she caught Nadia's wince. "What? This *is* all for Alex, isn't it?"

"It just seems a bit obscene to be going to one guy's house and trying to…" Nadia trailed off as she realised she didn't really know what verb to use to end her sentence.

"Snare another one?" Holly supplied with a grin.

"Hey, hey, hey, not snare; let's not get back on to the whole kidnapping and keeping in basements rhetoric," Nadia laughed, rolling her eyes. "I just want to look nice, okay? Mainly to see if it helps Alex to start seeing me in a different light. But also just because I want to look hot."

Holly laughed. "The very best reason."

"And you have definitely succeeded," Caro smiled, moving closer to instigate a three-way chinking toast of the wine glasses.

Chapter 15

Alex

Thankfully, Rory had deigned to tag along to the party in Brixton.

Nadia had said the night was set to really get going at eight, so Alex had decided that around 8.20pm was probably the optimum time to show up. They'd been waved in by the disinterested stranger who'd answered the flat door to them and immediately left to their own devices. Alex had clocked Matt from across the large, modern open-plan kitchen diner but Nadia was nowhere to be seen. He and Rory had duly taken up position in the only real gap between bodies, their backs to the wall and the cold bottles of Carlsberg they'd brought with them wet and slippery in their hands.

"Mate. This is a total sausage fest." Rory scowled around the room of mostly men as he tipped his bottle to his mouth. "Why did you drag me here?"

Alex rolled his eyes. "It's just a house party, Ror. I didn't promise you… whatever the opposite of a sausage fest is."

Rory grinned unashamedly. "An all-you-can-eat buffet?"

Alex snorted with laughter and most of the mouthful of lager he'd just taken sprayed over his hand. "I really have no comprehension about how you persuade women to go out with you, you know," he told his friend, shaking his head.

"It's because I'm so charming," Rory replied, deadpan.

Alex raised a sceptical eyebrow. "Yeah, sure. Anyway, Nadia should be here in a bit." He had considered texting her to ask where she was and what her ETA was, but he felt that might be a bit lame.

"Well, that's no good to me," Rory frowned. "Can't have her, can I?"

"No, you cannot," Alex answered immediately. "Wait," he back-tracked. "*I* know why you can't have her, but why do you think you can't have her?"

Rory looked at him like he was stupid. "Because she's your bird, isn't she?"

Alex gave a nervous laugh. "No. Even putting aside the fact that we are standing in her boyfriend's flat, I keep telling you – she's just a mate. Fair enough, she's one that I would lay my dead carcass down in front of as a barrier to stop you getting your hands on her. But other than that, she's not 'my bird'."

Rory just smirked as he took another drink from his bottle. "Sounds like she's your bird to me," was all he said.

Then, as if she'd been loitering on the landing outside waiting for just such an opportune moment, Nadia made her grand entrance. She had already made it halfway across the room, Caro and Holly trailing after her, before Alex's brain caught up with his eyes and he realised the woman he'd just been gawking at was actually Nadia. She had really made an effort; she looked completely knock-out gorgeous, wearing a soft-pink dress that span around her body a half a second behind her turns and movements, and with a hairstyle that made her look as if she'd just stepped off the set of a shampoo advert. Alex blinked a tad manically – as if by doing so Nadia would morph back into her casual, denim-clad self – clutching at the neck of his bottle of lager.

Matt, formerly lost in the crowd, appeared just as dramatically.

"Nads!" he cried, and for some reason Alex's skin crawled ever so slightly at the familiarity of it. "You look fantastic." Matt grabbed a startled-looking Nadia by one forearm and made a valiant attempt to dip her so he could kiss her; unfortunately Nadia probably hadn't realised that was his intent and remained ramrod straight, resulting in Matt simply hooking himself over her like an awkward hunchback and everyone in the room exchanging embarrassed smirks over their drinks.

"Matt." Nadia placed her palm flat on his chest almost as if she was pushing him away. "Hi."

A tall individual in a salmon-pink Hollister t-shirt sauntered over to the couple. Matt slapped him vigorously on the back and gestured grandly at Nadia as if he was offering this guy to her as a gift.

"This is Jez," he beamed. "Jez, Nadia," he concluded, which Alex found a little unnecessary at this point.

Nadia nodded politely. "Hi, Jez. Happy birthday." She motioned behind her and opened her mouth to present her companions.

"And this is Holly and Caroline," Matt introduced them before she could get the words out. Nadia's forehead creased in an ever-so-slight frown

"Hiya." The birthday boy grinned at each girl in turn. "Cheers for coming. What are you ladies drinking?"

Caro pushed forward, moving off and away towards the kitchen sides. "What have you got?"

Nadia

Nadia was already reaching into her bag for her phone to text him when she noticed Alex standing across the room, watching her with a weird look on his face. Rory was by his side, looking at her a tad more appreciatively. Great! Right dress, wrong flat-mate. Leaving Holly to field Matt and Jez, Nadia edged her way over through the mass of bodies to where Alex and Rory were squeezed against the wall.

"Hi," she beamed as she went up on her tiptoes to throw her arms around Alex's neck. She felt him hesitate, just for a second, before leaning in and returning her hug. She slipped back down

149

to her heels and smiled politely at Rory. "Glad you guys could come. Sorry we were late. We had to finish the bottle of wine we'd opened – they don't really let you take drinks in Uber taxis."

Alex smirked. "It took you three that long to finish one bottle of wine? I don't believe that for a second!"

Nadia nudged him playfully. "Hey! We were talking as well."

"Hey," Rory said, suddenly, gesturing with the hand that was holding his bottle towards the kitchen area. "I think your friend wants you." Nadia turned to see Caro, all but pinned into a corner by Jez, eyeballing her frantically over his shoulder.

"Oh God," Nadia sighed, heading to Caro's rescue. "Excuse me there, Jez, sorry," she said loudly as she squeezed her way in between them. "Caro, need help doing the drinks?"

"We brought that bottle of rum there, if you girls want to make something with that," came a voice from behind her. It was Rory; he and Alex had followed her across the room.

Jez was seemingly undeterred by the appearance of an audience at his attempt at seduction. "I've got a bottle of gold label tequila," he purred at a desperate-looking Caro. "It's some real good shit – I got it at the duty free – so I keep it in my bedroom." He grinned hopefully over Nadia's shoulders at Caro, who was looking vaguely ill at the thought of the duty-free tequila – or maybe it was at the thought of Jez's bed.

"I'm good with the rum," she insisted, reaching across for the bottle as she spoke. "Thanks anyway, Jez."

"Maybe later?" he tried, as Caro grasped Nadia's hand and attempted to make their escape, pulling her towards the pile of plastic cups on the far side of the kitchen counter. Caro sighed and turned back to their hapless host, taking him in from head to toe with an unimpressed expression on her face.

"I'm just… really not a tequila sort of girl," she finally said, tone exaggeratedly polite. By now there were clumps of nearby party guests eavesdropping on the exchange; it was obvious to anyone with a couple of brain cells that what Caro really meant was that she wasn't a Jez sort of girl. Even Jez finally seemed to twig that he was being taken the piss out of; his face hardened slightly.

"Come on," he pressed, moving to take the bottle of rum from Caro's hand. "It's good stuff," he insisted.

"I don't want your 'good stuff'," Caro snapped, her patience at an end.

"Hey," Rory interjected, suddenly interposing himself between Caro and her ardent wooer. "The lady said no," he thundered at Jez, and suddenly it was he rather than Alex who sounded as if he'd just wandered out of the nineteenth century.

Caro immediately rounded on him. "I don't need your input here, thank you very much," she barked. Rory shied backwards in alarm. Apparently giving up the pretence of wanting a mixer – or even a glass – Caro marched off in the direction of Holly, still carrying Rory's litre bottle of rum by its neck. Jez seemed to realise belatedly that most of his house guests had been watching that embarrassing little scene and his face and neck turned an interesting shade of red.

"Whatever," was his magnificent closing statement. He grabbed a couple of the plastic tumblers off the kitchen side and disappeared out into the corridor, presumably in search of his "really good shit" bottle of duty-free tequila and a more agreeable girl with whom to drink it.

Nadia turned to Alex, eyebrows raised. "Sorry about that," she said. She turned to Rory. "And sorry about Caro. She's just really not a damsel-in-distress type."

"Don't worry about it. I just don't like seeing women treated like meat is all," Rory explained, with a self-deprecating shrug. There was what sounded suspiciously like a disbelieving snort from Alex, but when Nadia glanced at him he was studiously staring out across the room and glugging down a large amount of his lager.

"Anyway, I'm glad you guys could make it," Nadia continued, brightly. "Sorry about your rum. But, it's okay!" She reached into her oversized handbag with a grin. "Cos I went stereotypical and brought vodka."

Alex

Two hours and most of the bottle of Smirnoff later, Alex began to wonder if he was a participant in a game that nobody had bothered to tell him he was playing. The ultimate aim of the game seemed to be annoying poor Matt. The guy was a bit of a tool, but Alex wasn't sure what the guy had done to deserve being constantly dragged to and fro.

"Matt!" Caro had called cheerfully, as Matt had squeezed his way over to sit on the arm of the sofa near Nadia. "Where have you been?" She'd linked their arms together firmly like handcuffs and pulled him back to his feet. "Give me the grand tour!" she'd demanded, leading him off before he'd even had a chance to agree (not that anyone usually disagreed with Caro).

And later: "Matt!" Holly had chirped, as soon as he had escaped Caro's unprecedented interest in a pretty standard three-bed, new-build flat and attempted to return to Nadia's side. "My glass is empty. Shall we go to the kitchen and see what there is to be had?" And so poor Matt had been dragged off – quite literally – once again, looking more than slightly perplexed.

Alex found he had to actively change the subject to bring Matt up at all. "Hey," he tried, whilst the other two girls were diverted by Rory, pitching his voice low, and moving in close to murmur in Nadia's ear. "Is everything okay between you and Matt?" He could feel warmth rising from the exposed skin of her neckline; it was like a sauna in the over-full room. A combination of the heat and the alcohol had flushed Nadia's cheeks as pink as her dress.

Nadia looked at him suspiciously, as if his question was some sort of trap. "What do you mean?"

Alex had been expecting an immediate denial, so he was slightly put on the back foot. "I mean, you don't seem very coupley tonight."

Nadia laughed, but there was no humour in the sound. "I've

told you a thousand times. As far as I'm concerned it's very casual, me and Matt." She gave that funny little laugh again and took a drink from her double-strength vodka and cloudy lemonade. "Is everything okay with you and Lila?" she asked, giving him a meaningful look over the rim of her glass.

Alex baulked. "What? Me and Lila? Where did that come from?" He sat back as far as he could on the uncomfortable sofa, trying to get out of Rory's eye line, just in case he was listening. He racked his brain; had he ever drank too much and confessed his inappropriate, unrequited and embarrassing affection for Lila to Nadia? No. No way he ever, ever would have. Not even after *ten bottles* of vodka. It was something he had kept so close to his chest for so long.

"Nothing." Nadia sighed to herself. "I just thought now that Rory's out of the picture you would have made a move or something." She rolled her eyes. "You've waited long enough."

Alex threw his remaining half-glass of vodka and coke straight down his throat before answering. "Hey, I need another drink," he announced loudly (once he'd finished coughing). "Come with me?" He phrased it like a request, but he knew Nadia would know it wasn't.

Nadia

Vodka was evil; pure liquid evil. She needed to learn to keep her mouth shut. She needed to learn that vodka was not her friend. Much like Alex wasn't likely to be if she couldn't extricate herself from this.

She trailed Alex as he impatiently made his way over to the kitchen area and grabbed one of the few remaining clear plastic tumblers off the side. "So," he said, conversationally, as he reached over to the sink to get some water, "What's all this you've got in your head about me and Lila?" He handed Nadia the water to drink, which luckily gave her a few moments to compose her thoughts as she took a gulp.

153

"Oh, I don't know," she said, airily. "Something I picked up, I guess."

Alex looked mildly panicked. "Picked up?" he echoed. "How?"

Nadia wasn't sure what to say. Because it was true that Alex had never given any outward sign of wanting anything more than friendship with the pretty, heart-faced, honey-blonde Lila. She'd never seen him touch her, or have a real laugh with her, that stupid, over-the-top one he did when he found something really and truly funny, a sort of guffaw that sometimes turned into a terribly unattractive snort. He didn't overly mention her in conversation, and he certainly hadn't seemed to be worried that since he'd met Nadia he'd spent less and less time in her company. If it wasn't for Matt telling her about it, she'd never, ever have guessed...

"I guess..." She looked at Alex straight, guilt prickling at her when she realised how concerned he was about this. "I guess maybe it was that you never seemed totally comfortable around her."

Alex tilted his head, confused. "I never seemed comfortable?" he repeated, incredulous.

Nadia laughed nervously. "You know. A bit edgy. Nervous." She bit back a wince as she saw Alex's alarm increase. "And so naturally I assumed you were secretly madly in love with her," she finished with a dramatic gesture and a laugh, hoping her poor attempt at humour would defuse the situation. Alex laughed too, but it was half a beat too late and way too forced. "Oh, I don't know, Alex. I'm drunk as hell. Don't ask me difficult questions. Either way, clearly I was mistaken." She mimed zipping her lips shut. "You won't hear from me on the subject again."

Her words seemed to mollify Alex. He stopped chewing his bottom lip to shreds and reached to pour his own drink of water from the kitchen tap. Nadia hesitated; she felt the vodka pushing the words up and out of her like bubbles. She needed to know.

"Unless you want to. Talk about it, that is."

Alex frowned at her over the rim of his plastic glass as he drank from it. "Nadia, I don't need to talk to you about Lila."

154

"Are you sure?" Why was she even pushing this? Nadia took another self-conscious drink of her own water. "It's just that… we're friends, aren't we?" She smiled weakly. "I just want you to know you can talk to me about things like that."

An exasperated smile began to tug at the corners of Alex's mouth. "Nads. My 'dear friend'." He grinned to soften the sarcasm, and plucked the empty tumbler from her grip. "Trust me, there's nothing to talk about. Me and Lila-wise, anyway. Okay, so I sort of fancied her when we met up again, you know, after uni. But obviously, Rory did too!" Alex rolled his eyes. "And that was that. Hardly the greatest love story of the century, right?" he scoffed.

Nadia felt a weird sort of dizziness that was a combination of vodka and relief. Matt must have misheard or misunderstood. Alex wasn't in love with Lila and this one small realisation made her feel inexplicable, like she could somehow stretch out and fill the entire room. It changed things. She could never have competed with a girl he'd known and wanted for so long, but now maybe. Maybe.

And it was in that moment that Nadia knew for certain that things with Alex had gone too far; there was no way back.

Alex slung his arm around her shoulders. "Come on then, *friend*, enough of this," he grinned again. "Let's go and try to liberate that rum from Caro, eh?"

Alex

He'd been feeling quite smug that he'd managed to head Nadia off and shut down the Lila conversation before it really began. He'd always known what he felt was unrequited, sure, but he hadn't quite anticipated that there was going to be a whole other level of super-unrequitedness that was Lila being single and *still* not being remotely interested in him.

But to be entirely truthful, these days – with all of Lila's belongings gone from the boys' Tooting flat and the corner of the sofa where she'd usually sat no longer feeling so empty – he was just starting to feel faintly embarrassed about the whole thing. It was pitiful, really, and Nadia's pity was something he was quite sure he wouldn't be able to bear.

As they moved back through the main room, which seemed to be growing denser with bodies with every passing hour, Alex felt Nadia hesitate. Matt was sitting on the sofa in the space they had just vacated, talking animatedly to Rory. Alex saw Caro and Holly catch Nadia's eye apologetically; there was definitely something going on here; he just wished Nadia would clue him in a little.

As if they felt his attention on them, Matt and Rory suddenly looked up at him. Rory's eyebrows came together in a small frown as he made eye contact with Alex. "What?" Alex mouthed across the room at his flatmate; Rory shook his head slightly. Not here.

"Alex," Nadia said suddenly, and he felt her fingers fluttering near his wrist nervously. Without thinking about it, Alex grabbed Nadia's hand in his and held them both curved into a ball against his chest.

"What's wrong?"

"I want to break things off with Matt." The words came out of her in a rush, as if she'd been holding them in for forever.

Alex blinked in surprise. "Okay." He looked at her, confused. "So what's stopping you?"

Nadia held his gaze for a moment, almost as if she was looking for something in his expression or waiting for him to say more. Finally she dropped her eyes. "I don't know," she answered, honestly, with a small shrug and a laugh. "I actually don't know."

"Excuse me?" Caro's suddenly outraged tone brought their attention back to the group on the sofa; Caro sounded even more posh when she was angry. Jez had returned – a whole lot drunker and a great deal more determined to convince Caro to join him for that tequila nightcap.

"Look mate, I don't think you understand English," Rory bellowed, standing up to his full height in an attempt to look threatening. Matt got to his feet a second behind him. "The lady isn't interested."

156

Jez had an ugly twist to his mouth that spoke volumes about his level of drunken frustration. "Lady?" he echoed, with a nasty laugh. "Just because she looks like a fat Pippa Middleton and talks like she's got a cock shoved in her mouth doesn't make her a lady."

There was a moment of horrified silence from everyone before Caro spluttered into indignant life.

"Seriously? Fuck you!" was her apt if not madly intelligent retort.

"Yeah, fuck you!" Rory parroted with a scowl. "What is your problem?"

"Who's saying I've got a problem?" Jez answered immediately, turning to Rory, his stance combative. "Are you making this a problem?" This was escalating far too quickly.

"Hey, guys, calm down," Matt tried, woefully ineffective.

"His problem is, clearly, that I would rather shit in my hands and clap than have sex with him," Caro pointed out, blisteringly, making sure that everyone remotely nearby could hear her. "Like any sensible woman. Nads?" Caro turned to face the stunned Nadia. "I think we're done here, yeah? I'll call a taxi."

And with that, Caro stooped to pick up Rory's still half-full bottle of rum, tossed her hair over her shoulder as she stood and exited the room – majestic in her high, high heels – before anyone had a chance to say any more. Rory stared after her, looking more than a little thunderstruck.

Holly stood too. "Nads?" she called, cocking her head towards the door. She eyeballed the spot over Alex's heart where his and Nadia's hands were still entangled. Alex felt Nadia's fingers suddenly flicker within his grasp as if she too was just realising how long they'd been holding hands and hurriedly let go. He wondered if Matt had seen. "It's time to go," Holly finished, flatly, the double-meaning of the phrase ringing obvious.

"I think we should probably get going too," Rory pointed out; Jez was still glowering aggressively. "Besides, Caro's taken all the bloody booze."

"I'll tell Caro to get a people carrier," Holly said. "You guys are welcome to come back to ours for a bit."

"You don't have to go, Nads," Matt suddenly interjected, looking rapidly between Alex and Nadia like an overwhelmed tennis spectator. "I... thought you might stay here tonight."

Nadia just sighed. "No, Matt. I'm going to go home. But you should come round tomorrow, maybe. We can get some food in and... talk."

Alex had watched Matt's face brighten all the way through Nadia's sentence, until the fatal final word. Even Jez was respectfully silent in the face of it.

"Talk," Matt echoed, trying to sound casual and failing miserably. "Yeah, sounds cool. I'll text you in the morning, okay?"

"Okay," Nadia smiled. "Let's head down," she told Holly and the boys. "Caro's probably got a fleet of taxis waiting for us by now."

At the very last possible minute, Nadia paused at the flat door. "Oh, and Jez?" she called back, into the open living space. Jez raised a bleary face from where he'd been resting his head on the arm of the sofa. "Happy birthday."

From out in the corridor Rory snorted with laughter at the epic sarcasm Nadia had managed to load her words with. "You arsehole!" he couldn't help but add with a shout, somewhat ruining Nadia's icy dignity, just as the flat door swung shut behind them.

"Well done," Alex turned round to grin at Nadia as they made their way down the staircase to street level. "But you do realise that you totally gave him the head's up there, right? He's probably going to turn up tomorrow and immediately tell you some bullshit about it 'not working out', just so he can get in there first and won't have to say he was dumped!"

Nadia laughed, and she already sounded lighter, freer than she had the whole evening, the whole month. "Honestly? I really don't care."

Chapter 16

Nadia

The sound of the front door closing echoed through the flat; Nadia finally let out the sigh that had been brewing.

On cue, Holly peered around the doorframe. "Is it safe to come out?" she teased.

Nadia shot her a withering look before turning back to the pizza she was trying to tear apart with her hands. She'd thoughtfully popped it in the oven before Matt had been due to arrive, assuming he'd want some sort of lunch. She hadn't got as far as using the wheel to slice it into segments before he'd legged it. The hot cheese was burning her fingertips.

"Did you hear all of that?" she asked.

Holly shook her head. "No. But believe me, I tried. I even considered putting my ear to an empty glass on the wall like they do on TV," she joked. "But it was just a lot of mumbling. So…" She moved to sit on the floor in front of the coffee table, legs crossed, and reached to tear off her own bit of pizza from the disc. "All broken off with him, then?"

"I think so. I mean, yes. I mean…" Nadia considered her response. "I think *he thinks* it was a mutual decision. So I suppose that's a success in itself."

Holly laughed, holding her hand over her mouthful of food.

159

"The big question is, did either of you use the phrase, 'it's not you, it's me'?" she quipped.

"But it genuinely wasn't him," Nadia argued immediately. "It's my fault, and I told him that. I told him I'd gotten carried away." She sighed, listlessly watching the melted cheese stretch out into thinner and thinner strings as she pulled the pizza apart. "But, to be honest, I basically based it around the fact that I shouldn't be starting any relationships of any kind at this stage, as I'll probably have been booted out of the country before Christmas. I pretended I thought it was pretty much a done deal, the deportation." Was it pretence? Nadia was never quite sure any more. "I thought that would sting a little less than 'I'm just not that into you'," she continued, with a wry smile. "Either way, it's done now." Holly frowned but Nadia ignored her, dropping the food back down to the plate without having actually eaten any. "Alex was right, though," she continued. "Matt did come in here fighting. I gave him the head's up last night that I wanted to *talk*. There wasn't any messing around; he didn't even have any lunch." She gestured at the rapidly cooling pizza.

"Means more for me," Holly pointed out, popping another chunk into her mouth.

"You know, for someone who was apparently quite into me, he sure couldn't shake himself off fast enough." Nadia shook her head. "It was like a rat off a sinking ship."

"Oh Nads, stop it. You're not a sinking ship." Holly rolled her eyes. Nadia decided not to press the issue; she knew Holly hated any mention of the fact that she might be deported. "So," Holly continued mercilessly. "What now?"

"What do you mean, what now?"

"You know very well I mean 'what now' with Alex. Does he know you're young, free and single?"

"Being as it's been about five minutes, and I've spent four and a half of them talking to you, no, he doesn't yet!" Nadia picked listlessly at the food in front of her again. "Besides, what is he meant to do with that information? Don't you think that if it was meant to happen between us it would have happened by now?" she argued. Now she no longer had the Lila thing to blame, being too far into the friend-zone was her go-to argument.

Holly was having none of it. "I just refuse to believe that man's not totally in love with you."

Nadia snorted with laughter. "And why's that?"

"Because, A, the way he looks at you..."

"Ahh, yes, 'the way he looks at me'," Nadia echoed sarcastically, settling back against the sofa. "That again..."

"B," Holly continued to list, ignoring her. "The way he's always angled to where you are. Like he's a big arrow, pointing at you all the time. And I mean that in a metaphoric, romantic way, not like, you know, a penis."

"Oh, God, Holly..." Nadia groaned, burying her face in the crook of her arm.

"He was holding your hand last night," Holly argued. "Why would he just randomly hold your hand?"

"He's a good friend," Nadia protested feebly.

Holly gave a snort of disbelief. "You two looked like you were standing at an altar about to get married."

Nadia dissolved into giggles. "Okay, okay," she conceded. "You win. He's clearly madly in love with me, but doesn't realise it quite yet. But the question remains: what am *I* supposed to do about it?"

"Go round there," Holly urged. "Ring him." She pushed Nadia's mobile phone across the coffee table so it skittered closer to her. "Tell him you're coming round later. Tell him you broke up with Matt because you like someone else. Smack him in the face with the hintiest hint that ever hinted. Because the man isn't an idiot. In fact, that's reason C as to why I'm certain he's crazy about you."

"Oh yeah?"

"Yeah. Because he'd *have to* be an idiot not to be." Holly stuck her tongue out playfully as Nadia screwed up her face again. "Go on. Call him. Come on, Nads," Holly urged, when Nadia had made no move towards her phone. "Life's too short," she finished sadly, the unspoken words hanging in the air between them: *your time might be running out.*

"We're doing 'Candy' on Thursday," Nadia said after a minute. "I'll talk to him then. See what the lie of the land is. Seriously!" Nadia insisted, when she saw the look of doubt on her friend's face. "I promise."

Holly arched an eyebrow sceptically. "Make sure you do." Satisfied, she helped herself to yet another piece of pizza. "I wasn't sure about him at first, you know," she added, as she picked off rogue peppers with her fingernails. "But I really like him now. You guys sort of *fit*, you know?"

Yes, Nadia knew; 'fit' was exactly the word for it. As a foreigner with an eccentric accent – somehow neither quite Russian nor English – Nadia had always felt just slightly out of place. But nowadays, everywhere felt like her castle, as long as Alex was there too.

She could almost still feel the weight of his hand upon hers, a ghost of the night before.

Alex

He was still puzzling out Rory's weird behaviour as he arrived home. Jez's birthday "after-party" back at Nadia's in Clapham Old Town had certainly left them both stupendously drunk, but that didn't explain Rory's recent attitude. He'd been an angry sort of quiet on the night bus back to Tooting in the early hours of Sunday morning, but Alex couldn't be sure if Rory was cross with Alex or cross with him. Either way, he'd spent all of Sunday closeted in his bedroom – sleeping off a bad hangover, for sure – but Alex just couldn't shake the feeling that something was off.

And now, this evening, Alex had turned his mobile phone on after work to a perfunctory text message from Rory informing him that he wouldn't be home that night and – mystifyingly – urging Alex to "enjoy his evening". Rory worked late so often recently that he'd completely given up all attempts at keeping Alex informed of his movements, and he'd certainly never before wasted time with textual well wishes; *what was going on?*

To be honest, Alex was quite looking forward to a quiet night in. It used to be that all his nights were quiet ones in, but since meeting Nadia his social calendar had somewhat exploded. He seemed to be spending more time out and about than ever before, perhaps even more than when he was a student back in Brighton. It was quite nice to realise that he had things like laundry to do and television to catch up on, rather than knowing he was just going to flounder to fill the empty hours of the evening until it was time to go to sleep and start all over again.

It was still stifling in the city – as "hot as Satan's arse crack" a heavily perspiring Donnelly had poetically dubbed it earlier that week – and so the first thing Alex did after shutting the flat door safely behind him was to kick off his work shoes and drop his charcoal suit trousers to the carpet with a satisfied sigh. If this summer went on for much longer maybe he *would* have to look into getting "suit shorts" for work after all, ha ha. He flicked his trousers up from the floor using his foot and caught them deftly with one hand before moving into his room and throwing them on the bed to deal with later. Time to put that overdue wash on, and then he'd see what he could cobble together for dinner from whatever was lurking in the freezer.

He walked through into the main part of the flat with a collection of indiscriminate laundry piled so high in his arms that he didn't notice her at first. He continued halfway through the living room towards the kitchen and had to double back, mouth stupidly slack, dumbfounded. Lila smiled in a leisurely way at him. She sat tucked into the corner of the sofa, a book on her lap, exactly where she always used to be. And Alex stood there – like some awful stunt double for Tom Cruise in *Risky Business* – wearing only a rumpled shirt, a pair of old boxers and comedy Simpsons socks.

Firstly – and mainly – he just wanted to full-on die of embarrassment. Then secondly...

"Lils!" He lowered his armfuls of dirty clothes down his torso in what he hoped was both a subtle manner and to a height that would conceal his groin. "What are you doing here? Rory's not home. Wait." He frowned at her. "How did you get in?"

Lila slowly put a bookmark into her paperback and slid it onto the coffee table before standing and moving towards him across the room. "Rory let me in earlier," she admitted.

"He's here?" Great! Another witness to this saggy-boxered humiliation.

"No." Lila's tone was meaningful, as if she was waiting for him to realise something. She came a little nearer and stopped, folding her arms across her chest, smiling at him like someone who has a secret, like someone who is more than a little nervous about something.

He just hoped she wasn't close enough to smell the slightly stale funk from his laundry.

"I'm just going to stick this in the washing machine," Alex blurted, shrugging his shoulders to gesture what he was holding, somewhat redundantly. "Hang on a second." He all but threw the clothes into the drum, barely sparing an instant to throw in a liquitab after it, deciding it was okay to forego the nicety of fabric softener under the circumstances. He exhaled as the machine started up with its low, watery grumble. He glanced back; Lila hadn't followed him. Then he glanced down, belatedly realising that he was – of course – still trouserless, and now without his dirty laundry groin-barrier – fuck!

"Need any help?" Lila called politely from the next room.

Alex sighed, resigned. "No thanks." He moved back into the living room. "I should probably get some trousers on, huh?" he joked weakly.

Lila smiled coquettishly, her eyelashes lowering shyly, strangely. "Sorry. It's pretty hot today, isn't it?"

"Yeah…" Alex agreed as he edged past Lila and made for his bedroom. He endeavoured to keep himself angled towards her, which unfortunately resulted in him entering the corridor walking like a crab; it just seemed rude to turn his boxered behind to his unexpected guest. The first thing to hand when he reached his room was a pair of tartan lounge pants lying discarded in a crumpled heap at the side of his bed. Alex hurriedly pulled them up his legs as he returned to the living room, and to Lila.

She hadn't moved; she was still standing in the middle of the wide room, one hand picking nervously at the fingernails of the other. The bright sunlight of the summer evening outside fell into the room in slants through the half-open window blinds and lit her up as if she was on a stage. She was, as usual, gut-twistingly magnificent. She was wearing a maxi dress that was slightly too long for her and bunched up against her toes, where her nails were painted a coral pink. She gave him another one of those enigmatically shy smiles she was suddenly so free with and Alex felt himself swallow tightly; she was so beautiful. He suddenly couldn't believe there was a part of him that had accepted he might not ever see her again. Which reminded him…

"So, Lils, what brings you here?" Alex forced himself to ask, breaking the spell of the silent moment they were sharing. "When we said we should 'do something' one day soon, I wasn't really expecting a home invasion," he joked.

"Rory let me in," Lila repeated. Alex waited for her to elaborate. She hesitated again. "Okay, Alex, I don't really know how to do this; so I'm just going to come out and say it, I think. The thing is, Rory told me that you have feelings for me?"

She said it so casually, like a question, that the panic didn't set in immediately; when it did, it hit like a sledgehammer.

"He said what?" A winded Alex struggled to order his thoughts. He couldn't feel less surprised if Lila had roundhouse kicked him in the chest.

Lila smoothed the flicks of the front of her bobbed hair behind her ears, a nervous trait he was familiar with. "He said you had feelings for me. That you always have." Her hands were still up,

165

cupped by her face, even though her hair was as smooth and neat as it was ever going to get. "Is it true?" she pressed, after a moment's more painful silence. "Do you?"

Over the past year, Alex must have pictured this conversation a hundred thousand different ways. In not a single one of them was he being waylaid whilst in his underwear.

"Where did Rory get that idea?" Alex eventually managed, in a pathetically strangled-sounding tone. Hurt immediately flashed across Lila's face and he felt like ramming his fist into his mouth.

"So, you don't, then?" Lila mumbled, taking an uncertain half-step backwards. "Oh. This is embarrassing..."

"No, wait, I didn't mean it that way," Alex countered desperately. "I just... I was just wondering why this is suddenly coming up now..."

"He called me on Sunday," Lila explained. She rolled her eyes. "It was mega-awkward. He sort of made small talk for a while, asking me what I'd been up to, how I was, like he cared..." Lila seemed to catch herself and swallowed the bitterness that had been building in her tone before carrying on. "Anyway, I challenged him; I was like, why are you really calling me, Rory? And he just sort of blurted it out."

Alex had been listening to Lila's monologue with a sense of rising horror. "Blurted what out?" he echoed.

"That you guys had been at some party, and that he'd got chatting to Nadia's boyfriend. The subject of Rory being newly single came up..." Here Lila rolled her eyes again. "And then apparently this guy was like, oh, Alex must be pleased and then it all sort of came out." She gestured vaguely. "That you'd, you know, liked me. You like me," she corrected her tense, looking up at him shyly for confirmation; Alex exhaled shakily. "Anyway, he just thought that I should know. In case I... wanted to do something about it."

And all Alex could think about was Lila the night of that house party. It was last year, the earliest point you could refer to as spring; the evening still had a fair bite to it. She'd always had long hair, her natural mousy-brown with a wave back at university, and he'd taken a few seconds to place her when she approached him with that sleek, pale bob. He hadn't seen Lila Palmer for years, and they'd shared alma mater memories over a pair of self-poured and over-strong rum and cokes. Lila had only known the younger Alex, the one with all the answers, with the fit girlfriend, the Alex who'd known her for three years and never bothered to learn her surname or what she studied. For that first evening of their reunion, Alex could be that guy again, even if it was just through that one girl's eyes. And he'd liked it; he'd liked it a lot. He liked Lila too. The new styling suited her, gave a bit of bite to her natural cuteness, all upturned nose and bee-stung lips.

Of course, Rory had thought as much too.

You know," Lila mused, dragging Alex back into the present; she was biting those bee-stung lips. "I don't think that Rory would have gone for me if he'd known you liked me. He's a good guy like that, I suppose. And you're, like, his best mate – and a good friend, Alex. Especially to me; always to me." Tentatively, Lila reached forward and brushed her fingertips across Alex's wrist.

Jesus. Was he being friend-zoned, even now? Alex's stomach jittered madly; what was Lila up to? Was he meant to try kissing her, or apologise for ever even thinking about it?

"So, where do we go from here?" he asked, twisting his wrist so that the sides of his fingers brushed against the back of Lila's, like the very gentlest version of holding hands.

Lila smiled softly, looking up at him through the veil of her eyelashes in that cute way she did. "On a date, I think."

Chapter 17

Nadia

"Okay, so!" Alex punctuated himself with a dramatic flourish of a French fry. "I've got news."

Nadia hurried up the chewing process of the mouthful of Big Mac she was working through so she could answer.

"Me too," she managed as she finished swallowing. "You go first." She was dying to see his reaction to the news about Matt being out of the picture, but wanted the time to savour it. Surely if he felt even the tiniest flicker of interest in her that way, she'd see it in his face as he digested the news? Okay, so the rammed Piccadilly Circus branch of McDonalds wasn't exactly the most apt place for a romantic epiphany, but at this point she would take what she could get. Besides, it was the best place to fuel up on alcohol-absorbing carbs before a night at nearby Closet.

Alex smiled to himself, dabbing another fry into the swirl of ketchup he'd squeezed into the lid of his burger box; Nadia wasn't sure if he was playing for time in order to increase the suspense or because he was trying to order his thoughts. She quite liked that about him, he was always so considered.

"Well, it's about Lila," he said eventually, the smile growing even broader on his face. The second mouthful of burger that Nadia had just taken suddenly turned to ash against her teeth. "It's really funny that you were asking me about her at the weekend, actually!"

Nadia somehow managed to swallow. "Oh, yeah?"

Alex laughed. "Yeah! Which reminds me, I need to thank your Matt. Turns out he's got a big fecking mouth, but it's actually worked out quite well for me." Alex pressed on, excitedly. "Well, as you might have guessed, I sort of downplayed the Lila thing at the weekend. I just didn't think there was any point hashing it over. I truly thought I wasn't even going to see her again, not even as friends. I wanted to start getting over her, so I thought it was counter-productive to tell you how I really felt. I didn't want you feeling sorry for me."

Nadia toyed distractedly with fries she had no intention of eating. "And so what's changed?"

Alex's smile spread even further. "I don't know yet. Maybe everything."

He looked so damn excited, so happy. Nadia steeled herself as she plastered a smile on her face. "Hold on there! Why don't you start from the beginning?"

"Well, like I said, Matt's got a big mouth. That night we all met? In Bison I sort of told him that I had a thing for my flatmate's girlfriend, and so when he met said flatmate at Jez's last weekend, he apparently couldn't help but spill the beans. Rory had had no idea. But then he thought about it and decided that he should see if Lila, you know, could ever be interested in me in that way, because seeing his mate and his ex-girlfriend happy seemed like a win-win to him. And, you know, have I ever told you? I knew Lils first; we were friends at university. But, anyway, so he called Lila and arranged for her to be in the flat when I got home from work the other day so we could talk it out."

Images of Alex and Lila writhing together on the boys' dark sofa, their bodies sinking deep into the cushions raced through Nadia's head.

"And so, you... talked?" she managed to ask.

"Yeah. Literally! We *just* talked," Alex clarified, belatedly realising what Nadia had been insinuating; he grinned sheepishly. "I was in my underwear for part of it though!"

Nadia couldn't help her startled laugh. "What!?"

"She, er, caught me by surprise…"

"Caught you with your pants down, one might even say!"

Alex laughed through his mouthful of food. "Indeed."

"And so you're what? Just going out with Lila now? It seems a little rushed…"

"Well, you haven't seen me in my underwear," Alex joked; Nadia felt her cheeks fire. "Nah, nothing like that, not really. We're just going to go out on Saturday night." He paused. "You and me didn't have any plans, did we?"

Nadia – who had been planning on suggesting that Alex came over Saturday night and they cooked something together – simply took another bite of her unwanted burger and mutely shook her head.

"So I need your help deciding where to take Lila for dinner. Somewhere nice, but not, you know, *too* nice. Where would your perfect first date be?" Alex asked.

Nadia gave a small smile. "Bodeans?"

"Ha, ha."

"No, I sort of mean it," Nadia insisted. She paused, the urge to help her friend warring with the desire to completely sabotage this inconvenient fledgling romance. "You don't need to try so hard. I mean, this girl already knows you. If you're not acting like yourself, she'll know it, right?"

Alex gave her a grateful smile. "You're right. I just still can't believe this. I've wanted this for so long. It sort of feels like a dream." He was the handsomest she'd ever seen him in that moment, with his cheeks flushed and his eyes shining. How could Lila not fall in love with him?

"Don't worry." Nadia picked up her Coke and swirled it so the ice cubes tumbled and rattled. "Something tells me that this is going to be the start of an epic romance…"

Alex

Clapham Common and its surrounding environs boasted several supposedly high-end burger joints, but Alex always felt that simply putting "gourmet" in the restaurant name didn't necessarily make them so. After a couple of days of indecision he decided to think totally outside the box.

"Covent Garden?" was the first thing Lila said when she arrived at the table, a teasing smile on her lips.

"I know, I know – 'north of the river'!" Alex laughed. He dropped his voice conspiratorially. "This is where the real Londoners live, you know."

"No, this is where the *tourists* live," Lila countered. "This place better be good; I had to avoid a creepy living-statue street-performer and walk across cobbles in these heels!" She flicked her feet out prettily to show that she was wearing three-inch stilettos.

Alex laughed. "Wowza! But it's appreciated. You being here *and* the great shoes, I mean." He took her all in as she sat down across from him at the little two-person table, quaint and chintzy, covered in a gingham oil-cloth. She'd obviously made an effort, which was a good sign. The front bits of her hair were pinned to the crown of her head creating a little sleek quiff, a hairstyle he'd never seen on her before, and along with the killer heels she was wearing a powder-blue mini-dress that contoured all the way down her body. It reminded him suddenly of a similar dress Nadia had, although hers flared at the mid-thigh and danced around her body as she moved.

"This place is lovely," Lila said, helping herself to a sip from the glass of tap water Alex had thoughtfully already ordered for her. "I hope you haven't gone to any trouble?"

"No, no trouble," Alex assured her.

"Are you sure? You know I would have been just as happy in a Pizza Hut!"

"In which case..!" Alex pretended to get up and leave, sending Lila into a fit of the giggles.

"No, no, we're here now!"

And Alex, who still, *still* couldn't quite believe that he *was* there, beamed at her. "Good. Because I've already ordered a bottle of wine."

Nadia

"Hey," Nadia greeted as she pulled open the flat door. "Thanks for…" She blinked; Caro was wearing a terrifically tiny red-and-black lace dress, heels and an unexpected amount of eyeliner. "Coming," Nadia finished weakly. "You look… Were you thinking we're going clubbing or something?"

"No," Caro answered shortly as she kicked off her shoes and made her way through to the living room, where she petulantly threw herself on the sofa, tucking her legs up underneath her (whilst pulling her hemline as far down as she could). Her mobile phone had remained in her hand all the while; she began sliding the pad of her index finger across its touch screen distractedly.

"Hey, I know I might have sounded pathetic and lonesome on the phone earlier, but you really didn't need to cancel a big night out to come babysit me," Nadia assured Caro as she followed her into the main room.

"I didn't. Don't worry." Caro finally dropped her phone to the sofa cushions and looked across at her friend with her expertly made-up smoky eyes. Nadia – in a pair of knee-length joggers without a scrap of makeup on – felt very underdressed. "So. Who's standing *you* up this fine Saturday evening?" Caro asked with a dry little smile.

Alex

The first bottle of wine saw them through discussing the weather (yes, it was still bloody hot), how their respective jobs were going (both meh in the extreme) and a gross-out YouTube video that had recently gone viral on Facebook (disgusting yet oddly compelling). It was polished off before their starter plates had even been cleared away and within two minutes of Alex motioning at the waiter, a fresh one was placed in their ice bucket; now *that* was Covent Garden-style service.

Far too used to Nadia – who he'd seen on more than one occasion drinking wine out of a pint glass – Alex clumsily over-filled their glasses past the little white line that indicated a socially acceptable level. Lila thankfully didn't notice and continued to chatter on, the wine blushing prettily high on her cheeks and in a ribbon between her collarbones.

"So," she changed the subject with a mischievous smile, as if she'd just sensed his attention wandering. "It's great that this isn't weird, huh?"

Alex decided he was drunk enough that he could play the blunt game too. "Why would it be weird?" he asked, picking up his over-heavy glass. "We must have had a hundred dinners together."

"Takeaway on your sofa with Rory sat between us hardly compares," Lila laughed. They both paused for an off-kilter moment, sipping awkwardly at their respective drinks, as if they were waiting for the spectre of the ex-boyfriend/best friend Lila's unthinking remark had conjured up to get bored with them and walk away.

"Fair enough." Alex conceded. "But I, for one, am glad – wait, make that *ecstatically happy* – that Rory's not sat between us tonight."

Lila returned his smile, reaching out across the table to give his hand a little squeeze, letting her fingers linger over his wrist, where his pulse jumped towards her.

"Me too."

"God, I should have said something earlier, shouldn't I?"

"I don't know about that." Lila moved her hand away and picked up her wine glass once more. "I mean, maybe it's better that we got to know one another again in a casual way. You barely spoke to me the entire three years at uni, sure, and then I think it took about three months of me dating Rory for you to start to hold a conversation with me!"

Alex choked a little on his mouthful of wine. "That's not true," he managed.

"Oh, it is!" Lila laughed, but not unkindly. "You'd always hide in your room when I came over, never came along anywhere we invited you... Rory said that's just what you were like nowadays, and not to worry. Said you'd had a bad break-up after uni. I said I'd heard. You and Alice, and all; I still have her on Facebook, you know."

Alex bristled immediately at the thought that his ancient heartbreak had been a topic of casual conversation for armchair psychologists. "I really don't think that's the case at all, Lils..."

"It's pretty obvious," Lila insisted gently. "You couldn't bear the thought of being hurt again, so you did the natural thing and kept yourself to yourself." Her eyes dropped. "It's something that I've had to struggle against recently. But it's important to get back on the horse, you know?" She beamed at him encouragingly and took another large gulp from her glass.

Alex – unsure whether to be insulted or delighted that he was apparently considered a horse worth getting back on to – studied Lila carefully. Maybe she was drunker than he thought. Mentally he urged their main courses to hurry up; the carby pasta bake that Lila had ordered would go some way towards soaking up her indulgence and ensure the conversation steered itself back to safer waters – waters that hopefully didn't feature Alice Rhodes, Rory Ryan or Alex's allegedly hermit-like lifestyle.

"But you weren't like that with Nadia, actually," Lila continued, and her tone carried the slightest sting of jealousy.

"What? Nadia?"

"Hmmm. You were trotting off on adventures with her before you even knew her last name. Took you over a month before you'd even come into your own kitchen for a glass of water if I was in there!" Lila's tone was jovial, but the little twist to her bottom lip was anything but. "I felt for sure you were going to end up going out with her, you know."

"What? Nadia?" Alex repeated, feeling utterly confused by the person that Lila was painting and calling himself. Surely he had never been so cringing around her? Surely Nadia hadn't caused that massive an impact on him?

"Yes, Nadia," Lila mimicked. "You're always with her. When you're not, you're talking about her. She reminds me of Alice, sometimes. Smiley. Social. You know," she waved her hand dismissively. "It seemed obvious what was going to happen between you two."

"Did it?" Alex asked, incredulous.

"Of course! Rory used to tease you about it all of the time."

"Rory teases me about *everything* all of the time," Alex pointed out.

Lila gave one of her little musical laughs. "Good point. But no, genuinely, we all thought it was, you know, on the cards."

On the cards; Alex had a sudden flashback. Nadia curled beside him on the floor of her flat; the going-threadbare carpet managing to itch him even though his jeans; the brightness of her nail varnish flashing on her fingertips as she dealt herself playing cards, worked them into intelligible piles; Nadia turning her face to his and telling him that she wasn't going to get what she wanted.

"I was really worried for you," Lila had continued.

Alex struggled out of the memory to catch up with the conversation. "What do you mean, worried?"

"Well, you know… she'd hardly be a sensible choice, Alex!"

Alex felt his shoulders stiffen immediately at the senseless insult to Nadia. "What do you mean?"

Lila's mouth formed a little "o" of surprise; she obviously realised she'd crossed a line, even if Alex himself wasn't entirely sure where or what that line was. "I don't mean it in a bitchy way," she assured him immediately. "I quite like Nadia. Like I said, she's fun. It's just that, well, she's going to be deported, isn't she?"

Alex gritted his teeth. "Not necessarily." It was something that, to be honest, had been playing on his mind more and more recently. Nadia should be receiving her court hearing date for her appeal any day now, and it was all uphill from there. She'd joked the other day that she wasn't ready, that her to-do list spread over countless more notebook pages, and that she was going to have to abscond from the system, live as a nationless nomad hidden in the mews of London…

"I mean, I won't have an identity, or, you know, a home," she'd laughed. "But at least I'd never miss a Candy at Closet night!" And Alex had laughed too, but the laugh had felt a little hollow and unpleasant inside his chest as he did so.

"She'll go in front of a judge soon," he continued, trying to sound confident, dismissive. "And she'll get her Indefinite Leave. I'm sure of it."

"But Rory said that you told him that probably wasn't going to happen," Lila pointed out. Alex cursed his pessimistic self of six weeks ago, the self who had stood there with his Border Control Enforcement hat on and known that Nadia simply didn't have a legal leg to stand on, and had explained to Rory as much.

"I reckon she's got a fair shot," he lied.

Lila obviously saw the lie in his face; she smiled sympathetically. "See, this is what I was talking about. You're close to her. I mean, not in the way I thought you were – obviously – as it turned out you liked me all along." She blushed delightfully, making Alex's stomach go a little funny. "I just mean it would have been a massive shame if you'd avoided relationships for like, half a decade, only to have your new girlfriend kicked out of the country!"

She had a point. Alex was already feeling vaguely sick to his core over the thought of Nadia being denied her Leave to Remain and having to go. He couldn't imagine how he'd be feeling if she was his girlfriend.

"Alice was always a laugh, but she was a bit of a bitch. Especially to you," Lila continued, assertively. "I never wanted to see you hurt again," Lila finished, fumbling for Alex's hand on the table top once again. "You don't deserve it. You're one of the good guys,

176

Alex. You'd never hurt anyone. You deserve all good things." And as she spoke, she lifted his loose fist and brought it to her mouth to place a kiss on his knuckles, the chill the wine had left on her lips pressing against his skin.

Nadia

"He's still not answering." Caro threw her phone to the carpet, where it bounced off its corner and came to rest under the coffee table. She raked her hair back off her face with her fingers, pressing the swell of her palms into her temples in frustration.

"He's probably with his wife," Nadia reasoned.

"No, no, she's away at her parents for the weekend," Caro insisted, her voice muffled by the fact that she had her arms up over her face. "That's why we arranged to go out."

Monty hadn't turned up at the Chelsea bar where they'd agreed to meet. He hadn't called and he hadn't answered his phone when Caro had eventually swallowed her pride (and two Passion fruit Daiquiris) and rang to see what was up. There was nothing from him: this great, terrible, foreboding nothing. And whereas Nadia had longed for Professor Fletcher to have absolutely nothing to do with her friend for months now, she could see how utterly miserable Caro was when it actually happened; it just made her hate him all the more.

Love changes you, so they say – how romantic. But nobody ever says that love can change your life for the worse, can turn you from a beautiful, confident woman into a shaking, phone-throwing mess. They should put *that* on the Valentine's cards.

"I know you think I'm stupid," Caro said suddenly, but there was no tone of reproach in her voice. "Hell, even I think I'm stupid. But I just don't want to have gone through all the pain I've gone through for nothing, you know? I need to believe that we're meant to end up together, me and him, otherwise it means I've just wasted my time, for nothing; been the other woman, for nothing; cried so hard I've felt like throwing up, so many times,

over and over, and always for nothing. And I just can't bear that."
Caro let her arms drop down into her lap, her hands hesitating
there for a moment, before she moved to retrieve her phone.

Alex
Although he was absolutely stuffed, it felt like a three-course sort
of evening, and so Alex insisted that they order dessert. After some
convincing, Lila agreed to share one, so Alex did that terribly kitsch
but heart-warming thing of asking the waiter for "two spoons,
please" with a knowing smile. And so the pair finished off their
delicious but pretentious chocolate soufflé and the dregs of bottle
of wine number three, and headed out into the summer night.

Lila was swaying slightly on those high heels of hers, but seemed
steady enough as they meandered their way down the Strand,
packed with its usual Saturday-night mixture of tourists and
native Londoners, who – like them - apparently didn't know any
better. The pavements outside the pubs and bars were thronged
with people smoking, or queuing, or simply enjoying the balmy
evening. Alex had to take Lila's elbow as these blockages forced
them to walk in and out of the road, laughing as they raced back
over the curb of the pavements as taxis neared and beeped their
horns angrily. He still had her elbow as they arrived in the grey
expanse of Trafalgar Square, having headed in that direction by
some sort of silent accord.

The lions sat quietly on their high plinths, only obvious as black
hunched shapes against the indigo of the clear night's sky. Despite
the busyness of the Strand and Charing Cross itself, the Square
was relatively peaceful, mostly just couples strolling arm in arm,
craning their necks as they took in the surrounding architecture.
Couples like us, thought Alex, realising that Lila had at some point
curved very prettily into his body as they walked and talked,
making them into a pair of parentheses, although he didn't know
what – if anything – they were circling. The nerves that Alex had
successfully evaded all evening suddenly bloomed in his stomach.

178

"Did you know that the lions are made out of bronze melted down from cannons seized from enemy ships after the actual Battle of Trafalgar?" he found himself saying. It was a neat little bit of trivia. When he and Nadia had spent the afternoon in the Square after their abortive trip to the National Portrait Gallery they'd spent at least an hour looking up information on their phones and reading the most interesting facts aloud to one another.

"Wow, that's really interesting," said Lila, in a tone that suggested she was being polite. She stopped walking and curved around to face him, still linked, his hand in the crook of her elbow. "Thank you for a really great night."

Alex gave a lopsided smile. "Are you just trying to change the subject away from pointless war history?" In response, Lila mutely drew her free arm closer, grazing her hand in a line across Alex's hipbone as she did, causing his abdomen to stiffen into rock underneath his thin shirt. This was actually happening. Above him, the lions stared outwards across London and the stars battled dimly against the light pollution. Down here, Lila Palmer was now officially in his arms and he could feel the heat off of her skin and watch her wet her bottom lip with her tongue with excruciating slowness.

And it felt a little like fate, that moment. That the good things that people had been saying he had been due for for years were finally arriving. That if Lila had never gone out with Rory for so long, she would never have had the opportunity to get to know him, to give him a chance to take her out for dinner, to kiss her underneath lions and stars.

Channelling an assurance Alex could have sworn the past five years had throttled out of him, he took Lila by the waist, felt the dimples at the base of her spine through her thin, tight dress as he slid his other palm across her back. And then he did what he'd wanted to do ever since that pretty blonde girl he used to know had walked up to him at that house party the previous spring, and kissed her.

Chapter 18

Alex

Rory had assured him that he didn't have a problem with it, but Alex couldn't help but imagine that things felt rather strained in the flat. To add insult to injury, even Nadia was quiet this week. She wasn't ignoring him per se, but she was taking ages to reply to his messages and not exactly being receptive to his suggestions of meeting up.

But of course, now there was Lila. He hadn't seen her since the weekend, but his lips still felt bruised. That was hardly surprising; he'd kissed her for so long, so desperate for it to feel like how he'd imagined it would. Alex exhaled petulantly at the memory. He knew that nothing could ever live up to fantasy, and that the Lila in his arms would never be the same as the Lila he'd put up on that pedestal. But still, after everything, after getting the sense that the stupid fates were finally aligning for him, he guessed he couldn't be blamed for maybe expecting something *more*.

His mobile phone burst into life, its cheery ringtone startling Alex out of his disquieting chain of thought. He reached for it guiltily, assuming it would be Lila, but checked himself when he saw the caller name on the screen display.

"Holly?" he greeted, not bothering to mask the curiosity in his tone; he didn't think Holly had ever actually called him before.

"What's up?"

"Hey, I've only got a minute," she began, without preamble. "I'll be home soon."

"Okay…" Alex said, nonplussed. Good for her?

"So what's your plan for the weekend, then?"

"My plan for the weekend?" Alex repeated stupidly; it was Thursday night, and as far as he knew he hadn't been involved in any plans with the girls over the next few days. He'd been hoping to maybe take Lila out for a picnic on the Common, to feed her fat genetically-modified strawberries and drink wine from plastic cups, try again to make her lips taste like the love he was sure he'd been feeling for almost a year.

"Wait, have you not arranged something with Nads?" Something was up; Holly sounded unreasonably cross.

"No, I hadn't; why, what's the big deal?"

"That little liar, I'm going to be having words with her," Holly ranted, more to herself than anything else.

"Holly! What's going on?" Alex pressed.

"I'm away in Birmingham for a work conference this weekend," she admitted, as if that explained everything.

"Okay." Alex paused. "That's sad and all, but I'm sure Nadia can handle being alone in the flat for a couple of nights. Look, I might be busy Saturday but maybe me and her can do food on Friday or the cinema on Sunday, I'll call her now…"

"It's her birthday," Holly interjected. "And you didn't even know? God, what is she playing at?"

Alex's stomach flipped over unhappily. Shit, Nadia's birthday. He'd never actually known when it was; she'd never referenced it, it wasn't on her Facebook. Why hadn't she told him? He would have thrown her a party, taken her anywhere she wanted to go. Was this why she was avoiding his calls? He hadn't seen her for a whole week, not since last Thursday's Candy at Closet; it was the longest they'd spent apart since they'd met.

"Is she at home?" he asked Holly, grimly, already moving into the hall to grab his keys from the console table and shove his feet into his shoes.

"Yes, she's in," Holly confirmed.

"Okay, I'm coming round now. I promise she won't be alone on her birthday, Hols, don't worry."

There was a heavy silence on the other end of the line before Holly spoke again. "It might be her last one here," she said, in a small voice. Alex winced. Out of all of them, Holly went out of her way the most to never mention the potential deportation. "I tried to get out of the work thing, Alex, I really did. But I thought she had made plans with you, so I didn't feel as bad."

"She will have plans with me," Alex promised. And he was almost done formulating those plans as he reached Carrington Avenue, ready to take his suddenly infuriating friend to task.

Nadia

She loved travelling, no matter what the medium was. She knew she looked a bit like a child as she pressed herself up against the train window but couldn't quite bring herself to care; she just continued enjoying the gold and green blur of the fields stretching out from the train tracks speeding past, as huge and expansive as the feeling in her chest: freedom, adventure.

The pair brunched on a combination of homemade sandwiches already warm inside their clingfilm and over-priced crisps and chocolates from the refreshment trolley. Nadia taught Alex all of the card games that growing up at a boarding school had left her crazily good at: hearts and whist and shithead, the last of which she was the undisputed champion of. By the time they were slowing down as they went through Hove, Alex was getting worryingly close to winning a hand, and so as much as Nadia felt she could have stayed on that train forever, she was secretly relieved it was almost time to disembark.

Like most coastal towns, Brighton was hilly and unreasonably steep, with the train station some way out from the centre of things. Even though Alex was carrying her holdall bag for her, Nadia was still slightly out of breath by the time they reached the bed and breakfast. The door was painted a fresh mint green with a heavy brass knocker, shabby chic and utterly charming, with old-fashioned leaded windows framed by white curtains, so old and washed so many times they were as soft and shapeless as down.

The whole weekend break was so last minute that there had been no way that Rory could get the time off work and, likewise, Caro had several seminars that Friday afternoon that she couldn't miss; they'd be joining them in the morning. But for now it was just her and Alex.

He threw himself down on one of the rickety twin beds; its ancient iron frame squealed in protest. "So what do you want to do first?" he asked, grinning at her. "Shops? Aquarium? Beach? Pier? Chips?"

Nadia laughed, sitting down gently on the opposite bed. Hers too rattled rather alarmingly, but the sheets were clean and the mattress soft and she was just so wonderfully happy there in that cheap little room. Tomorrow she'd be moving into a similar one down the corridor with Caro to make room for Rory to bunk in with Alex, but for tonight they'd be sleeping with barely a metre between them. She wondered what Lila thought about it, and knew she'd never bring herself to ask.

"You tell me, you were local here for three years," she pointed out.

Alex turned on his side to face her, propping himself up slightly on one elbow. "Exactly. And those are your options. Shops. Aquarium. Beach. Pier. Chips. And chips usually do come last," he advised in a matter-of-fact tone. "Because you'll probably only vomit them up if you eat them before going on the rides at the end of the pier."

Nadia screwed up her face at the thought. "Good to know!"

Alex gave her a lazy salute, touching one finger to his brow bone. "Local knowledge."

"Come on then." Nadia sat up and slipped her feet back into the flip-flops she'd only just kicked off.

"Where to?" Alex sat up too, twisting and stretching his arms behind him and up to the ceiling, making the shape of his torso strain against the fabric of his t-shirt and a pale corridor of skin appear between its hem and his jeans. Nadia barely swallowed the sigh that rose up inside her. This really would have been the most perfect romantic weekend. Too bad she was the only one of them with romance on the brain.

"You brought me to the seaside," she shrugged, grabbing her little across-the-body-bag from where she'd thrown it down on the bed. "Let's go see the sea."

Alex

Nadia appeared to realise her rookie mistake very early on. They headed down the first set of stairs to the beach that they came across; the rough, grey concrete steps reminded him of the ones by the Thames. Almost immediately Nadia was slipping jerkily as she attempted to walk across the smooth dark stones in her loose shoes. He grabbed her by the elbow to steady her as she went over on her ankle. She looked up at him, laughing a little helplessly, the sheet of blonde hair that he really should have warned her to tie back whipping across her face in the wind.

"When I was a student, I saw girls doing this in five-inch heels and blind drunk," he teased her. "Step up your game!" Nadia stuck her tongue out at him and – using his body for balance – moved to take off her flip-flops altogether. "No. Try and keep them on," Alex urged her. "There's shitloads of broken glass on this beach."

Nadia rolled her eyes dramatically as she bent to slip her shoe back on. "And you couldn't have taken me to Bali for the weekend, why?" she asked him, straight-faced.

Alex felt the dregs of his misgivings, that he'd somehow done something to upset Nadia, wash away under the tide of her gentle teasing. She must be scared out of her mind. No matter the outcome of the appeal hearing, how her life was going to play out was going to be decided one day soon, decided by a stranger in some whitewashed conference room.

She'd flat-out refused to come at first. On Thursday night she'd glared down both Holly and Alex, trying to play down the importance of her birthday, insisting she'd just wanted a quiet weekend in. What was the big deal? It was only after Alex had shown her that he'd already used an app on his phone to book their train tickets on his walk to her flat that she'd started to relent and he saw the excitement suddenly take root in her smile. She'd mentioned she'd never been to Brighton, and as an alumnus of the local university, who better to take her there than Alex?

They didn't end up going shopping, see the Pavilion or visit the Aquarium in the end. They just walked the beach for hours, Nadia eventually getting the hang of how to place her feet on the rocks, eating fat chips, sharp and soggy with extra vinegar, the way they both liked them. Alex dragged out all of his best stories from his university years. He told her about one particular prankster he'd lived with as a fresher, whose idea of the height of comedy was to clingfilm across the toilet bowls. He explained how he'd studied for his final year exams on this very beach, sitting with his mates, hunched around one of those disposable barbecue foil trays – completely illegal and ridiculously ineffective, but seeming a good idea at the time. They'd fed the dying coals little strips of paper from the margins of their revision notes for hours before giving up and tossing the still-raw sausages in the bin.

He showed her how bloody amazing he was at skipping stones across the water, taught her which stones to use – the flatter and smoother the better, not too heavy, but with enough heft to travel a fair distance. He told her about how on his first date with Alice he'd taken her to walk along the pier, thinking that the retro romance of it outweighed the cheesiness. Alice had told him that there was a legend that couples who kissed at the end of the pier would be together always, and he'd grinned and claimed her mouth with

185

his, pressing her up against the barriers that were all there was between them and the grey ocean beyond, unpremeditated and assured, the way he'd done everything in those days.

And when it was finally dark enough that the pier lit up in all its gaudy, flashing glory they automatically picked their way back along the windy beach and made their way there. They changed a five-pound note into 10ps, piled it all into the games machines in the arcade and somehow came out in credit. Nadia contorted herself and got completely in the way of tourists as she took photos of the lights, the rides overhead, the darkening swell of the sea in the background, asking his opinion on which Instagram filter looked the best, mocking him as an artistic Philistine when he admitted he couldn't see the difference between them.

They changed their pocketfuls of arcade winnings into ride tokens, and rode the worst of them until they genuinely felt as if they might be sick. Alex was pleased to discover that Nadia's favourite ride was his own: the Waltzer right at the back of the pier, and so they spent their remaining tokens just on that one, laughing stupidly every time the momentum made their bodies crash together, their heads whip back to the thin padding of the headrest.

Finally, Nadia pleaded no more and they wandered to the very end of the pier, at the rear of the noisy ride, only a few feet from where Alex's fated first kiss with Alice Rhodes had occurred. Nadia plonked herself down on the ground, straightening her back against the pier-end railings, her hands busily working as she dragged her fingers through the knots the sea-wind was blowing into her hair; she'd been doing it on and off all day, swearing she'd remember to put a brush in her handbag for the rest of the weekend.

Alex leaned with his arms flat against the top of the barrier, looking across the night-time sea, calm and still beneath him, but churning far out in the distance. He hadn't realised how he'd missed it until he'd returned: the smell of the water and fried junk food on his clothes, his hair being slightly tacky from the misting salt water. He'd left to make a life for himself in the capital city, he remembered; but being back here where his adulthood had begun, he couldn't say that he'd managed a good enough job.

"Hey," Nadia said, pulling him out of himself. He smiled down at her. He'd had such an ace day. He knew it more and more the more time they spent together; he flat-out adored this girl. He could make a sort of peace with the shitty years he'd spent merely existing after graduation – it was because of them that he'd met Nadia. She'd been the unexpected sunshine into the otherwise rainy bank holiday that had become his life.

"I've always wanted to ask you," Nadia continued, her face slightly pinking with unexplained shyness. "Your arm."

"My arm?" Alex repeated, nonplussed.

"Yeah." Nadia gestured at her own shoulder and he realised immediately what she meant.

"Oh." He felt stupid. "This?" He rolled up the sleeve of his t-shirt a little way to reveal the offending dark line on the curve where his shoulder became his arm.

"Yes." Nadia got to her feet and came for a closer inspection. Alex jumped slightly as her fingertips grazed his skin, tracing ever-so-lightly along the mark. "What is it, a tattoo?"

"It was meant to be." Alex wanted to roll down his top and cover the stupid thing up, but he couldn't with Nadia's hand there. "I basically chickened out at the very last minute – literally."

She smothered a laugh. "Sorry," she said, contrite.

Alex laughed too. "No, it's okay. It's just rather embarrassing. It was a knee-jerk reaction after uni, after Alice…"

Nadia nodded slowly; her fingertips were still there, feeling cool against his flushed skin. "What was it meant to be?"

"Words. I mean, a quote. From my favourite film." He shrugged. "It seemed like a good idea at the time."

"Tattoos usually do," Nadia teased. "What was the quote?"

Alex hesitated. He would have never told her in London, he

would have made something up. But out here it almost didn't seem as stupid as it had done. "Make your life extraordinary."

He waited for her to laugh again, but she didn't. She looked again at the little mark that was meant to have become an M and nodded slowly. "That's a good quote." She looked up and met his eyes. "*Dead Poet's Society*, right?"

Alex broke into a grin. "Right."

Nadia bit her lip lightly. "Alex," she said again, as though she had another question for him.

"Mmm?"

And then as if it was the most natural thing in the world, she lifted her face to his and suddenly Nadia was kissing him.

Chapter 19

Nadia

Caro's eyes were as wide as her mouth.

"No! You didn't?" she squeaked. The occupants of the three nearest tables all turned around to eyeball them shamelessly. Nadia felt her face flush even darker; maybe she had been talking a little loudly there by the end…

"I'm guessing that the rest of this story isn't so great," Caro said, tilting her head sympathetically as she stirred the remainder of her half-forgotten latte. "Or I wouldn't be sitting here hearing it."

Nadia and Alex had met Rory and Caro off the train in from London with slightly manic smiles stretched over their faces. Grabbing her friend by the arm before she'd even properly got through the ticket barriers, Nadia had babbled about her urgent need for coffee – despite the sweltering mid-morning temperature and the fact that she had had two cups at breakfast – bundling Caro into the nearest Starbucks and telling Alex and Rory that they'd see them back at the B&B a little later on. And then, with lattes they didn't really want cooling on the table top between them, Nadia had filled Caro in on last night's epic lapse of control.

"So, was it super-awkward? Did he pull away?" Caro pressed, voice sympathetic.

Did he pull away? Nadia had lain awake all night preoccupied with that very question. Had he pulled away first? Had she? Maybe they'd both realised at the same time and moved apart together. She just didn't know; it had been so damn quick – a sheet lightning of a kiss – nothing but lips and a handful of seconds.

Alex

Rory literally crowed with delight.

"You dog!" he said, reaching over the expanse between the twin beds to smack Alex admiringly on the shoulder. "I knew it was just a matter of time." He paused, looking over at the weekend bag he'd half unpacked whilst listening to Alex tell his tale. "Do you want me to get another room?"

Alex raked his hair through his hands, stressed to the max. "No, it's nothing like that. It was just... a friendly kiss."

Rory arched his eyebrow scathingly. "A friendly kiss?"

"Yes."

"A friendly kiss on the lips from a super-hot girl?"

"Something like that," Alex managed through gritted teeth.

Rory laughed. "I need me some friends like that." He shook his head as he continued unpacking.

Alex had only just about registered what was going on by the time Nadia had pulled away, the sea air rushing in cold between them where they'd just been pressed close. He'd just stared at her for a moment, punch-drunk and suddenly noticing things like how the freckles across her face were almost bleached out in the artificial lights of the pier, and the way those lips he'd just been kissing were slightly parted still, as though she was finding it hard to breathe.

And then, finally, she'd laughed: a sound so goddamn normal that it broke the spell.

"There you go," she'd smiled, pressing her index finger to his chest, right between his ribs. "Now we'll be friends forever."

"What?" Alex still feeling sideswiped by what had just happened, wasn't thinking quickly enough.

"You said it yourself. People who kiss at the end of the pier stay together forever," Nadia had shrugged, turning her face to the sea, fidgeting with her hair again, completely normal, as if she hadn't just dropped a grenade into his chest cavity and walked away.

Nadia

He'd been looking at her as if she'd just gone insane, and maybe she had. She couldn't even blame being drunk – an always useful go-to excuse – as they hadn't had a drop of alcohol. It had just been so damn romantic, what with the lights and the sound of the sea and Alex being all mellow and open to her in a way she'd never felt him before. She'd kissed him on instinct, for one crucial second not thinking of the consequences, unanchored from any future.

But he hadn't taken her in his arms, hadn't sought out her tongue with his, hadn't pressed his long, lean body against hers like she was dying for him to. Maybe it had been her who'd pulled away first after all, unable to take his physical rejection. Even now, twelve hours separating her from the moment, Nadia's heart ached at the thought. It had ached all night and kept her lying awake, knowing from his uneven breathing across the tiny room that Alex was doing the same, and that for one careless instant she may have ruined the best thing she had.

"I think I got away with it," she told Caro, trying to force herself to be optimistic. "I played it off as a friendly thing."

Caro looked doubtful. "A friendly thing?" she echoed. "This was a proper kiss, yeah?"

Nadia waved it off, as though it wasn't actually the huge deal it was. "No tongue. Barely five seconds, I reckon. It was nothing."

Caro arched an eyebrow. "Nothing," she echoed. "Five seconds?" She paused. "Sweetie, it sounds like you didn't really give him much of a chance to, you know, *react* all that much, did you?"

"Well…"

"And did you say he's sort of going out with that Lila girl now?" Caro insisted. "I don't think Alex is the sort of guy to really kiss

191

one woman whilst he's involved with another."

"Yes, but…"

"It's like when you were worried because you were seeing Matt but you had feelings for Alex," Caro continued to argue. "It might be the same sort of thing."

"Caro!" The rise in volume of Nadia's voice caused the adjacent tables to turn around again. Caro fell silent. "It was a huge mistake, okay? I'm a bad, bad person. He's been in love with Lila for months and months and he finally gets somewhere with her and then I come along and try and throw a spanner in the works. Some friend I am." She pushed her hair back from her face impatiently, pressing the heels of her palms into her temples as she did so. She felt vaguely panicked, as though everything was starting to spiral out of control.

Caro just looked at her pityingly. "I don't think that the fact you kissed him is the huge mistake at play here," she muttered, stirring her unwanted coffee distractedly once again. "And for what it's worth, I'm pretty sure it was probably you who pulled away first…"

Alex

After dropping Nadia a text to tell her they'd gone down to the sea, Alex and Rory headed out, stopping at the off-licence en route. They sat with their backs to the damp sea wall, where nobody could see that they were illegally drinking on the beach and sat in a thoughtful, companionable silence with each other and their beers.

Alex wasn't sure what Rory had going on to be so thoughtful about, but to be honest he didn't really have the head space to spare on his mate that afternoon. His mind was still firmly tethered to last night, and to the pier, which loomed dowdy and innocuous off to their left, shabby in the sunlight. In his head he stretched out that brief brush of lips to last for years, searching for the meaning in it, for what had triggered it, and what had stopped it.

He was pathetic. One casual, friendly peck on the lips and he was in sudden freefall, raking back over months of simple

192

friendship looking for something more. All night he'd replayed the moment over and over, and in all his variations he kissed Nadia back, pulling her closer, closer still, burying his fingers in the pale mass of her hair. And all that imagining had started up an ache in his jaw, in his chest and a hunger so persistent that it was only sheer, shameful cowardice that had stopped him from crossing the yawning space between their twin beds.

And he knew, with a sick sort of certainty, that this was what he'd expected from Lila's kisses.

We'll be friends forever, Nadia had laughed, dancing away from him as the bomb went off and the ache started up and friendship was forced completely out of Alex's mind.

"It's not a good idea, you know," Rory said gently, as if he'd been quietly following Alex's chain of silent thought to its end.

Alex didn't bother to pretend he didn't know what Rory was on about. "Why not?"

"Why not?" Rory echoed. "It would be quicker to give you the reasons for it, to be honest." When Alex didn't make a move either to argue or to agree, Rory sighed. "Well, just to start with… Look, I like the girl – you know I do – but she's a complete flaky mess right now. And you know it. She's about to be deported." At this Alex opened his mouth to protest, but Rory barrelled onwards. "You know it's the truth," he insisted. "And she's all over the damn place about it. She's with Matt, then she's not, then she's kissing you, then she's bullshitting about how you guys are BFFs forever? She's hot and cold and she doesn't know what she wants and she's in a panic and she's all over-emotional and stuff, yeah?"

Alex rolled his eyes. "Could you be any more patronising? In a minute you'll suppose it was her time of the month."

Rory shrugged. "The truth hurts. Essentially, that girl is one giant hot mess right now and you need to steer clear. Worst-case scenario, you sleep together and it gets mega awkward and you lose your friendship. *Best case* scenario, you guys fall madly in love and she gets banished from the damn country. Not exactly win-win here."

"Rory, she's my friend! I can't just randomly kick her out of my life!"

"Why not? It was pretty 'random' the way she entered it in the first place, wasn't it?"

Alex thought about that afternoon all those months ago, when he'd held the application form of Nadezhda Osipova in his hands and hadn't really cared – not about the faceless Russian girl, not about his job, not really about anything. He'd never told Rory about it – and knew he could now never tell Nadia – and so that fateful little moment would probably always remain a cold little secret in his core.

"And also, of course, there's Lila." Rory swiped at Alex's shin with the hand that wasn't holding his can of beer. "What's the deal with that? I put all my personal shit aside and practically delivered her gift-wrapped for you because I *thought* you were madly in love with her."

"I am," Alex protested. "I mean, I genuinely thought I was, at least."

"Those are two different answers," Rory pointed out with a knowing quirk of his eyebrow.

Alex buried his head in his hands. "I know," was his muffled answer.

"If you want my advice," Rory continued.

"Do I have a choice?"

"Only bad things will come from you forcing this kiss thing with Nadia. You'll ruin your friendship, and you'll ruin things with Lila. And I really think you guys could have a shot of being good together, you and Lila. She's a really great girlfriend."

Alex raised his head to shoot his friend a look. "This coming from the guy who unceremoniously dumped her."

Rory shrugged, unconcerned. "She wasn't right for me. She's much better suited to you. She was a bit too… high maintenance for me, I think. But that would be okay with you. You wouldn't mind, you know, putting in the hours."

Alex stared at Rory as he described his relationship with his ex like some sort of job, or duty. And there was a little worming of guilt as he realised that he sort of knew where Rory was coming from. With Lila there was always the inescapable sense of obligation: to flatter and entertain, to be bright and funny and fill all the silences. It was the polar opposite of how yesterday had been, on that bright, smooth beach with Nadia, of how all their days together had been. Nadia brought out the chatty, witty colour that had always been the bedrock of his personality, so it wasn't very often that they sat in silence – but when they did it was as natural as the talking.

No wonder the sense that something was missing with Lila had left him muddled and wanting. His heart had been looking for the same kind of comfort it had found with Nadia.

And Alex's stomach crunched in on itself as he realised with dismay just how much he could come to regret not kissing his friend back.

Chapter 20

Alex

Alex watched from his place in the bar queue as his friends dominated the dance floor of Lola Lo, acting like the teenagers they hadn't been for years. Nadia, holding aloft what was left of her tropical cocktail, was wearing her hair loose and it span round her like a cape as she danced. She was fresh and casual in a strapless lilac tunic paired with her usual denim shorts, a complete contrast to the prowling Caro, who was certainly getting her fair share of attention in her leopard-print mini- dress. Rory held guard, scowling down any opportunist men who looked as though they might be thinking of coming over.

"Now, don't think you're going to get drunk and shag Nadia tonight," had been Rory's doleful warning as the two boys were getting ready to go out. "Because I'm not letting you guys have this room. In protest I will remain, even after things get squelchy, even after –" Alex hadn't heard the full extent of how far Rory was willing to go, as he'd thrown a pillow at him to make him shut up.

Potential shagging aside, Alex wasn't entirely sure how he'd managed to get through the evening thus far. He just wanted to grab Nadia and shout at her, or shake her, or kiss her, or something; anything that would quiet the appetite his lips suddenly had for hers, or sate the quaking cowardice that was holding him hostage.

He risked another painful glance over at the still-dancing Nadia, pale under the strobe lights, tilting her body back in his direction like a challenge, her neck taut and long and immediately bringing to mind all of the places other than lips a person could be kissed…

An impatient woman with a mildly terrifying afro pushed past Alex with a huff; he'd missed his cue with the bartender. Bodies surged to fill the space behind him that the woman had vacated, pressing in close, trying to get in front of someone they clearly thought was a vague idiot – pushing, pushing.

And Alex felt the warm snap that was his patience coming to an end. He drew himself up to his full height and brought his arm down like a crashing tree between the woman with the afro and the man next to her, using his forearm to physically claim his little piece of the sticky bar, using the rest of his body to block the pressing mass of bodies behind him. He'd been queuing for over ten minutes already, for crying out loud, and he *wasn't having it*. For once he wasn't going to be the guy who was pushed around.

Rather anticlimactically, Afro Woman barely seemed to register Alex or appreciate that he was having some sort of epiphany. She just scooted up slightly to allow for the presence of his arm and continued half-shouting, half-mouthing her order at the bartender over the thump of the music. And Alex decided that those last ten minutes were wasted, as he actually didn't want the drinks any more.

The mass of bodies on the dance floor even seemed to part for him as he made his way back across to his friends. Nadia had since finished the dregs of her cocktail and got rid of the glass somewhere – he hoped she wasn't too thirsty; she looked at him quizzically as if to ask where the promised round of drinks was. He didn't answer her silent question. He just took her elbow and lightly moved her arm out of the way so that he could get his around her waist. He didn't know the song that was playing, but it was about friendship and being strong and being there when it counted, and he took it as a sign.

Nadia didn't even look startled as he pressed her body closer to his, using his free hand at the base of her spine. She just closed her eyes and let him spin her away and in again in time with the music, her cheek colliding softly with his collarbone, her hand sliding up to rest there. And Alex remembered the way they'd danced together on the night they met – on that tiny, sticky dance floor in Bison & Bird – like this, but not. And he thought about that initial little bit of daring – the first he'd had in so long – that had pushed him to follow her into the night; and the second, where they'd sat together on the swings and he'd decided he'd quite like to know this girl – even if it meant eating questionable meat. What was one more little nudge of courage?

Nadia had opened her eyes again and was looking up at him expectantly, still pressed close, dancing with him on instinct, even through the track change. The flashing lights shot colour across her face. Alex moved his hand up and along her neck, feeling where her skin was flushed and heated, and slipped it around the back of her head, moving his thumb from the corner of her mouth to her earlobe in one stroke. Nadia closed her eyes again, and Alex took it as the invitation it undoubtedly was. He could smell the pineapple and citrus on her from the cocktail she'd just finished as he moved the inch that was all there was between them.

He always moved his mobile phone from his back trouser pocket to the front one when he was in places like this, believing it would be harder to pickpocket from there. And so the text, when it came, vibrated as much against Nadia's hip as it did his thigh. Nadia's eyes snapped open and met his, and he saw immediately that she assumed – as he did – that it was a message from Lila. He saw the bobbing at her throat as she swallowed, once, and slipped away from his hold unfathomably fast, stepping away towards Caro – had the other two really been so close that entire time? – picking up dancing with her where she'd left off, as if the last two minutes had never happened.

Nadia

Caro was so desperate to get to the ladies to digest what had just happened – or at least what had very nearly happened – but Nadia felt cemented in place. Even when Caro walked off the dance floor towards the toilets, Nadia didn't follow, couldn't follow. Alex was standing off to one side, offensively still amongst the whirling dancers around him, replying to his text message. The uplight from the phone's screen showing that his face was flushed and the twist of his mouth a guilty one; that mouth that had so almost been upon hers...

Alex looked up as he finished with his phone and slid it back into his pocket. Nadia wasn't quick enough in looking away to avoid the eye contact. And for a moment he looked for all the world as if he was about to move to take her up in his arms again and Nadia felt that by-now habitual weakness for him urging her to let him.

A box of brightness flared through the fabric of his jeans as his phone screen lit up with Lila's reply; Nadia grit down against her instincts and turned away.

And then later, back at the B&B, when Alex, wearing a hopeful expression, had asked if she fancied a midnight walk along the seafront, Nadia just said she was too tired and went to bed.

Alex

He had to hand it to Rory and Caro; they had taken it upon themselves to make sure that there were no awkward silences on the journey home and were performing their task admirably. They never shut up. Somewhere around the rolling countryside of Haywards Heath Rory even tried to strike up a game of I-Spy.

True to type, Caro had an Uber taxi ready and waiting for them in the bays outside Victoria Station. Alex went for the gentlemanly approach and sat on one of the flipseats that faced backwards, his knees knocking against Nadia's as he sat, and for the fiftieth time that day they avoided each other's gaze. Rory ignored the other flipseat, choosing instead to wedge himself in between Caro and Nadia.

Alex watched Rory and Caro effortlessly flirting with one another – watched Nadia watch them too – and envied how simple it could be for them. They could flirt, mess around, part ways; nobody was going to get hurt or left behind. He wondered – not for the first time – if he should have just snogged Nadia that very first evening they'd met. There'd have been no Matt, no complicating friendship, no wasted time.

Nadia's shins brushed against his knees again as she swapped over her crossed legs, her face still turned studiously out of the window, and Alex hated himself a little bit.

Caro's posher neighbourhood was closer, so her flat was the first drop-off. Her neighbourhood was almost off of a postcard, with grand three-story Edwardian houses and wide, tree-lined pavements, each house in the terrace with a little sweep of steps up from the street to the uniform black front door. The only thing that was not identical was the slump of a figure and the square of a suitcase outside Caro's…

At first Alex thought it might be a homeless person, but as the taxi neared and slowed the neatness of the person's clothes put paid to that theory. Then suddenly Nadia, the only other person in the taxi who'd been looking out the window, gave a sharp gasp.

"Caro." She turned to her friend and cocked her head urgently towards the house.

Caro was so entrenched in her conversation with Rory that she took a moment to realise that her attention was being diverted. She leant forward in her seat to get the right angle to see out of the right-hand window. Her face quivered with at least five undefinable expressions as she noticed the man waiting at her door and froze.

Nadia

"What's up?" Rory asked immediately, craning his neck to see out of Nadia's window as the driver finished his parallel park and Nadia heard the click of the door locks being disengaged. Caro remained rooted to her seat, staring at Monty, who apparently hadn't yet noticed the huge black Uber car idling nearby and just remained staring dolefully into the middle distance.

She met Alex's eyes for probably the first time since their near-kiss in Lola Lo. He knew something was up, but didn't know what he should be doing about it. Nadia had never told him about Caro's affair, deciding it wasn't her story to tell. She shot him her best "don't worry" look and turned back to Caro.

"Do you want me to come in with you?" she asked her friend. "I can stay."

"He's got a suitcase," was all that Caro said in reply, still staring across at her lover.

Rory tried again. "What's going on?" he asked, looking from one person to the other questioningly, even at the driver, who had turned around in his seat wondering why nobody was exiting his car. Caro pulled her tote bag with her weekend stuff up onto her lap and reached blindly for the door handle.

"Caro," Nadia repeated, full of foreboding she didn't quite understand.

"I'll call you later," was all that Caro said as she exited the taxi with no further leave. Monty had finally noticed her, standing up to his full height as she ascended the steps towards him. And the last thing that Nadia saw as the taxi pulled away around the corner was Monty flinging his arms around Caro as if it was him and not her who was the one arriving home.

"Who was that?" Rory was still craning his neck to look behind them, even though the car was well on to the next road by now. And then he said something that surprised everyone. "Was that that Monty guy?"

Nadia eyeballed him. "She told you about Monty?"

"Yeah, on the train down on Friday," he scowled. "So that was him? He looked even more of a complete tool than I imagined."

"Wait, why am I the only person in the dark here?" moaned

Alex. "What is going on?"

Nadia turned to him impatiently. "Caro's boyfriend. Her tutor. Married. With a kid."

"Complete tool," Rory helpfully summarised again.

"Okay. Gotcha. And so, what, he's left the wife and kid?" Alex asked, doubtfully.

"He'd never leave his wife," Nadia answered, shaking her head emphatically. "Never."

"Well I think the huge suitcase says otherwise," Alex pointed out.

Nadia pulled her phone from her handbag as if Caro was likely to be calling her any moment. "I hope she's okay. Just when I thought she was starting to get over him. He goes completely AWOL for a couple of weeks and then pulls a stunt like this?" She shook her head again and lapsed into an agitated silence. She kept a worried eye on her dark and silent phone for the remainder of the short journey through the South London backstreets to Clapham Old Town. The windows of her flat were closed up tight, the blinds fully down – Holly couldn't be home yet.

Nadia slipped out of the car, sliding her weekend bag along behind her and thanked the driver politely. Then she said goodbye to Rory before finally turning to Alex, the embarrassment lingering and palpable as gum stuck in her throat. He too had got out of the car and was motioning for her to pass over her bag, as though he was going to carry it upstairs for her.

"Oh, I'm fine," she insisted immediately, flustered, pulling the bag up and onto her shoulder for good measure. "Thank you for this weekend," she smiled. And then, all too aware of Rory and the impatient Uber man rubbernecking at her, Nadia lightly went up to her tiptoes and kissed Alex on the cheek. He hadn't shaved at all whilst they'd been in Brighton and his stubble prickled at her lips like a warning.

"It was my pleasure," he replied, a little hoarsely, as she pulled away. "I… hope you had a happy birthday?" Nadia just nodded, not trusting herself to say more. "See you later?" Nadia just nodded again, and made her escape into the silent, stifling flat.

She'd already been home for a couple of minutes and was going to and fro opening all the windows to get some air circulating before she even noticed it. She must have stepped clear over it when she came home: that perfectly sharp-edged white envelope lying on the mat.

Chapter 21

Alex

Did you have fun in Brighton?? Lila's text read, its tone impossible to gauge (there was, for once, no helpful smiley face for context).

Although, considering he'd not actually told her in advance he was going to Brighton – the place where they'd originally met and been students together – and presumably she'd found out through Facebook, maybe not that impossible...

Alex considered the message for a minute or two, knowing that Lila was clearly expecting a speedy and appropriately ingratiating reply. And then he stopped himself. A year now spent doing this: drafting out perfect emails, perfect text messages, three-quarters of which Lila would usually never reply to.

He'd used to think it was enough. He'd never realised he was so wrong, how the truth of love was a person who could simultaneously be enough whilst still making you need more and more of them, for always. And whereas he used to study the planes and angles of Lila's face, looking for meaning in her flippancy, straining to hear all the things she wasn't saying, now it was just Nadia, and it was easy.

Except, nothing was ever that easy, was it? What they'd all been dreading, Alex maybe most of all: her hearing date had come in the post. And they were out of time; *he* was out of time...

So he wouldn't reply to Lila's text message. He'd call her and arrange to meet up. There was too much to say, too much that was too important to get right. Because if there was one thing that Lila deserved after a year battling for Rory's attention, it was a guy who could give her his whole heart – and Alex knew that guy would never be him.

Nadia

Nadia leant out of the way as Caro hefted a steaming serving bowl of homemade paella over her head and onto the dining table. She inhaled appreciatively: Caro was a woman of many talents. Even though the cause for this impromptu little dinner party was achingly transparent, Nadia wouldn't complain if it meant she got to partake of a four-course meal and all-you-can-drink wine.

"Hey," Caro tossed her hair over her shoulder as she straightened and called back into the kitchen area. "Can somebody please open that 2004 Pinot?" She smiled at Nadia. "The man in the wine place said it would be perfect to go with a seafood paella."

Nadia grinned and moved the empty glass that had held her arrival Prosecco nearer. "Sounds good to me." If Caro thought that this is what it would take to keep her friend's spirits up, Nadia definitely wasn't going to dissuade her.

"Caro," Holly said suddenly, nodding to send Nadia and Caro's attention over to the kitchen, where a weary-looking Monty and an abused-looking Rory were going through every single drawer and cupboard in search of the corkscrew.

"In the small drawer under the microwave, sweetie," Caro called over to Monty. "The corkscrew is a very important tool in this house; it's important that you know where it is, now you live here and all!" Monty smiled amiably at her as he struggled with the cork; Rory stalked back over to the dining table and threw himself back down in his chair next to Alex, who shot him a look emblazoned "behave yourself".

Yes, Alex was on his best behaviour tonight, and that apparently had to extend to his grumpy flatmate as well. In fact, Alex had been on his best behaviour ever since Nadia had called him up and told him she'd had her court appeal date through in the post. She'd practically heard it in the sudden silence down the other end of the phone: the moment where he'd switched gears and became this careful, polite, quasi-stranger; it was almost as if he'd said goodbye to her already.

"Nadia?" Monty drew Nadia out of her introspection. He was standing behind her chair, proffering the bottle of seafood-friendly Pinot questioningly. Nadia smiled the affirmative and pushed her glass nearer for him to fill, which he did, before moving on to Holly. Nadia watched him as he made his way gentlemanly around the table, making sure everyone had exactly the same measure of wine. She should feel happy about his presence – Caro certainly was; Monty had been the exception to the rule and had left his wife for his mistress. They were going to have to keep it a bit quiet for the next few months, just until Caro's dissertation was fully submitted, but still, it was an about-turn that Nadia could have never dreamed of for her friend.

Monty continued the gracious host act, remaining standing until everyone had been served from the central bowls of paella and salad before slipping into his seat at the head of the table, Caro to his left, Rory to his right and facing Holly and Ledge, who each had a corner of the far end. Caro's six-seater dining table was *not* coping well with the influx of a live-in boyfriend. Neither were its occupants; the conversation was slightly stilted, nobody too sure what to make of the fact that the man they'd been demonising for months was suddenly the guy topping up their glasses. Caro tried valiantly to keep the chat flowing, eventually turning to reliably opinionated Rory and his favourite topic: current affairs.

"Sweetie," Monty interrupted eventually, having listened to Caro wax on about politics for five full minutes. "Come on, now. You just don't understand what you're saying."

Everyone's eyes swivelled to the top of the table; Alex actually dropped his fork.

"Of course I know what I'm talking about. I read their manifesto and everything," Caro tried, after a moment's embarrassed silence.

Monty just smiled patronisingly at her and continued eating. "You're just regurgitating things that were said on last week's *Question Time*, though, aren't you?" he challenged once he'd swallowed his food. "The thing is, when you're a grown up with grownup obligations you'll realise pretty quickly that the world isn't as black and white as all that."

"When she's a *grown up*?" Rory repeated, incredulously, looking between Caro and Monty as if he was watching a tennis match. "What are you mate – all of five years older than her?"

"Seven," Caro corrected quietly.

"Seven, then." Rory rolled his eyes. "Whatever."

"I'm just saying," Monty insisted, leaning back in his chair to take everyone in. "When you have a mortgage and nursery fees and real financial pressures and actual responsibilities, you won't have much time for any of this bullshit, pie-in-the-sky political ideology, let me tell you that for nothing."

The room remained silent, not really knowing how to react to Monty's breathtakingly offensive stance that their lives were somehow less important than his just because they were a handful of years younger. Nobody said anything at all. Nadia bit down on the urge to howl at him, not wanting to ruin the already awkward evening completely. Across the table she saw Alex's fist tighten against the tablecloth and knew he was struggling too.

Alex

Alex could feel Rory actually bristling beside him, the atmosphere in the room darkening a shade further. Across the table Nadia was clearly fuming too; Alex could see the flash of white between her lips that was her gritting her teeth. Someone should say something! He should say something…

"And this is why politics isn't polite dinner chat," Holly chimed, faux-cheerful as she tried to get the conversation back on an even keel. "Shall we open another bottle of wine, Caro?"

"Er, yeah, okay." Caro got quickly to her feet, the serviette she'd had draped over her lap slipping to the floor unnoticed. "I'll get some." She moved across to the kitchen side lightly enough, but Alex noticed how her usually confident hands shook and fumbled as she worked the corkscrew. He saw that Nadia had noticed it too, could read the indecision on his friend's face like a book; did Caro want comforting, or would she hate it if her friend drew attention to her embarrassment in front of her tactless lover?

"Here, Caro, give it here." Caro shot Alex a nervous look over her shoulder as he made his way over to her. "I think your hands are a bit greasy," Alex added, a nonsensical but perfectly apt excuse. Caro's anxious expression slipped into a subtly grateful one as she handed over the wine bottle and the corkscrew.

"Yeah. Thanks. I'd better wash them," she agreed, moving to the kitchen sink and rinsing her already clean palms under the tap. Alex popped the cork with a practised twist and tug and turned back to the table.

Monty got to his feet. "I'll do that, mate."

"Nah, you're alright." Alex didn't even look at him as he rested one hand on the back of Nadia's chair and used the other to fill up her empty wine glass. She tilted her head back and gave him a tiny smile that made him have to really concentrate on the pouring. Man, it was hard to avoid all the elephants in this room. Monty remained standing, awkward and lanky, thumbing the swell of his glass. Caro diligently avoided looking at anyone as she dried her hands on a tea towel. Rory sat swung right back in his chair, glaring at Monty as if he was the antichrist. Holly studied the congealing remains of her paella and Ledge merely looked confused. Alex plonked the bottle down in front of them so that they could serve themselves.

Monty began stacking up the dinner plates, scraping the leftovers messily between them as he did so. "Dessert, anyone?" he asked.

Alex looked at Nadia's tight face, Caro's still-fidgeting hands. "I think I've had enough," he answered, in a cool voice that left no illusions over what – or who – he'd had enough of.

Nadia

There simply wasn't going to be enough time between Caro's front door and the bus stop to adequately express how she was feeling, so Nadia decided to just stay silent. Rory didn't seem to have the same concerns and had started mouthing off the moment they hit the pavement.

"Cock!" he practically spat. "Complete cock."

"Rory," Holly frowned. "He's not that bad. I mean, he's always going to have this stigma because we all know he cheated on his wife…"

"And jerked Caro around for a year," Ledge added, arching his eyebrows.

"But he's sort of doing the right thing now," Holly insisted.

"What? Leaving his wife and infant child?" Rory asked incredulously.

"Lots of people get divorced. It doesn't make them monsters!" Holly tried.

"It's not him having had an affair that I take issue with," Rory argued back immediately. "It's the fact that he's an arsehole. He should be crawling around on his hands and knees and kissing Caro's feet and thanking the fucking stars above, not ragging her out in front of her friends."

"Caro can handle herself, Rory."

Rory just looked at Holly, shaking his head slightly. "Were you in the same room as me or not? Because *that* Caro was definitely not handling herself. And I don't like it."

And Nadia knew exactly what he meant. Not once in the seven years she'd known her had she ever seen Caro's jaw tremble like that, her fingers so nervy on the stem of her wine glass. Nadia didn't think that there'd be very many more dinner parties at Chez

Caro for the foreseeable future.

"He sure has got his hooks into her," Alex said suddenly, conversationally, as if he'd been listening to her thoughts and waiting for a pause in which to speak. Nadia noticed with a start that the two of them had fallen into step, into a pair, striding off ahead of the loiterers just as they usually did. The conversation they weren't having – the one they'd probably never have, now – marched along in the space between them like a third person.

"Do you think we should say something?" Alex continued.

"No. I know her. She won't hear it. It will just make her angry," Nadia replied sadly. "I think we just have to be here for her, and hope it, you know, runs its course. Like any nasty virus."

"Be here for her," Alex echoed. He looked down at their feet moving against the pavement, not at her face.

"Yup. I'll just have to tell the Home Office that I simply can't leave. My friend needs me." Nadia managed a weak smile. Alex finally looked up.

"She's not the only one who needs you here, you know," he said, quietly. Nadia's breathing hitched up in her lungs and she watched as Alex tugged at his lower lip with the edge of his teeth. He was nervous, gearing up to say something; maybe they'd be having that conversation after all? He didn't care that she could be deported in two weeks' time; that she could very well be the epitome of a lost cause; he didn't care about perfect Lila Palmer. He felt the same way as she did. He knew that a fortnight together was better than a never.

"Nads, I can't come to your hearing," Alex said eventually, looking away as he did. "I can't be a character witness for you."

That ricocheted off so many layers that Nadia had to take a few moments to fully absorb it.

"Can you... not get the time off work?" she asked; it was the only reasoning that seemed to make sense to her. The hearing was set for a Thursday afternoon.

Alex hesitated again and Nadia braced herself.

"No, it's not that. Or, well… It kind of is to do with work."

Realisation dawned. "Oh. It is because you work for the Home Office?"

"Yeah. But it's not just that. Nadia, I may have… downplayed my job slightly."

Nadia raised an eyebrow. "You're actually the Home Secretary?"

Alex laughed awkwardly, even though her joke hadn't been funny. "Not quite. But I do work in Immigration. And, the thing is… well, you should know that… it's not a big deal but… my name is going to be included on the list of officials who handled your application."

Nadia's faltered, her stride immediately broken. Alex whirled around to grab her hands, keeping her moving next to him, ahead of the others.

"I really am basically just an admin monkey, I haven't lied about that," he insisted earnestly. "It's nothing sinister, I promise. It's just I sorted your application when it arrived in my department. I passed it on."

Nadia just stared at him, stared at their hands clasped together.

"I could have rejected you out of hand, you know," Alex babbled on, perhaps nervous that she wasn't saying anything; she didn't know what to say. "But I liked you. Even then, I liked you, Nads."

Nadia stirred. "This was before we met?"

"Yes, just before. About a week before." Alex rubbed his thumbs nervously across her knuckles, giving her a feeble attempt at a smile. "Isn't it a small world?"

Nadia glanced behind. Ledge, Holly and Rory were only a few feet behind them. Holly clearly knew that something was up. She tried to catch Nadia's eye, but she turned back to Alex, whose face fell slightly as she pointedly extricated her hands from his.

"Why did you never tell me this before?"

Alex rubbed his palm against the back of his head, mussing up his hair. "I don't know. The usual. I didn't want to come off creepy. Did it really ever matter? You knew I worked for the Home

211

Office. I never lied to you, Nadia."

Nadia barked a short, humourless laugh. "No, I suppose you didn't."

"Anyway," Alex continued, awkwardly. "My name and office designation will be included in your appeal notes bundle and I don't even know if you would have noticed, or seen it, but…" He exhaled. "I thought I should actually come clean, just in case."

"How big of you," Nadia snapped. She hated this. Her stomach ached with the hate of it. It was like when she'd found out about him secretly being in love with Lila. Just when she thought she had a handle on Alex Bradley, he shifted away like sand underfoot. "Okay. So you can't be a character reference for me. Okay. Can you not even just come? As my friend? In support?"

Alex was already shaking his head before she'd even finished the sentence. "Nads, I can't. I could lose my job."

"You hate your job."

"Come on, Nadia," Alex tried, but his 'don't be like this' tone only served to infuriate her further. "I will help you all I can, you know I will. I just can't physically be there on the day."

Nadia felt her jaw set, felt the steel there. "Don't worry about it," she clipped out.

Alex groaned, reaching for her hands again and pulling her to a stop in front of him. Their three friends came to an immediate, unsure halt behind them.

"Give us a second, guys?" Alex asked, not looking at them.

"Everything okay?" queried Ledge.

"Everything's fine. Just finding out that Alex can't come to my appeal hearing because he was one of the Home Office Immigration officials who *handled my application*." Nadia watched as Holly's mouth dropped open in shock and Rory's tensed up in a wince. "And now I'm hearing a load of bullshit about why he can't be my character witness. But it's fine." She waved her friends on down the road. "Carry on. We'll only be a minute." This last sentence she shot as a warning at Alex.

After a hideously awkward moment of indecision, the trio carried on down the road, Holly looking back over her shoulder reluctantly. "He's not some sort of crazy stalker, is he?" Nadia heard her ask Rory as they moved away and out of earshot.

Nadia pulled her hands away from Alex's for the second time that night and moved to lean against the nearby front garden's brick wall.

"I can't believe you," she said, after a moment.

"Nadia, I'm really sorry. I was going to mention it, and then I sort of didn't, and then it had been so long that it would have been too weird to suddenly blurt it out…"

"Not that." Nadia shook her head. "Although you must have known all along it would come down to this."

Alex shrugged. "I guess I never expected to…" he trailed off. "Become such good friends with you," he finished, after a minute.

"Well, I'm sorry!" Nadia growled.

"Don't. Don't say you're sorry." Alex was pressed up close to her so quickly, she hadn't even registered his movement; he crowded her against the wall, the bricks damp and cool against her back. "Don't ever say that." He took up her hands and placed them flat against his collarbones, as if he could force her into hugging him. "I'm sorry. I know you hate secrets and you hate liars. I'm sorry."

"I just feel like a prize idiot," Nadia managed, after a moment; she left her hands where he'd placed them. She could feel the heat of his skin through his t-shirt, against her palms.

"Never. Not ever. That'd be me." And if he'd sensed her softening towards him, Alex hugged her. It was a proper hug; his face was buried between her neck and her shoulder and his arms tight around her waist. "But don't give up on me," he murmured against her skin.

Nadia waited for him to pull away, as he usually did, but he didn't. She sighed. "Oh, Alex. I guess I just thought… we were a little closer than that."

At that Alex did pull back, looking at her searchingly. "Nadia.

It's not that. You know, though? You know how I feel. About everything. About you..?"

If he felt the same way that she did, Nadia thought to herself again, he'd know that a fortnight together would be better than a never.

"But I don't," she answered, honestly. She was tired of it, tired of the conversation that was always underneath the conversation they were actually having. "I don't know how you feel, Alex. And now there's just no time."

Alex tightened his grip on her waist. "There will be time. We'll have all the time in the world because you're not going anywhere. I want to help you. Let me help you."

"How are you going to help me when you can't even be in the room for the hearing?" Nadia asked with a sad smile.

"I'll figure something out. Do you know how many ILR applications I read through a day? Feels like a billion," he clarified with a dry laugh, after Nadia mutely shook her head. "And yours is the only, only one I ever remembered after I got home. And then, a couple of days later, you're sitting opposite me in the pub. And then we're on the Tube together, we're breaking into playgrounds together! I really think, Nadia Osipova, that the universe wants us to be together."

Nadia almost felt like she could cry as she heard Alex voicing her own secret thoughts. "But what about Lila?" she managed to force out.

Alex gave her a little smile; unreadable, maddening. "What *about* Lila?"

"Have you… finished with her?"

"Well, there wasn't really anything to finish. But yeah."

"Oh." Nadia pinched her lips together to stop a wholly inappropriate smile from spreading across her face.

"So, you see," Alex continued, as if Nadia had never interrupted, never mentioned Lila, "the universe would never, ever send you back to Russia. The universe wants you to stay right here. Next to me. And when you've dealt with this appeal and you've got your Leave to Remain, then you and me are going to have a very long talk about all the other things that you apparently don't know I feel," Alex finished with a grin.

"Guys!" Ledge hollered at them from the bus shelter at the far end of the road, gesturing with exaggerated motions behind them. "Bus! Move it!"

And Alex took up her hand again with a grin and began to jog, keeping just ahead of the approaching headlights. Nadia laughed as her flip-flops smacked and slid on the pavement, feeling her heart beating hard and sharp and certain.

Chapter 22

Nadia

Caro's bedroom always felt like an oasis of calm. Artfully distressed French furniture – just the right level of shabby chic – looking as if it had just been pulled from the pages of interior design magazines, carpet the faintest of eggshell blues. But that day there were things that jarred. It wasn't the growing mountain of clothes in the centre of the king-sized bed – that was par for the course for an activity like this. It was in the little things. In the pair of dark chinos slung carelessly over the back of a chair. Contact lenses sitting in little round pods on the vanity unit, when Caro had perfect eyesight. A new heaviness in the very smell of the room.

Monty was at work. Nadia didn't let herself wonder if she'd have still been as welcome around here if he hadn't been. She just let Caro do what Caro did best and busied herself fingering the expensive fabrics and marvelling at the styles and colours as things were thrown at her from the depths of the walk-in wardrobe. This was serious. They were building Nadia's court hearing outfit.

And dissecting Nadia's love life, of course.

"So you just left it like that?" Caro repeated for about the third time that morning. "With so much unsaid?"

Nadia felt her face go pink. "It's not that it was unsaid. It just…"

"Wasn't said," Caro supplied dryly when Nadia left her sentence

216

hanging a shade too long. "I see."

"You know what I mean."

"Well, he broke up with that bit he's been hankering after for yonks for you. If that's not love, I don't know what is!" Caro laughed, causing Nadia to flush further.

Nadia distracted herself by holding up and shaking out a metallic silver blouse with ornate buttons – a bit showy for her purposes. She moved it across to the 'no' pile. "Do you have anything a bit less… exciting?"

"No. I'm an exciting sort of gal."

Nadia reached up on reflex to snag the acid-yellow silk top that Caro was throwing at her out of the air. "Seriously, Caro, I'm thinking nice sensible dress and blazer here."

Caro was back in the depths of the wardrobe. "You want to make an impact!" was her only retort.

"Perhaps, but I don't think I'm going for the sort of impact that neon provides," was Nadia's tactful response, as she loosely folded the yellow top and placed it atop the "no" pile.

"So, you're just not going to talk about it until, what, next week?" Caro continued as if Nadia had never changed the subject. "How can you stand it?"

"I'm trying to stay focused, is all. *You* are not helping with that, by the way."

"I only signed on to help with the clothes," Caro replied smartly. "How about this?" She held up a plain wrap dress in a soft, deep grey – the colour of smoke in the dark. Nadia reached out to touch the hemline.

"It's beautiful," she agreed. "Much more what I was thinking."

Caro moved closer to the bed, dropping the dress gently so that the material pooled in Nadia's lap. "Okay, then." She patted Nadia on the shoulder in a way that reminded her of something her grandmother used to do. "You're going to look great. And it's going to be fine."

"It's going to be fine," Nadia echoed automatically.

"And then, lucky girl, you'll be getting the visa *and* the man," laughed Caro, moving away to scoop up the "no" pile in her arms. "This has been a really good summer. I'm so glad we're both loved up at the same time!"

Nadia watched her friend move back into the wardrobe, tasting the comment she wanted to make inside her mouth, barely managing to swallow it back. "Uhuh."

"Now we just have to find someone for Holly!"

And there it was: an opening.

"True." Nadia ensured that the utmost nonchalance was in her tone. "What about Rory?"

There was a definite pause. Even the hangers that had been rattling on the rail swung to a halt.

"No," came Caro's disembodied voice. "Not Rory. Not Rory and Holly."

"Really? Why not? I think they'd be cute together," Nadia pushed.

"Nah." Caro emerged looking harried. "Holly's too sweet for him. He needs someone with a little more… bite," she finished, with a jut of her jaw. Nadia smothered a smile.

"I thought you didn't even like Rory."

"I like him fine." Caro needlessly smoothed down her bedsheets with agitated fingers.

"You know, I thought in Brighton that there was a little some-thing, something going on between the two of you…" Nadia pressed.

Caro shot her a look loaded with warning. "Nothing went on between us. I was with Monty."

"Well, you weren't, though, were you? Not that weekend, anyway. You hadn't heard from him for a month."

Caro's face shuttered and Nadia knew she'd gone too far. "Well, it all turned out well, didn't it?"

"I suppose…"

"Look, I know you don't like Monty, Nads." Nadia blinked – she thought she had been quite subtle. "You've never liked him. But

218

I love him. And he loves me. He *left his wife for me*. This is the real thing. So you're just going to have to learn to deal with it."

In for a penny. Nadia raised her head to meet her friend squarely in the eyes. "Is it the 'real thing' because you love him? Or because he left his wife for you?"

"What does that even mean?"

"It means I don't want you to feel obligated. You were getting over him when he turned up at your door – don't deny it, you were. You had a great time in Brighton. There were sparks with Rory, there were." Nadia insisted, when Caro opened her mouth to protest. "Monty messed you around for the longest time. Have you forgotten it all? I haven't. I don't think I ever will."

The room fell into an uneasy silence. Caro broke it with a heavy sigh.

"Like I said, you're just going to have to learn to deal with it," she said, her tone pronouncing the matter closed. "Come on," she commanded, lifting the grey dress off Nadia's lap once more and shaking out non-existent wrinkles. "We still have to do accessories."

Alex

Alex had spent six weeks studiously avoiding all thought of his annual appraisal. He turned in his self-assessment forms twenty-two minutes before his meeting; the look the HR Administrator shot him assured him his negligence was well noted. He couldn't quite bring himself to care. What was Donnelly going to do about it, fire him? If he did it would certainly solve a problem.

But, to Alex's surprise, it wasn't Donnelly and his paunch that awaited him in the small meeting room. It was the Head of the Department, Sarah Jenkins, she of the high heels and higher expense account, who Alex had exchanged awkward small talk with exactly once, at his second Christmas party. He faltered in the doorway and her quick, pale eyes caught his stumble, flicking up from the sheath of papers she'd been studying.

"Alex. Good to see you. Please, take a seat."

Alex obediently plonked into the chair opposite her. What was going on? To get the big boss doing his appraisal meeting he was either about to be promoted or fired, and he had to admit that the former was much less likely than the latter...

"Where's..." His manager's actual first name sailed clear from his head. "...Donnelly?" he finished weakly. Sarah Jenkins gave him another of those wickedly quick looks.

"I'm handling some of the annual appraisals for *Michael's* team this year, where he's thought it appropriate to get me involved," was her succinct answer. Alex began doing the maths in his head: how long would his savings cover rent and food?

"So, Alex." She didn't smile. "You've been with us for a fair few years now. Graduate fast-track, weren't you?"

"Yes ma'am." Alex instantly hated himself for the ma'am, but Sarah carried on regardless.

"University of Brighton lad, weren't you?"

Alex blinked. "Yes."

"Same as me.

Alex blinked again. "Oh." He wasn't sure what he was meant to do with that information. Bond over shared reminiscences of vomiting outside the student bar?

"You know, a lot of the graduates from your intake year are on level eight, or even seven by now." Yes, he knew.

"I was up for promotion in this stream." Alex scratched his jaw awkwardly, felt a rough patch he'd obviously missed whilst hurriedly shaving that morning. "Donn – Michael didn't think I was quite ready yet."

"To be frank, Alex, Michael doesn't think that you're ever going to be ready for management here."

Alex swallowed down the hot embarrassment. Although it was true that the thought of spending the rest of his life crawling up the Home Office ladder made him want to beat himself to death with his computer keyboard, it still sucked to hear that he sucked.

"Have there been complaints about my work?" he managed

eventually.

"No Alex, you're missing the point. You're a very able administrator, and a very well-thought-of member of the team. It's more that you seem to have little interest in being anything more. You haven't displayed the ambition we'd expect in someone of your calibre. If you only did, you could go far with the organisation."

And Alex pictured himself, at forty, at fifty – barely controlling a team of self-obsessed twenty-somethings who thought he was a prick; his own ever-growing paunch straining against his own collection of identical TM Lewin shirts; complaining loudly about how much his kids' private school fees cost him, how his wife was getting fat and never cooked for him any more. He'd known from his first day here that he didn't want to go far, go *anywhere* with this organisation. He just had never known where else to go.

Sarah Jenkins leaned closer to him, her elbows on the table. "Do you disagree with this assessment, Alex?"

Alex met her eyes. "No. I don't." He could practically hear his P45 being printed.

Sarah Jenkins smiled for the first time. "Okay." She straightened the papers in her hands and placed them neatly down on the desk. "Have you considered other career paths within Her Majesty's government?"

"I… hadn't really thought about it, to be honest." Surely it would be more of the same? The Foreign Office, GCHQ and the SIS; it would just be a different desk, a different shade of the same non-fulfilment.

"Well, that could be food for thought, then." Sarah capped her biro and shifted in her seat. "Did you have anything that you wanted to flag in this meeting?" she asked Alex, almost as an afterthought.

"Um. No."

"Okay then. You have a good week Alex. But do come to me if you ever want to talk about your options."

"So, I'm not, in trouble?" Alex blurted out as Sarah Jenkins rose to her feet. She stared at him as if he were mad.

"Of course not. Like I said, you're a model employee. It's just that you could be even more. We just want you to achieve your full potential, be the best that you can be and all that!" The ghost of Alex's aborted tattoo finished the refrain of clichés, mocking him: *Make your life extraordinary.*

Alex returned to his desk and sat staring at the industrial, impersonal grey background to his computer, waiting for the clock to tick through the afternoon.

He wished again that he was one of those people who knew who he was, knew what he was for. Back at university, when he'd been untouchable, life had seemed to be one giant buffet. He'd had his requisite degree, his beautiful girlfriend, a ring in his pocket and a small amount of savings in the bank – he'd figure everything else out.

And so maybe it was that confidence, and not his heart, that had taken the biggest kick to the nuts back then. Oh his heart had taken a fair punch, for sure. Even now, if he walked past a woman wearing that same floral scent that Alice had always worn he ached a little for that lost love – but the sheer shock of it had spiralled through him; maybe it was spiralling through him still.

You love me more than I can ever love you, Alice had told him, on that last afternoon, looking apologetic, but not as apologetic as he thought she should. And maybe he'd been subliminally thinking that nobody ever would. And as the years had drifted past and his friends had drifted away, he'd somehow never realised that he was living a self-fulfilling prophecy.

He'd always blamed Alice Rhodes, told himself she'd pulled the rug out from underneath him, derailed his perfect life. But it was becoming clearer and clearer to this older and wiser Alex, that maybe he'd done that to himself.

Alex sighed, shooting a glare at the clock on the wall that seemed to be getting no closer to five-thirty. At least he was seeing Nadia that evening; the thought made any afternoon seem more bearable.

Nadia

"I think that the most important thing is just to stress that you don't think you can have a comparable life back in Russia," Holly was saying. "Say it's a culture clash. Say you don't agree with the politics. Say anything."

"She can't claim to be a political refugee, or in fear for her life," Alex argued. He shot Nadia an apologetic look. "Her parents are middle-class suburbans. She speaks the language. None of that is going to fly. You're just going to have to persuade them of the extreme emotional damage it will cause you to leave the city that's the only home you've ever known. That's our angle here."

"Can we not pretend you're a lesbian?" Ledge suggested brightly. "They're not too keen on gays, the Russians, are they? You could be a refugee from discrimination."

"Ledge, be serious!" Holly gave her cousin a censorious glare.

"No, I mean it, it's actually brilliant!" Ledge continued, warming to his theme. "We just have to convince them that Nadia drinks from the furry chalice..." He was cut off, unfortunately not in time, by Alex hurling the sofa cushion into his face.

"I think we're going to have a hard enough time dealing with the boyfriend called Matt who didn't, then did, exist, and now doesn't again," Holly pointed out, shooting a glance at Alex. "And the whole quasi-relationship status in general, to be honest." Nadia watched Alex rub the back of his head awkwardly.

The weather had broken slightly; it was dark and spitting stinging shards of rain outside, a good evening to have arranged to stay in, get a takeaway and go over the logistics of the appeal hearing.

Caro had been meant to bring the wine and notes she'd made talking to a lawyer friend of her father's. Two hours ago she'd emailed over the notes along with the excuse that she wasn't feeling very well and wouldn't be making it. It could have been true, of course – there was a first time for everything – but would that be too much of a coincidence?

"This has got Monty written all over it," Holly had agreed, without even being asked, after Nadia had passed over her phone so she could read the email. "Do you remember that time she insisted on coming with us to that gig when she had the mumps?"

"Look, I know the law." Alex was still arguing. "And under Article 8, which it specifically mentioned in her appeal letter, we have to prove that on balance it is unfair to remove Nadia from her private life here. And considering she doesn't have a career here, or family, or…"

"A boyfriend?" Holly chimed in, after Alex's pause had grown embarrassing.

"Well, a partner of more than two years' standing, whom she would preferably be living with," Alex countered. "Without any of those things, we're really going to have to ham up the friendships, your social life, your inherent Britishness, do you know what I mean, Nads?"

Nadia was too busy dealing with the squirm of hurt that had raged up in her throat as the man she thought herself in love with pitilessly listed all of the deficits in her life. He seemed to belatedly realise that and melted back from Scary Home Office Guy to normal Alex, touching her upper arm sympathetically.

"Don't worry, it's all good," he assured her. "You *are* inherently British. I just want you to be as prepared as possible. It's no walk in the park, this process." He looked around the room, at her motley collection of character witnesses, minus Caro, of course. "You need to all be as prepared as possible. The judge could ask you anything. Short, succinct answers. Don't ramble. Don't panic."

"Alright, Judge Judy." Ledge rolled his eyes. The familial resemblance to Holly was always strongest when he did that. "We get it. This is important to us as well, you know." And Nadia felt a little burst of love for Ledge and Holly, her oldest friends, the ones whose family used to have her for the school holidays when she couldn't go back to Russia, who had been with her every step of the way, and now stood beside her still, raging against the dying of the light.

Alex's face had softened too. "I know that." He looked around the small living room again. "You'll all do great. I know it." And Nadia loved him a little for his sweetness, but couldn't help but hate the fact that he wasn't going to be there all over again.

Chapter 23

Alex

"She couldn't be from a worse country, mate," was David's damning conclusion. "It's red hot with the Russians lately, with all that's been going on over the last year or so. They're not even really giving them travel visas, let alone Leave to Remain." He sipped a little of the office canteen's crap coffee and grimaced. Alex grimaced too; he'd been expecting it, but it was still painful to hear it straight from his esteemed colleague's lips. David worked in the sector of the Home Office that dealt with the courts; if anyone had his finger on the pulse of what Nadia's appeal reality was, it was him.

"But she's been here since she was a kid," he found himself defending her, always dredging up those last few droplets of hope from somewhere. "They might not consider her in the same way that they would other Russian national adults."

David was already shaking his head before Alex had even finished his sentence. "I know, I read the file. So, this is your girl, right?" Alex hadn't said anything in his original email that suggested he and Nadia were more than friends. God! It must be practically tattooed across his face. He simply nodded. David shook his head again. "Messy, Alex, really messy…"

"Is it going to help or hinder her case? Being involved with me? If I stand up in front of the judge?"

"You don't live together. You haven't got any history. The judge won't consider you a serious enough relationship under Article 8. It's not going to make a blind bit of difference to the appeal. It could, however, get you fired. You're meant to declare relationships with foreign nationals you know, Alex, which of course means you're not supposed to have them at all. It could void some of your security clearances."

Alex raked his palms back over his hair, covering his eyes with the heels of his hands. "Yes. I know." He sighed. "It's just, I've barely 'declared' the relationship to her, how could I have done it to the office?"

David arched an eyebrow as he took another sip of sub-standard coffee. "That sounds like the sort of story that needs telling over a beer, not a weak-ass Americano," he said. "You free this evening? Could grab a swift one after close of play."

Alex blinked. Years he'd worked in this place, years, and this was the first time a colleague had ever extended a social invitation to him. Having said that, to be fair, he'd never got further than nodding politely at David when they shared the lift. Maybe asking for his help, inviting him down for a coffee had broken some societal barrier?

"That would be really good," he said, sincerely. "But I'm going to see Nadia tonight."

David nodded sagely. "Trying to get in as much time with her before she has to go?"

Alex swallowed. "Something like that."

"I feel for you, man. We'll catch up after it's all over, then." After it's all over and she's gone, he means, Alex thought. David stood up and clapped him on the shoulder. "Good luck with it."

Nadia

Nadia had already begun quantifying her life in hourly segments. Eight days until the court date. The next Wednesday evening she had would be the night before the appeal and she'd probably be a lot less relaxed.

You wouldn't think it was getting on for eight o'clock at night. The Common was carpeted with bodies, ties loosened and shoes kicked off, the bright orange of Sainsbury's carrier bags of hurriedly purchased picnic food a constant refrain against the bleached, dry grass. Nadia had brought a couple of the little square scatter cushions from her living room and so reclined in relative comfort, her head on one, an arm thrown over her face to block out the brightness of the evening. She could still sense Alex next to her – a solid, warm presence. The last time they'd lain out on the Common together they'd topped and tailed on the picnic blanket, giving one another an extremely polite amount of personal space. This time they turned their faces in towards one another and it was much, much better.

Now they'd maybe, kind of, *almost* had the conversation, it was a different type of tense between them. Like the kind a moment before you stepped out on stage, before you'd quite crested the drop of the rollercoaster; it was excitement and apprehension and everything this long summer had been, all at once, all rolled up into one unstinting feeling. Off to the west, Nadia could just about make out the playground where they'd had that first conversation, the one they'd never been able to have with anybody else, about life and loneliness and swinging over the bar.

Alex had been a little manic these past few days, constantly talking appeal strategy, a one-man-army against her deportation, never letting up. But in the thick, heavy heat of the evening he'd grown quiet, his breathing even, and he dozed peacefully next to Nadia, reminding her of the time he'd fallen asleep in the cinema and she'd half-pressed her lips to his. So many near misses, almost-kisses. And now, here they were, lying together companionably – almost at the end, but not yet – not quite yet.

And although Nadia regretted not having more time with Alex, and although she knew she'd regret having to leave him – if it all went south, and she had to – she could never regret all of these perfect little moments, the sort of moments that together make a rope, that make a happy life. And whilst, perhaps, new moments wouldn't feel as extraordinary without Alex, without Holly and Caro and all her friends, life would, of course, go on, and on, and Nadia could always keep that with her, for ten years, for fifty: all the way until the end of the rope.

It had always been one of her favourite things: sitting out on the Common. Now it could be a perfect memory.

Alex

When Alex roused the Common was almost deserted; it was almost fully dark, and his neck and shoulder blades felt a little as if they'd been cemented in place. But the first thing Alex saw when he opened his eyes was Nadia, casually asleep, her chin tucked into her chest and her body arced to his, one leg of hers sandwiched between his two. And he knew that he loved her, simply knew it, in the way that you know your own name. It didn't rush in all at once; it was as though it had always been there, waiting patiently for him to notice it.

And he knew he couldn't lose her across the sea, this woman who'd changed him, changed his life, the sunshine that had come out and dried up all the rain. Alex lay there, stock-still – not wanting to wake her yet, not wanting to break the spell of the quiet, darkened Common – and began to bargain with the faceless universe. Come on. Please. You brought us together. Don't screw us over now. Please. I'll do anything.

The strident beep of a taxi on the faraway road came blasting, almost like an answer; Nadia jerked awake, sitting upright and rubbing her face quickly with her hand.

"Wow, conked out!" she laughed. "Embarrassing. What time is it?"

Alex consulted his watch. "God, it's like ten!"

"Ten?" Nadia pulled herself to her feet and stretched languorously. "We'd better get going, then."

Alex watched her from below, fascinated by her, by every little thing, by the way she stretched her arms up behind her head, and the way it pulled the hem of her dress further up her thighs. "Go where? Home?"

Nadia grinned, bending down to collect her throw cushions and stuff them into a plastic bag. "Let's hit the swings!"

Nadia

Ledge's housemate was on holiday, so they were round at his place in Earlsfield, Ledge having waited weeks to get to proudly show off his entertainment system set-up to Rory and Alex. Nadia and Holly were much more interested in the bottle of apple Smirnoff he'd got in for them.

It was like so many other Saturday nights, except, of course, that it was the last one before the appeal.

And Caro wasn't there.

From the stilted text conversation Nadia had had with her the day before, she deduced it wasn't so much that Monty was stopping Caro from going anywhere, but rather that he *insisted* on coming, and Caro was all too aware of Monty's rather low popularity rating. Nadia could see the reasoning behind her friend not wanting to make waves until everything was a bit more settled, but still, the thought that one of her besties wasn't there with her on this last precious weekend rankled, and she put her mobile phone away in her handbag without replying to Caro's most recent message.

As Ledge had apparently thought the best thing to mix apple vodka with was Apple Tango, Holly was in the process of making up a batch of extremely apple-y drinks. Nadia took a sip of one and laughed.

"This reminds me of when we used to sneak random bottles of spirits in to the dorm and mix it with Tizer from the vending machine down the hall."

Holly made a face. "Eurgh, yeah. A personal low point was Drambuie and Tizer, I seem to recall."

"Ah, Hols." Nadia stopped her best friend in her tracks, catching her round the waist and putting her head on her shoulder. "I hope I get to send my kids back here to boarding school and that when I do, they meet best friends at least half as amazing as you."

Holly grabbed up Nadia's hands, a serious look on her face. "You won't have to send your kids back here to boarding school, Nads. You're going to be here already. They can go to normal school and come home to their lovely mum at night and see their Auntie Holly every weekend."

Nadia shook her head sadly, determined to get this out, let this person know how much they meant to her. "Holly..."

"Holly, nothing!" Holly dragged Nadia into a hug that bumped their chests together fiercely, driving away the words Nadia had been gearing up to say. "You're not going anywhere. If I need to chain myself to you, like a Greenpeace protestor to a tree, so be it." Nadia felt the heat and blur of tears in her eyes but blinked them away, surrendering herself to the bear hug. "So be it," Holly repeated.

"Okay, Hols," was all Nadia could say.

Two hours later everyone was feeling faintly nauseous on the sugar-sharpness of their drinks. The conversation circled around lazily, nobody really wanting to talk "appeal" again, or discuss Caro's predicament. Nobody had been quite bothered enough to set up the Rock Band game that they had discussed fifteen minutes earlier. It was easier just to be.

The vodka munchies had dictated that the Hungry House app got fired up and boxes of dirty fried chicken ordered in, but everyone was rather surprised when the flat buzzer went off twenty minutes later. That was supersonic speedy for a London takeaway on a Saturday night. Ledge scooped the handful of notes and small change that made up everyone's share of the bill and loped off downstairs to the main door of the building to collect the food.

They heard Caro before they even saw her; she apparently could smell them before she saw them. "Christ, is that apple?"

Nadia struggled to her feet from where she'd been wedged into the sofa between Alex and Rory. "Caro?"

"Good thing I picked this up en route." Caro waggled the bottle of Sauvignon she was holding by its neck and headed straight through the open-plan living area for the kitchen cupboard she knew held the glasses. Nobody spoke whilst she filled a wine glass and turned back to face them; they sensed she had more to say. "So. Monty's wife called me." She swilled the wine around in her glass as if it was brandy.

Nadia and Holly exchanged a cautious look. "Just now...?" Nadia asked.

"Earlier."

"Are you okay?" Rory blurted. Caro shot him a look of soft surprise at the interjection.

"I'm fine," she assured him. "Just, needless to say, this is not my first drink today." Caro gave everyone in the room a slightly sharp smile and then, to their intense horror, burst into tears.

She'd almost recovered by the time the girls had bustled her into the relative privacy of Ledge's slightly musty bedroom. Caro swiped at her wet cheeks angrily, as if the tears were acting outside her control.

"I'm such a mug," she said, over and over, clutching on to her wine glass as though it was a life-preserver. "I'm such a mug. I'm such a fucking horrendous cliché."

"Hey, are you heartbroken here or embarrassed?" Nadia asked, trying to lighten the mood, gently taking the over-full wine glass away from her friend and placing it down on Ledge's bedside table. "What happened?"

Caro was silent for a moment, clearly composing her thoughts. "I knew things weren't right. I'm not an idiot. That we didn't work in real life, you know? We couldn't cook dinner together, or just crash in front of the TV, all that usual stuff. It felt weird. Like we had to be sneaking around, snatching an hour here and there – always just in bed with each other, never really talking. I thought it would get better. I thought, Jesus, this man has *left his wife and child* for me. If that's not love..." She gave a deep, miserable shrug.

"You felt like you owed him," Holly summed up perceptively.

"Something like that."

"So what did the wife have to say for herself?" Nadia couldn't help but ask. "Did she rant and rail at you? Funny how they never blame the man as much as they do the other woman."

Caro had started crying again, silently now. "Nothing like that. She called to talk to me. She sensed I didn't know the whole deal. She was worried he was taking advantage. She was right."

"The whole deal?" Nadia repeated.

"*He never left her for me*. She kicked him out." She started almost laughing. "He turned up at my door because he didn't have anywhere else to go; he was homeless. It wasn't that he loved me. He never loved me." And although Caro was still crying, she sounded almost relieved.

"He probably did," Nadia said, kindly. "But not in the way that you deserve to be loved, that you will be loved one day, Caro."

"He's an absolute idiot, who didn't deserve his wife, or you," Holly concurred. "You made a lucky escape. The both of you."

"I know," Caro admitted, "I know. But it still freaking hurts."

Mutely, Nadia handed her friend back the wine glass. "I can imagine."

"And, of course, I've got four more months left of him teaching me," Caro added, ruefully. "That's going to massively suck."

"Can you talk to someone about it?" Holly asked.

Caro covered her face with her hands. "No, no. After tonight, quite frankly, I never want to talk about it again."

"He shouldn't be able to get away with it," Holly pointed out, angrily.

"He hasn't," Nadia pointed out softly. "He's lost everything, hasn't he?"

"And actually, as I don't think the daily commute between his parents' house in Derby and central London is going to prove very easy, he might be forced to give up his job, too. He can't afford to rent anywhere on his own, not on his salary, and he doesn't really have any friends he can crash with," Caro said. She just sounded sad now – tired and sad. Nadia ached for her. What a waste of a year, a waste of time and love and hurt that would have been better spent elsewhere. She'd never again be completely the Caro she'd been before she met Monty and become so many new things: the forbidden fruit, the other woman, the doormat. At least she was free to become more new things – better new things – now.

"Can I stay with you guys tonight?" Caro asked suddenly, taking a small sip of her drink. "We had it out and everything and I told him he needed to be packed and gone by the time I got home, but…"

"Of course!" Holly told her. "You can stay as long as you like."

"But I think in the meantime we should definitely put our boys to good use," Nadia grinned.

"Our boys?"

"Yes. The ones who are clearly standing in the hallway earwigging." Nadia raised her voice. "Hey, guys? We've got a job for you." The bedroom door opened immediately, the boys not even having the grace to pretend they hadn't been right outside it.

"You want us to go over and make sure he's gone?" Rory asked Caro without preamble. "It would be my pleasure, trust me."

"Throw us your keys," Alex added. "We'll go now and hurry him along."

"It's alright, guys, you don't have to go right this second. I don't want to spoil your evening," Caro assured them.

"Seriously, it would be my *pleasure*," Rory repeated. "Make with the keys."

The flat buzzer sounded rudely and suddenly, startling them all.

"Maybe after the food," Ledge laughed.

Chapter 24

Alex

Nadia had stressed that she wanted to keep it very casual. There'd be enough bread and circuses at the courthouse in the morning, she pointed out; all she wanted was a quiet night in. She wasn't expecting to get much sleep. She mainly just didn't want to be alone.

Although Monty had been long gone by the time the three boys had turned up at Caro's place – their metaphorical guns blazing – Caro had remained living at Holly and Nadia's. Her junk was scattered everywhere, driving the more minimalist Holly slightly insane, but Nadia had confessed that she found the background bickering distracting, almost calming, and was loving having her two best friends underfoot. And underfoot they were, barely leaving Nadia's side for a second, almost as if they thought that if they left the room, they'd return to find her gone, disappeared away like a magic trick. She'd laughed about it when she told Alex, but it was a sad laugh, incomplete.

It was well into September but the heat refused to die and the evening was still as light as midday outside, as if the sun was refusing to set on this summer, this final evening. There would be other evenings, of course; even if it all went to shit tomorrow Nadia would still have twenty-one days' grace to leave the country.

But, either way, there would never be another evening like this, one where she was still uncertain, floating in hope.

When Nadia came back from serving drinks she squeezed in next to Alex on the sofa, her body slotting precisely against his as she continued chatting casually – grinning up at him as she passed him a new bottle of beer – and the idea that she might one day not be right there seemed completely unfathomable to him.

But although she was chatting and smiling and drinking, there was an edge to Nadia tonight, a palpable panic beneath the jokes, like a hummingbird's heartbeat. It was almost catching; nerves yawned inside Alex's chest, empty and sharp, no matter how much beer he poured in to fill it.

Caro and Rory sat across the room, sharing both a bottle of red and the oversized beanbag, flirting outrageously, as if they were aware of the fact that they needed to be an entertaining distraction, or maybe they just didn't care. Holly and Ledge did their best, too, keeping up a rattle of conversation.

They'd made quite a good six, somehow, out of nowhere. Ages ago, before he really knew them, Nadia had told him that she wasn't sure if Holly and Caro would remain friends without Nadia there between them, and Alex knew what she'd meant. Nadia was the heart of everything. He'd never be in a room where she wasn't missed. He threw yet more beer down his neck in a valiant attempt to plug that cavernous hole.

Ledge left for home early enough to make the last train, but Rory and Alex hung doggedly on, not quite wanting to let the night end, not just yet. But as the hours crept towards dawn, Alex knew they'd have to go. The hearing wasn't until two in the afternoon, but still, they all needed to get as good a night's sleep as what was left to them. Nadia, yawning, was starting to stack the washing up in the sink and he popped quickly across the hallway to use the bathroom.

He was straightening the hand towel on its rail as he opened the toilet door, so he didn't see her straight away, and jumped when he did; Holly was standing in the gloom of the corridor.

"Sorry," she said, sotto voce. "Didn't mean to scare you."

"Well, don't lurk around like some sort of toilet ninja then," Alex laughed back, going to move around her and back into the lounge.

"Alex." It was more her tone rather than the hand she brought up to his side that paused him. "Can I talk to you for a minute?"

Alex blinked. He hadn't expected a belated "what are your intentions?"-type conversation from Holly of all people. "Yeah, sure, what's up?" He'd automatically dropped the volume of his voice to match hers.

"I need you to be straight with me, here." Holly wrapped her arms around her torso self-consciously.

"Of course. Seriously, what's up?" Alex asked resignedly.

Holly's voice had dropped so low, Alex strained to hear her. "What are her chances? Be honest."

Alex felt rather as though someone had just dropped a bucket of iced water over his head. "Her chances?" Holly wasn't fooled by his obvious attempt at stalling. She just stared him down in stubborn silence. He sighed. "I don't know, Hols. I work for the Home Office, yes, but it's not like I'm a judge who sits on the hearings."

Holly's frown increased. "You said you'd be honest. I just want to be prepared, okay? And ready to be there for her. It's not like you're going to be."

That last dig hit its mark. Alex bristled. "You really want to know?" Fine. Why should he be the only person eaten up by this? "It's not good. It's not good, Holly. But you know that. You're not an idiot. You know she ticks none of the boxes. You know that Russia is like the persona non grata of the UN right now and so she pretty much couldn't be from a worse country. You know that the government is being judged on its immigration stats and that it can't stop people from the EU from coming in but it can stop her. How do *you* think tomorrow's going to go?"

Holly didn't speak right away. She looked the queerest combination of sick and relieved. The hallway was horrifically silent. Alex could hear clattering and banging and Caro raising her voice in the living room, loud as usual, breaking the spell of angst. Regret smashed into him like a truck.

"I'm sorry..." he began immediately.

"What for?" Holly interrupted, with a sad smile. "You're only being honest."

Caro tumbled into the hallway, smacking her palm flat against the light switch. Holly and Alex both flinched as the space flooded with brightness.

"You guys" Caro half-shrieked, half-growled. "What the hell is your problem?"

Alex looked at Rory for clarification as he brought up the rear, but he looked as livid as Caro.

"How was that an appropriate conversation to be having?" Caro continued, glaring at them.

Holly suddenly looked even sicker. "You could hear us?"

"WE'RE NOT DEAF," Caro bellowed. Maybe Alex hadn't been as quiet as he'd sounded in his own head after all.

"Neither is Nadia," Rory added, gesturing behind them to the living room and Alex belatedly recognised what those sounds had been; the way the flat door's letterbox clattered a bit when you opened and closed it, Caro's voice raised in slight panic as she called her friend's name. He barrelled past them into the living room, confirming it was empty.

Alex whirled back round to Rory and Caro. "Where's she gone? Why'd you let her run off like that?"

"Hey, this isn't my fault!" Caro argued back. "And it's not like she ran off crying. She just said she needed some air and to be alone. To be quite frank, I didn't fucking blame her. You're drunk and you're loud and you're a bloody pig, Alex."

"I think you've spooked the shit out of her, mate," Rory concluded disapprovingly.

Wordless, Alex made his way to the huge sash window that had been open all night, allowing the breeze and ever-fast rumble of traffic from the city at all hours to circulate the stuffy flat. He hung his whole body out, staring through the pre-dawn blur west towards the high street, north towards the Common. Holly was trying to call Nadia, but her forgotten mobile phone just rattled and buzzed against the top of the coffee table.

"Shit," she said, jabbing End Call. She looked at Alex. "We have to go find her. Do you know where she'd go?"

Nadia

Nadia stepped off the night bus and took in a lungful of fresh air after a half-hour journey of smelling the vinegary chips the homeless man at the back of the bus had been ploughing through.

It was almost four in the morning but Nadia was far enough into the city now that people were still bustling past her, crowding and rushing as usual, not paying the blonde girl the slightest bit of notice as she descended the stairs to the right of the bridge, extra careful on the steps in the half-light. Funny how her quiet place was in one of the busiest parts of the city.

It had been surreal, almost, to hear Holly half-whisper the question that Nadia had been dying to ask Alex herself – weirder still to hear Alex answer it so baldly. But she didn't blame them. She blamed herself. She blamed denial. She should go back. They'd be worried. And yet...

It was almost like going into shock. All of the air inside her body had rushed out, leaving her bones creaking and her heart shaking, cold and alone in the suddenly certain knowledge that this time next month she would be living a different life: that the Nadia Osipova she'd been would be no more than a ghost or a memory. What would happen to the Nadia who lived with her best friend in Clapham Old Town, who ran laughing into the Underground, always just about making the last Tube; always made Candy at Closet every month without fail; the Nadia who fearlessly walked the banks of the Thames at low tide, keeping one eye out for buried treasure; the Nadia who Alex Bradley had

239

fallen for. Not one second of that Nadia's life had been nothing.

She wasn't ready to leave London. There were still streets she hadn't walked down, museums and galleries she hadn't wandered through, must-go and must-see places she'd never made it to or seen. She'd never done the ice-skating outside of Somerset House at Christmas, or visited the Olympic Park, or seen *The Mousetrap*. She hadn't seen Caro fall in love or helped Holly find a better job. She hadn't truly kissed Alex, not the way he deserved it, down to his toes, with everything she could manage to put into it.

Nadia perched on the first cinder block she came across, staring out across the water, so still in the darkness that the line between the water and the far bank was an almost indistinguishable blur. The moon was on its way down, fat, full and butter-yellow and so, so close it was almost as if it was sitting atop the curve of the river, just there – as though she could walk right up to it. She wrapped her arms around herself against the wind off the river; for the first time in months she felt chilled.

At least her last London summer had been a glorious one – in all ways – one she'd always remember as a string of endless sunny afternoons with glorious friends; non-stop laughter; stomach-churning, knee-trembling, lip-biting falling in love; the man who'd always be her greatest What If…?

Suddenly decisive, Nadia pulled her handbag across to her knees and scrabbled around inside for the notebook and pen she always carted around but never actually used. She knew exactly the sort of distraction, the sort of catharsis she needed tonight.

Alex

It wasn't the first place he looked, purely because he hadn't imagined she'd travel all the way to Blackfriars in the small hours the night before her appeal hearing. But when he hadn't found her at the swings in the middle of the Common or nursing a coffee at the twenty-four-hour greasy spoon up by Stockwell he'd finally guessed where she'd gone and jumped on the first night bus heading north of the river. She'd wanted some air and some quiet, she'd said; there were only so many places in this city you could get anything approximating that.

He saw her almost immediately when he got down to the level of the bank, both her hair and the material of her skirt were glowing pale in the half-light and fluttering in the wind off the water, only a little way down the river. She was on one of the inexplicable huge grey cinder blocks, hunched a little over her own knees, unaware of his approach or anything else around her: tiny, alone. As he got closer he could see that she was twirling a biro over her knuckles, saw her tense when she finally heard the crunch and shift of the stones under his shoes and glanced up, ready to take flight.

"Okay, so, I'm the biggest rat bastard in the world, right?" was Alex's weak attempt at humour. Nadia pushed her hair back behind her ear and clutched the notebook she'd been writing in close to her chest.

"Well, I suppose it's hardly your fault that the country of my birth isn't currently respecting international borders," Nadia conceded after a moment. "I guess I'm not very good at running away, huh? You found me pretty easily."

"Wasn't the first place I looked," Alex admitted. "I didn't think you'd jump postcode."

"You were enough of a rat bastard for that." Despite her harsh words, Nadia moved over on the cinder block in mute invitation for Alex to sit down.

"Nads, I am so, so sorry. Holly is too, of course. The last thing we wanted to do was upset you."

"But there's the thing," Nadia sighed. "Because I am upset. And I think I get to be. I'm upset that somehow it's okay for a bunch of lawyers and politicians to decide that I don't get to keep living my life. That because, by a complete accident of birth, I happen to be Russian – instead of Polish or Romanian, or whatever – that my relationships, my career, *my life* is up for debate. That I have to

241

see my friends upset and stressed out on my behalf, whispering in corridors and dreading tomorrow almost as much as I am. Having to lie to me and tell me that everything's going to be okay when they are manifestly not."

Nadia finally took a breath; it was a deep one. "Alex. I'm not upset with you. I'm upset because tomorrow I am going to be given a deportation order. And things aren't going to be okay again for a very long time."

Alex marvelled at her; fighting words to the end, not even the smallest crack in her tone, just calling out her impotent rage across the river at the faceless people who were doing this to her.

"Alex." She turned to him, her face purposefully overly close and tempting. "I've just got to ask. I've got to. I'll hate myself forever if we never got around to having this conversation. If I wasn't going…" Alex knew the time for patronising and protecting her was over and swallowed down the words of comfort that swelled in his throat and let her finish. "If I wasn't going, do you think… do you agree with me, that it could have been magic between us?" She said it like the simple question it was at heart, her tone as open as her face, not wanting anything more from him at this eleventh hour than the truth.

Alex's response was to slide his hand along her jaw, to send his fingers up under her hair, feel the heat of her and the way she automatically pressed her cheek against the curve of his hand as if she couldn't help herself.

"It already is," was his answer, the easy truth that had always been there, before he drew her in that final inch and kissed her, and it was nothing like before, soft and unsure. It was too, too many things at once: thrilling and familiar; solid and tremulous; an ending of sorts, for sure, but a beginning as well. And Alex knew that if he kissed Nadia Osipova like this every day for the rest of his life it would never be enough, but it would be a start.

When they had to draw apart for breath Nadia started to laugh. "I thought we weren't doing that yet?" she giggled uncontrollably.

"I thought we were waiting?"

Alex shrugged. "Waiting was a stupid idea," was all he said, before he pulled her mouth back to his, already starving for her again. He couldn't even gauge how long it had been when Nadia pulled away again.

"Wait, wait," she laughed again; inconceivable – Alex wasn't wasting another minute. "I've got something for you," she continued, reaching down for the notebook that had slipped unheeded between them. She neatly tore out the top piece of paper and presented it to him with a cute little flourish. It was a list, bullet-pointed and neat in Nadia's small, loopy handwriting. In larger underlined text, the title: *Alex's To-Do List*.

Alex looked up, confused. "What is this?"

"Well, the whole reason we even became friends is because I got you involved in my London Bucket List," Nadia explained. "And how you didn't have enough to do, and I had way too much," she smiled. "Well, that doesn't have to stop for you when I'm gone. In fact, it shouldn't. So, ta-da!" She repeated her flourish. "A brand new to-do list – all yours. And you can call me on Skype all the time and tell me how it's going." For the first time that night Nadia's voice wavered slightly into sadness.

Silently, Alex read his instructions.

Update your CV, get job-hunting!!

Go speed-dating again (with Rory?)

Go back to Brighton and send me selfies from the end of the pier

Finish your tattoo

Keep going to Candy's for me – don't forget, first Thursday of every month

Kiss first

Kiss often

Eat an entire Jacob's Ladder ribs (plus sides) on your own

Buy a beanbag

Stay friends with Holly and the others

Actually make it all the way round the National Gallery

Save up your money and annual leave and come see me in
Russia

Alex swallowed and steadied his voice. "Okay, so," he started conversationally. "Point taken about the needing-a-new-job thing. The tattoo... we'll see. Candy is a given. The Jacob's Ladder on my own I still don't believe is physically possible..."

"You have to at least try," Nadia reprimanded gently, and Alex knew she didn't just mean the giant ribs.

"I will," he promised her softly, folding the list small enough to slip into his jeans pocket and turning his efforts and attention back to Nadia and the little breathy noise he'd discovered she made when he kissed her just right.

Nadia

They brought the witnesses in one by one.

First her well-meaning but bumbling manager at the Oxfam store, who rambled through a few points about Nadia's philanthropic spirit and admirable work ethic before being dismissed to the seats at the rear of the room.

Ledge was her first character witness, awkward in his suit but sincere in his words. Caro was next – all fire – and Holly the last – all steel – both effusive in their love for her, their belief in her worthiness, their desperation for her to stay. When the Home Office lawyer finally finished with Holly after a bored-sounding and peremptory cross-examination she almost stumbled on the way to her seat, clearly overwrought. When she got there, Nadia saw Alex pick up Holly's hand and hold her arm close. It had been too late to get him in as a character witness, but at least he was there, his presence there – even though it was practically a resignation – making her that little bit more fearless in turn.

And after the Home Office suit finished delivering his closing argument, biting words that stripped her down to nothing more than a nationality, Nadia – who had never been able to afford her own lawyer – stood up in defence of herself. And she told the judge how much she loved the city, the country: how she truly felt British down to her bones, and about how when she dreamed she dreamed in English, never in Russian.

She explained how she had plans to put her bilingual skills to good use, how she'd like to work in government, if they ever granted her nationality, how she'd like to make a difference. She told her how she'd never been without Holly, how they'd gone from the boarding school dorm – always adjacent beds – to their nothing-special but special-to-them two-bed flat on the affordable side of Clapham Old Town.

She admitted that she might not be married or living with a boyfriend, but she had one, and it was love all the same, and felt a rush of pride as she got to gesture behind her to where Alex was sitting, breaking all the rules to be there for her, remembering how he'd reached to touch her face, just once, before they were taken into the room and how strong his strength had made her feel in turn.

And even though she knew it was a scream into the void, and that her leaving was a foregone conclusion, it was almost all worth it just to get to stand there and show this stranger sitting in judgment that Nadezhda Osipova – nationality Russian, date of birth 10th September 1988 – was so, so much more than that.

Epilogue

21 DAYS LATER
Holly had been to the WH Smiths in the airport and was stuffing another few Mars Bars into Nadia's hand luggage. She knew they were Nadia's favourite, and Nadia hadn't had the heart to tell her that she could still get them in Russia. Instead she just kept talking about their plans for Christmas – Holly was going to take two weeks off work and, politics permitting, was going to travel over. So it wouldn't be too long. It would never be every day, not again, but there was WhatsApp and there was Skype, and there would be sometimes, and they'd love each other just the same.

And then, in the New Year, Caro would have to be next, but judging from the way that she kept dramatically clutching Rory's hand, hiding her tearful face against his chest, they might be more of a package deal by then. Nadia smiled. That was fine by her; in fact, it was rather convenient. Funny how things work out. When life gets it right, it's its own kind of magic.

As if he'd sensed she was thinking of him, Alex turned away from his conversation with Ledge and smiled at her. It had been a bit of a rush, but in the end someone high up at his office had pulled some strings and the red tape had magically fallen away. And so for now there was a two-year work visa and a job at the British Embassy in Moscow dispensing practical advice and assistance, a job that conveniently came with a tiny little city-centre flat. So, they were exchanging Trafalgar Square for Red Square, and Alex had admitted he was already swotting up on interesting trivia to impress her with. Nadia wondered if anyone ever did any mudlarking on the banks of the Moskva River; she was excited to find out. A whole new city of adventures spread before them, and she intended to make the most of every single one.

Alex shared a secret smile with his girlfriend across the heads of their friends and felt it again, that feeling he'd had since the day he'd read through Miss Nadezhda Osipova's application form, that he was – for once – *exactly* where he was supposed to be.

Nadia had cried and cried and asked him over and over again if he was mad, if he was sure, if he loved her enough, and his answers were the most effortless yeses anyone could ever give.

He knew it wasn't going to be easy, but nothing that worth it ever was. And if life was a path with a hundred directions, then every one of them had led right here.

It would be scary, and it would be hard, sure, the two of them forging one brand-new life, together, but at least Alex could be sure that it was going to be an extraordinary one.

Nadia Osipova's Hidden London

Hello! My name is Nadia Osipova, and I'm a Londonholic.

I've lived here my entire adult life, and I love it all: the tourists, the expensive, inauthentic food, the crowded pavements, the 'minor delays' on the tube... Haha, I'm joking (sort of) – but it is the truth that since the news of my potential deportation, I've been feeling extra fond of the Old Smoke. Because it's true: "when a (wo)man is tired of London, (s)he is tired of life; for there is in London all that life can afford." Or something like that.

But London isn't all Buckingham Palace and museums and boating on the Serpentine (although that is very nice) – in my years here I've discovered that the ancient city has many secrets... And here are my Top 15!

1. Embedded in a case set into the front of a rather shabby WHSmith on Cannon Street is the 'London Stone', the ignoble remnants of a once much larger limestone object, because... REASONS (that had already been forgotten by Tudor times). But it is generally accepted that the Stone came to London with the Romans, although some prefer to believe it formed the altar in a temple founded by Brutus, the Trojan refugee who was the mythical founder of London a thousand years even before said Romans. Level three on the romantic scale

is that London Stone is the stone from which the legendary King Arthur pulled the sword Excalibur. However it got here, legend has it the destruction of the stone is meant to herald the destruction of the city in turn!

2. London is famous for its grisly histories and ghost stories – for a couple of quid you can join tours that will take you round all of the ghoulish sites. But they probably won't include the tale of London's weirdest ghost – the chicken ghost of Pond Square. As the story goes, Francis Bacon (yes, he who pops up in films about Elizabeth I quite a lot) was hurrying through a snowstorm in January 1626 when he suddenly came up with the theory of refrigeration (as you do). Eager to test out his idea he quickly purchased a chicken and slaughtered it before stuffing the carcass with handfuls of snow to see if it preserved the flesh. Wonderfully ironically, Bacon never lived to find out: the day out in the snow meant he contracted a severe chill, which eventually became pneumonia and killed him a couple of days later. But it's not Sir Bacon's disgruntled spectre that haunts Pond Square – there have been frequent reports for hundreds of years of a ghostly chicken who appears from nowhere to race in circles around the square, frenzied and flapping, before disappearing as suddenly as it arrived. So if you're at a loss around Highgate one evening, maybe go for a stroll around the Square, and see if the chicken appears for you...

3. London may be an amazing city, but it's seriously lacking in beaches, am I right? Well, if you traverse all the way to the western end of the Central Line you'll find a reservoir complete with artificial beach nestled near Ruislip Woods. The old reservoir was renovated into a lido for swimming and boating in 1933 and although the pollution eventually got so bad that going in the water was banned, there is a paddling area and now the water is said to be considered

again to be an "acceptable standard" (!) for inland bathing (should you be that desperate). Most people just enjoy the walk – it takes about an hour and a half to leisurely stroll around the water, but there's also a charming miniature railway run entirely by volunteers to take you most of the way round the lido in style.

4. Full of the typical grandeur and romance that the Victorians imbued the dead with, Highgate Cemetery is one of the world's most famous graveyards, but most Londoners don't even know where it is. The avenues of death entomb poets, painters, princes and paupers, including (most famously) Karl Marx, the novelist George Eliot, the man who invented the modern postal system and the one who invented cinematography! You can easily get lost in the winding paths, gazing at the gothic majesty of typically-dramatic 19th century tombs – but nowadays the cemetery is most famous for its supposed vampire. Girls looking for their Lestat/Edward/Salvatore brother, jump on the Northern Line now.

5. People most often go to Crystal Palace to go to the, er, Crystal Palace, which is fair enough. But if full scale models of dinosaurs are your thing, don't forget about Crystal Palace Park itself, an old Victorian pleasure ground. A delightfully random set up with one lake where you can boat and one where you can fish (and never the two shall meet), sculptures of extinct animals (the Bromley council website describes them as, tongue firmly in cheek, "the Victorians' answer to Jurassic Park" – in very unVictorian fashion, bring your smart phone to access a free audio tour), a landscaped maze and a small zoo (if you prefer your animals not yet extinct).

6. If you head as north as North London gets, you'll arrive in Enfield, where the ancient Plantagenet kings had a hunting

ground. Hidden away in the parkland that now covers the area is an island surrounded by a man-made moat, known since time immemorial as "Camlet Moat". Archaeological digs have unearthed that there used to be a substantial castle on the site, already established by the time the Romans were here. Unsurprisingly, Camlet Moat is a centre for spiritualists and Druidic activity and many believe that this was the site of the legendary Camelot. A wraith-like "grail maiden" is meant to appear to the worthy! Whatever your thoughts on King Arthur, the walk through the park and around the island is a magical way to spend a loose afternoon.

7. You can't help but notice the Windmill International – its sign is pretty unsubtle. It was once known as the Windmill Theatre and remains best known to this day for the introduction of nude *tableaux vivants* in the 1930s. Before the introduction of a little nudity the club was haemorrhaging money – people really weren't feeling variety shows anymore – and so the owners eventually decided to take a leaf out of the Moulin Rogue's playbook and brought in the ladies. However, to get past the Lord Chamberlain's censorship, the girls had to remain completely stock-still, as if classical statues (as that was their argument – how could nude statues be morally objectionable?). Cheeky soldiers on leave used to bring in mice or spiders in their pockets and throw them onto the stage in the hopes that the girl would scream and run around a bit, but the 'Windmill Girls' were famously stoic. So was the theatre itself. "We Never Closed" they claim proudly, even now; performances at the Windmill continued even at the height of the Blitz. Today (after a brief stint as a cinema/casino), the Windmill is now a pretty standard table-dancing club. Still, it's nice to celebrate the history of the British appreciation of a nice pair of tits (even while being bombed by the Germans).

8. The Palace of Westminster is pretty iconic around the world – even if some Londoners don't even know it's called that. It's more commonly known, of course, as the Houses of Parliament, which has met there since the thirteenth century. The Palace – the largest in the UK – has eight bars, six restaurants, 1,000 rooms, 100 staircases, 11 courtyards, a hair salon and a rifle shooting range (as you do). There's also been a long-held myth that nobody is permitted to die within the grounds of the Palace (presumably if you show up looking a bit peaky they rush you off in an ambulance sharpish). This has probably come from the fact that as the Palace is (officially if not in practice) a royal residence, so anyone who dies there should receive a costly state funeral. But the absolute best thing about the Palace of Westminster is that the lifts have, to this day, hooks inside them for hanging up your sword. In fact, floor markings in the Commons Chamber have been designed to be a safe two sword lengths apart. You know, just in case the debate starts getting too hot.

9. The Underground map has got to be one of the most iconic London images of all time. There are about 270 stations on the network – but there are also an additional 40 lost or 'ghost stations'. These points were usually closed due to poor user numbers – now their street-level facades are repurposed into branches of All Bar Ones, or Pizza Express, but the subterranean platforms and tunnels remain… If you know when and what, you can catch glimpses of the old platforms from your tube windows – sometimes they're still tiled, the station name proudly emblazoned. The most famous and least-dead ghost station is Aldwych, closed in the 90s due to chronic underuse, but still used today whenever TV or film companies need an archetypical "tube platform". These quaint little pieces of history may not be around for much longer, though; Transport for London is actively seeking investors to turn several former stations into bars, clubs and restaurants. Try and grab a peek

of them in their shabby, abandoned glory before that happens (and after it does, go there for cocktails, naturally).

10. Fans of J.M. Barrie's *Peter Pan* series will probably know that the Darlings, like Barrie himself, lived around Kensington Gardens and this is precisely why Barrie chose to place the bronze statue of Peter he'd had commissioned there. The statue was erected in secret one night in 1912, appearing as if by magic to delight the children on May Day morning. Not everyone was feeling it though. Questions were asked in the House of Commons about whether an author should be permitted to promote his work by raising a statue of his main character in the middle of a public park! The children, however, loved it, and kiddies are seen climbing up the base of fairies and woodland creatures to get closer to the boy that never grew up to this day! Nowadays they can even use their smartphones to scan a barcode on the nearby plaque and get a personalised call back from Peter Pan himself! In time, all representations of Peter moulded to the statue's version, and there are copies of it in cities across the world.

11. Go to the Embankment and crane your neck to check out Cleopatra's Needle. It's nearly 3,500 years old and its twin can be found in New York City. Pillaged from Luxor, Egypt and brought to London at great expense, the Needle was re-erected in 1878. Entombed in the pedestal there is said to be a time-capsule that contains (among other things) cigars, a razor, a portrait of Queen Victoria, a bus timetable, copies of 10 daily newspapers, and pictures of 12 "English beauties of the day". The 'Cleopatra' part is a complete misnomer, as the monolith was already a thousand years old by the time she was born. And, of course, like any Egyptian artefact worth its salt, the needle is said to be cursed – at the very least it was the first monument in London to be hit by an air-raid during World War I. While you're there, also spare a thought

254

for the two bronze sphinxes who flank the monolith. They were installed 'backwards', so they are gazing at the needle rather than guarding it, rumour has it because Queen Victoria found that way round more aesthetically pleasing.

12. While you're checking out Shakespeare's Globe Theatre (because, come on, you *have to* check out the Globe), don't forget to take a peek at the Ferryman's Seat. Back in the day there was only London Bridge in use if you needed to get from South to North London on foot. Not that convenient. So, the taxi drivers of their day, the ferrymen, lined up on the shores to take punters from one bank to the other. The South was where all the fun was – the brothels and the theatres – and often ferrymen would be asked to wait around whilst their fares partook of the Southwark delights. Men waiting around needed seats. And that's what this is, an ancient granite 'bench' where a hard-working ferryman could rest his weary bones after a hard row across the sludgy Thames. It's the last one left in London. I wouldn't try to sit on it.

13. Take a trip east, to EC4, half-way between London and Tower Bridges, and there – right in the middle of the city – you'll find the atmospheric ruins of an ancient church, St Dunstan-in-the-East. Originally built by the Normans around 1100, the church was already old when it was damaged in the Great Fire of 1666. Like most of London it was patched up with the help of Sir Christopher Wren and managed to hobble on until it had to be shored up again in the early 19th century. Then in 1941 the church was severely damaged during the Blitz – amusingly, it was the older part of the church that faired the better, with Wren's tower and steeple surviving the impact whole. The decision was made not to re-build, and in the 70s the ruins were opened as a public garden, a beautiful bit of green seclusion in the very heart of the city.

14. Go and visit Big Ben. I bet you're thinking that sounds like the most touristy thing ever, and that I'm trying to catch you out, because of course you know that "Ben" is the great bell and NOT the tower itself (that's the Elizabeth Tower). But did you know that guided tours are free and available to all UK residents? The catch is that you have to write to your local MP and ask really, really nicely to get on the list – and with a maximum of 10,000 people allowed each year, that's quite a long list...

15. The seven noses of Soho. The hidden ears of Covent Garden. No, I've not gone insane. This is actually a thing – and legend has it they give good fortune to those who find them all! Scattered around Soho are seven sculptures of shnozzes. Back in the nineties there were originally over thirty-five of these installed by the artist Rick Buckley in reaction to the controversial introduction of CCTV (noses "under the noses" of the cameras – geddit?). The prank was not publicised and so urban myths grew up to explain the random noses. The nose inside the Admiralty Arch was said to have been created to mock Napoleon and that the nose would be tweaked by cavalry troopers from nearby Horse Guards Parade for luck when they passed through the arch. Fellow artist Tim Fishlock followed up by installing hidden ears around Covent Garden ("the walls have ears".... geddit??). There are two that are reasonably easy to find on Floral Street, but most are still awaiting discovery...

Happy exploring!

Nadia x

Turn the page for a sneak peek at Erin's
bestselling debut, *The Best Thing I Never Had*

The Best Thing I Never Had

ERIN LAWLESS

Prologue

February 2012

Nicky took the proposal in the same undemanding way in which it was offered. You know I love you, he had said, followed by: please – twice. It was like receiving a promotion when you were the only applicant in the running; she was grateful and excited, sure, but she couldn't really say that it had been 'unexpected'.

She stretched restlessly in bed the morning after – one day into being twenty-six years old, one day into being engaged – watching the dust dance in the slant of dawn from the skylight window. She watched as the fixtures and furnishings of the little studio flat grew pale and distinct and – rather disappointingly – looked just the same as ever. Beside her Miles lay sprawled on his front.

Nicky pulled her arm behind her head and thought back to the first bed they had shared; a single, he had not been able to sprawl then. So that first morning they'd woken spooned together, a curiously intimate position for a one night stand. He'd kept his hair longer then and it curled around his cheek and tickled at hers. She'd lain there, cramped and uncomfortable, and wondered how to get him to leave without seeming rude.

She had been laden down with Tesco bags that evening, her housemate opening the front door for them, when they both caught sight of the post-it note at the same time. Nicky had dropped one of the carrier bags to the ground and reached to peel it off the glass of her window; a little blue ink heart on the yellow square, stuck facing inwards to her bedroom. And, just in case she had hoards of men leaving hearts stuck to her window, Miles had thoughtfully added an M and an x for a kiss in the corner.

She still had it, somewhere, in a box with old text books, perhaps.

* * *

Leigha had, as her mother always put it, done very well for herself. She had her nails done every two weeks and her hair every four – whether they strictly needed it or not. Home was a minimally furnished leasehold apartment in a Georgian mansion block off the Gloucester Road, which she spent very little time in.

So, true to form, she wasn't at home when she got Nicky's text: she was in the office and already on her second latte and paracetamol combination of the morning. She read it three times before fully absorbing the content and breaking into a lazy smile.

Dear Nicky. She couldn't remember the last text she'd had had from her, couldn't put a finger on the last time they would have seen each other. Leigha rarely ventured out of London these days. Nicky belonged to a different place, a different time; one where she used to sleep until noon, ironed her hair poker straight every day without fail and, as a rule, only drank fruity cocktails – as wine used to give her a headache.

But still, here it was in black and white on her Blackberry screen: Nicky was calling in a years-old promise and Leigha was called to be a bridesmaid.

Dear Nicky, she thought again, absently, as her attention flicked back to her computer screen. I must give her a call after work.

* * *

Sukie was vaguely aware of her phone going off from downstairs but persuading her two particularly unwilling teenage sisters into their uniforms and onto the bus was taking up the majority of her attention.

Twenty minutes later, the table had been wiped clean, the dishwasher stacked, the laundry put on and Sukie went back to bed, tugging her mobile free from the charger cable as she climbed in. She felt a flicker of anticipation as she read the text. Always a little quicker off the mark than Leigha, she could immediately follow Nicky's thinking.

She tilted back on her pillow to better see the cork board that hung at the head of her bed. A digital photo printed out on paper, so many years ago now that the ends were curled completely over on themselves: herself and her three university housemates, all in pastels, pale, thin arms looped around and around one another like the rings of a magic trick. Sukie knew that if she had received a text asking her to be a bridesmaid, then Leigha had as well and so – it could be assumed – had Harriet.

Sukie fired off an appropriately excited and congratulatory response to Nicky and dropped her phone to her bedside table. She pulled herself up to her knees and reached to smooth down the curling edges of the photo. Harriet smiled out from the middle of the group, one arm around Sukie, one arm around Nicky. Sukie brought her hand away and the white edges sprang back.

* * *

Johnny cast a desperate look at the closed en-suite door. Was it worth a dash to the communal bathroom up on the second floor? Risk running into one of the abundant flatmates? No, surely she'd be out soon. He shuffled from foot to foot on the spot. What had possessed him to stay the night? He knew this would happen. He was going to be so late for work and look like shit to boot.

There wasn't even a clock in here. He grabbed his mobile from the bedside table and turned it on. 08.38. Fuck.

He was so distracted that he read the text that had popped up twice before he really registered its content. When it did hit home, he sat down heavily on the end of Iona's bed, scratching at the stubble on his chin absently.

At that moment Iona came out of the bathroom in a cloud of warmth and steam, her body and hair wrapped in matching hot pink towels.

'I'm so glad you're here to get me up early,' she spoke through her yawn, as he dashed past her into the bathroom and shut the door. 'I've really got to get to the library by eleven. '

Eleven! Bloody lazy students. Johnny made a face at his reflection as he wiped the condensation off the mirror with the flat of his hand.

* * *

Harriet read the text whilst waiting for the lift, her mobile in one hand, a cardboard tray of Starbucks' coffees balanced in the other.

During their last dinner together, back before Christmas, Nicky had drunk too much rosé and confided in Harriet that she expected a proposal within the next six months. Miles had, at long last, finished his PhD and would finally be making money. What better way to express his gratitude to the girlfriend who had upped-sticks and moved across the country with him – then financed five years of him researching one of the more obscure battles of the Wars of the Roses – other than purchasing an appropriately sized diamond with his first few doctorate pay cheques? Harriet had thought Nicky was damn right to expect it.

She automatically pressed Reply, backed out of the Reply screen to read the message through once more, pressed Reply again, and paused.

She had herself almost convinced; surely, after almost five years, she was the only one stupid enough to still be thinking about it?

Things could never be like they were before, but maybe, at the very least, they could stand there for one day in identical dresses. They could share old smiles, clasp arms and sing along to old songs. Maybe Adam would seek her out, look at her up and down in that old way he had of looking at her that she would never forget.

Harriet began to tap out her reply with the side of her thumb: Of course, of course I will be your Maid of Honour!!

* * *

Adam had his text from Miles the night before. He had felt his iPhone buzz in his suit trouser pocket – apologised to his companion for bad date etiquette – and read the text with appreciation.

'She said yes!' he grinned at his date, on an automatic impulse to share the moment. She stared at him blankly, thrown by the sudden change in conversation. 'My mate's proposed to his girl,' Adam clarified. 'I'm going to be best man!;' and suddenly she was off, talking a mile-a-minute about all the weddings she had attended over the last year, and wasn't it funny how everyone seemed to be getting married lately?

It suddenly struck Adam that there was finally going to be a wedding. He'd spent months knowing Miles was going to propose on Nicky's birthday. He'd even gone ring shopping with him, helped him book the chapel on their old University campus. Now the ring was on the finger, quite literally speaking, and they were all on countdown for an Easter wedding.

After the purchase was complete they'd gone for a pint, the ring with its respectable diamond quiet in its plush black box on the table in front of them. Miles had scratched under his chin in that nervous way he had. 'I assume… she'd want… the other girls. You know, as bridesmaids?'

Adam had taken a long sip from his pint while he arranged his answer. 'I guess'. There was no point pretending he didn't know which other girls Miles was referring to.

'So it will be, like, a reunion,' Miles had said carefully, taking a long draught of his lager himself.

'To be honest mate, it's about time,' Adam had answered, and had meant it.

He drew his attention back to his date, describing the halter-neck bow that had been on her dress for her sister's wedding. Her arms were held up above her shoulders, bent backwards at a strange angle as she laughed at herself for not being able to articulate what she meant. She looked very soft, very sweet, and suddenly Adam felt an impractical urge.

Let's leave the rest of the bottle – he wanted to say to her – let's go for a walk along the river. Let me tell you a story, from when I was young and stupid.

'That sounds really nice though,' was what he said instead, re-filling her glass with wine.

PART ONE

September 2006 – June 2007

Chapter One

September 2006

The Nokia rumbled against the table; Nicky was up like a shot, grabbing the phone and pulling the charger cable taut against the screen of the TV. Leigha immediately made inarticulate sounds of protest through a mouthful of dinner.

'Miles?' Harriet asked.

Nicky didn't bother to take the phone off charge, instead reading the text message standing slouched against the wall. Her mouth twisted; she tapped her thumbnail against the side of the phone nervously before looking up at her three housemates, who were looking back at her expectantly, eating momentarily forgotten.

'He's found somewhere,' she said finally, though she still chewed absently at her bottom lip.

'Hurrah,' Sukie replied, with probably a little more feeling than was tactful. Leigha shot her a quick look.

'Cool, nearby?' she asked Nicky, who had placed her mobile back on the table without sending a reply. Nicky's lip-chewing intensified.

'The high street, actually.'

'Wow, that's lucky!'

'It's above the estate agents,' Nicky interrupted, before the impression that this was a good thing could cement.

'Well, that doesn't mean it's not still really convenient,' tried Harriet.

'It's with two blokes he's never even met, and they're undergrads.'

'Oh no, however will he cope? It's not like he's dating one. It's not like he's just been squatting in the house of four all summer.' Sukie rolled her eyes, helping herself to some more rice from the foil takeaway container on the floor.

'It's only three hundred, and that includes some bills,' Nicky continued – although nobody had asked – 'so maybe we'll still be able to have something put away by graduation.'

'Not if you keep getting Chinese takeaway,' Sukie said through a mouthful of rice. Nicky ignored her and returned to her place on the sofa, looking about herself for her fork.

'When does he move in?' Harriet asked, tilting her head back to better see Nicky's face from where she sat on the floor in front of the sofa.

'He can from tomorrow.'

'Means I can start walking around in my underwear again!' Sukie laughed.

'Yippee,' mumbled Nicky, pulling her fork from the gap between the sofa cushions.

* * *

So, here he was, back for his final year at university. It seemed like no time at all since he'd been an embarrassment of a Fresher and now it was the beginning of the end.

Shaking off the rather uncharacteristically maudlin chain of thought, Adam immediately made himself at home, giving the most cursory of goodbyes to his damp-eyed mother (always emotional during the return-to-term farewell) and lugging his suitcase up the stairs, leaving it unopened just inside the doorway to his bedroom, where he was pretty sure it would remain until at least Reading Week.

The room smelt warm and musty from being shut up the whole summer but otherwise looked and felt much the same. At the foot of his unmade bed was a neat pile of envelopes, post that had arrived for him over the summer. Adam suddenly felt a little flare of annoyance at the presumption, the embarrassing politeness, at what he assumed to be the work of his new housemate.

He and Johnny had harboured serious hopes that their landlord wouldn't be able to let the box-room after their mate Mike sodded off on his placement year in industry, and their third year would just be the two of them. Of course, it was too much to hope for, that the guy'd be able to overlook the rent being short by a couple of hundred quid each month, and unsurprisingly, he'd rustled someone up. All Adam knew was that it was a guy, a postgrad, and his name was Miles.

It transpired that Miles was indeed embarrassingly polite, just the sort of guy that would sort a stranger's post for him and leave it in a neatly right-angled pile in his room. Nice enough, but he seemed so terribly old and serious; when he was at home he was closeted in the tiny box-room studying. Not that he was often at home. Because what Adam and Johnny found most irritating about Miles Healy was that he wanted to be there even less than they wanted him there.

Miles, it came as surprise, had a girlfriend, Nicola, who lived down the road. He'd spent the summer living there with her, being fussed and cosseted over without having to pay a penny towards rent or board; by all accounts, quite a jammy git. Miles' abrupt deterioration in circumstance to a rather damp, lacking in furniture, second floor flat above the estate agents' on the high street was purely down to the girls' landlord belatedly working out that he had an unofficial tenant. It contravened the tenancy agreement, he blustered, and Miles was out on his ear. It was two weeks before the start of term and every last measly room in the main town and the neighbouring student village had gone; apart from, of course, their box-room. Probably something to do with the fact that it hadn't had a carpet. Or a window that opened.

And eventually, after a tactful few days for the boys to acclimatise to one another, the girlfriend arrived, with a housewifely smile and a casserole in a Perspex dish. Johnny and Adam were – surprised. She was dirty blonde, tall and coltish, with a shy, unexpectedly pretty face.

'Talk about Legs Eleven!' Johnny whispered to Adam the second Nicky's attention was on serving out the food. Adam subtly held up his two middle fingers in agreement: their private sign for 'that bird has cracking pins'.

Nicky had let the boys dominate the conversation, interjecting here and there to encourage Miles to tell specific anecdotes, keeping the beer flowing, nurturing what had initially felt reasonably formal into easy chat. And then, at the end of the night, as Nicky pulled on her shoes, Miles hesitated.

'I think I'll stay here tonight, pet,' he said, haltingly, looking over at Johnny. 'You need to show me this so-called "dream team" on your Pro Evo!'

'Ah, mate, it's a work of art!' Johnny had been banging on about the particular merits of his carefully crafted digital football team the entire evening. 'I'll bring my Playstation downstairs.'

Nicky smiled to herself as she finished tying her laces. 'Okay, love. See you tomorrow?' Miles gave her a distracted smile and kiss on the forehead before bounding up the stairs with Johnny to help him disconnect his console from his bedroom television.

'It was nice to meet you, Nicky,' Adam said politely, upon being left alone in the lounge with the girl. 'That dinner was great. Feel free to come back, any time!' he teased.

Nicky laughed. 'Oh, I'm sure you'll be seeing me around!' She paused at the head of the stairs that led down to street level and the flat's front door. 'We're having a party, me and the girls I live with, across on Dell Road? A sort of "back to school" sort of thing.' She used her fingers to mime satirical quotation marks. 'On Saturday. You guys up for it?'

'Er, yeah.' Adam stepped back to let Johnny through, trailing a quagmire of black cables. 'We'll definitely try to make it.'

Deciding that it was infinitely cooler to turn up a couple of hours late, making it seem like they'd had 'another thing' on, Adam and Johnny had sat in their lounge drinking Carlsberg and playing Pro Evo for the first half of Saturday evening, before pulling on their shoes and making the five minute walk into the heart of the student village.

The door was open, with people spilling out into the front garden. A slight, Oriental girl looked up at them quizzically from where she was sitting on the crumbling garden wall – mid-way through bringing a cigarette she had bummed from her companion to her lips – but didn't seem bothered enough to object to their entering the house. They pushed past the bodies congregating in the hallway and at the foot of the stairs, coming through to a large, open-plan kitchen–diner. Adam nervously adjusted the bottle of cheap wine he was holding by its neck.

A brunette girl in a dark pink skater-style dress had turned away from her conversation, throwing her hair over her shoulder as she did. She smiled at them.

'Beads!' she said, very matter-of-factly.

'Sorry?' Adam thought he must have misheard.

'Beads,' the girl repeated, her smile growing wider. 'And a punishment shot. You don't come late to our parties.' She had turned to a shoe box on the kitchen worktop which was filled half-way to the top with necklaces of plastic beads, delved her hand deep into the clicking mass of them. She untangled two necklaces, draped them around his and Johnny's necks and was turned back to the worktop in a flash, the short skirt of her dress flirting around her upper thighs as she twisted.

'So, who do you belong to?' she asked conversationally, pouring

273

generous measures of Sambuca into two comedy shot glasses.

'Er, Miles,' Johnny answered, quickly. 'Er, I mean, not that we, I mean-'

'He's moved into our flat,' Adam supplied, with a touch more poise. He shot the rosy-faced Johnny a look.

'Aha!' the girl said, looking back at them with renewed interest, spinning the lid of the Sambuca bottle tight against the flat of her hand. 'Well, welcome guys. I'm Nicky's housemate. I'm Leigha.' Then she held out a shot glass to each of them like a handshake.

'Hey. Adam,' Adam said, taking the shot without complaint.

'Johnny,' Johnny introduced himself in the most nonchalant tone imaginable, whilst his fingers fumbled as Leigha passed over his shot glass; he had to suck the spillage from between his thumb and forefinger.

'And this is Harriet,' Leigha gestured behind her to the girl she had been talking to when they arrived, who had been leaning against the fridge and smiling a small smile throughout the whole exchange. She was petite – downright boyish in frame, especially standing next to her curvy friend – with dark, dark hair cut short at the nape of her neck.

'Hiya,' Adam nodded to the girl politely, which Johnny echoed before downing his shot as manfully as he could manage and handing the empty glass back to their hostess, whose attention had already drifted across the room.

'I recognise you,' Harriet said. Adam looked at her quizzically. Their campus was a small one; after two full years, it wasn't too unlikely that she might know his face. 'You do English with me,' she finished. It wasn't a question.

'Er, yeah.' Adam searched her face again; she had eyes as dark as her hair. He didn't recognise her.

'You guys!' Nicky was suddenly there, her fair hair in a fat plait over one shoulder, and clearly slightly drunk as she launched into a series of clumsy hugs. 'You made it!'

'Yeah, we thought we'd drop by,' smiled Johnny, although he

turned his head away to watch as Leigha moved away from them across the kitchen and started to converse with somebody else, the girl who'd been smoking in the front garden, who turned a liquid gaze upon them.

'So, you're the fresh meat,' she said, baldly, as she stepped closer to them. Adam blanched and laughed nervously.

Nicky, swaying on needlessly high heels, spoke before he had a chance to retort. 'Johnny, Adam, this is Leigha, and Harriet, and Sukie.' She gestured with a lazy flick of her hand to each of the girls who were gathered around them as she spoke. 'My housemates,' she finished, with an indulgent smile.

'Okay, so everybody knows everybody,' Sukie said, impatiently. She reached behind Johnny for the half-empty bottle of Sambuca. 'I thought we were here to have a party, not a debutante ball.' She began to form a line of sticky, empty shot glasses ready for the stream of Sambuca that was yet to come. 'Now, is anybody up for a game of Twenty Ones?'